MW00977719

WHITE LIGHTNING

WHITE LIGHTNING

Lucy Claire Jones

with Michael Marcades, PhD

PENIEL UNLIMITED

Published 2021 PENIEL UNLIMITED, LLC

PENIEL UNLIMITED, LLC
Dr. Michael Marcades, Founding President / Executive Editor
Kelly Marcades, CFO / Marketing Director
321 Avalanche Avenue
Georgetown, TX 78626
http://penielunlimited.com
michaelmarcades@gmail.com

ISBN: 978-1-7367185-0-6

Cover Design by Daniel Whisnant
http://suissemade.com

Copyright © 2021 by Lucy Claire Jones

All rights reserved. No part of this book may be reproduced in any manner whatsoever without written permission except in the case of brief quotations embodied in critical articles and reviews.

First Printing, 2021

ACKNOWLEDGEMENTS

To my children - who show me that superheroes hide in
ordinary people, every day, all the time.

To my mom and dad - who fostered my love of reading and gave me
loads of books in multiple genres
from the moment I could read,
and who taught me that language and communication take many
forms.

To my brother, my sisters, and my friends - for their support and love.

To my editor and publisher - Michael, for believing I had a story worth
sharing and providing
pivotal guidance along the way.

And finally - thank you, everyone, for opening this book.

CONTENTS

CONTENTS

1

The Awakening

Over the last hour the early morning cloud cover thickened enough to block out the pale blue Louisiana sky. Rain threatened and thunder rumbled lazily out over the ocean, but Jackson didn't notice. He was concentrating on the boar hunt. Jackson spotted the boar digging in the mud about an hour earlier, but one split second before he could squeeze the trigger the wind shifted. He fired, and the bullet grazed the boar's shoulder. The injured, angry mammal took off running. As he pushed through stands thick brush, it was easy for Jackson to follow the path of broken, twisted branches and falling leaves left by the boar's panicked flight.

The boar was now so fueled by fear and pain that the muggy air was perfumed with a pungent mix of the animal's musk and sweat. Jax (as his friends called him) had been hunting all morning and had come close to shooting the boar twice before. This was one frustratingly elusive boar. It seemed to know exactly when Jackson stilled his breath to pull the trigger because that's when it would dart to a different location. But Jax wasn't in the mood to lose; he was determined to get the boar.

Jax promised Evangeline a boar for her wedding dinner years ago. They were bound together like real life siblings since they were toddlers. Without being asked, Jackson had taken on the role of Evie's (as he called her) protective older brother. Before either of them had ever dated, he promised to bag a boar for her wedding feast, and he wasn't going to disappoint her now.

Mamere (his grandmother), was part of that plan. She had an almost magical way with food and could turn that boar into prize-winning boudin. Jax's mouth watered and his stomach growled just thinking about it. Focused on the task at hand, Jax paused at a fork in the path and closely eyed the intersection. Both trails seemed equally disturbed. One path sloped down to the left while the other rose upward and to the right over a small hill. The breeze shifted ever so slightly and Jax was caught full in the face with a heavy dose of the boar's musky fear. Though tall and heavily muscled, Jax sprinted effortlessly up and over the low rise. As muted low rumblings of distant thunder became bolder and more threatening, Jax – unshaken by the evolving weather danger-realized suddenly that he needed to pick up his pace if he was going to catch that boar before it rained.

Shirtless under his favorite pair of overalls, the sweat glistened on Jackson's dark caramel-chocolate skin. A bright orange hunting cap hid the bulk of an unruly tumble of naturally relaxed curls that would have otherwise fallen to tangle with his eyelashes. Sturdy work boots completed his hunting attire. Switch those boots out for tennis shoes and he was wearing what he wore almost every day: t-shirt and jeans.

Briefly pausing near the crest of a little hill, Jackson listened again for his prey. He shrugged his shoulders to shift the sling he carried like a backpack and felt another river of sweat trickle down between his shoulder blades. Then...

There! thought Jax. He saw a dark flash as the boar scampered up yet another lightly wooded rise.

Jax heard the sighing crash of the boar's bulky shoulders tearing through the brush to his left. He immediately took off running. Jax could almost *taste* the boudin as visions of feasting collided with the scent of raw animal fear souring the air. Quickly clearing the little hill, he followed the swath torn in the terrain by the boar's wild flight. A slow smile spread across his chiseled face as he thought, *This is as easy as it gets!* Jackson *loved* to hunt.

The path ripped and spun crazily down the hill before dropping into shadow. Jax paused at the base of the hill to listen. At first, he heard nothing over the noise of his own swift, deep breaths. He slowed his breathing and heard the lighthearted music of a creek. He stayed quiet a moment longer and listened more intently. His patience was rewarded when he heard the snuffling of that sharp-tusked boar. He slid deftly into the gloomy shade toward the sound. His dark skin helped him blend into the deeper shadows that were elongated by the ominously overcast sky.

Jax was light on his feet despite his size and made only the smallest whisper of noise. He ducked under a tunnel of wild vines and into a tree ringed clearing where he came to an abrupt halt. His mouth dropped open in shock! He could hardly believe his eyes. There, surrounded by the wall of dense foliage, were three very large, rusty, metal barrels. Coiled copper tubing connecting them clearly identified the contraption as a still. Deep green moss cupped the distilling barrels like large, gnarled fingers, as if trying to grab them and pull them down into the earth. Twinkling blue and white flowers littered the moss like stars on a green sea. Jackson had never seen anything like it before.

"What...moonshine!?" he asked out loud before he could stop himself.

He guessed that at one time it must have been a pretty impressive operation because of the unusually large barrels. Jackson hunted in this part of the bayou all his life but had never come across this still before. It captured his attention and he momentarily forgot about the boar.

The noisy creek was fed by a little spring that bubbled up and ran down the face of a low rock wall. Dropping into a sluice attached to the wall, the gurgling water sped away from the craggy face toward the center of the clearing. Hanging over a shallow dish of pebbles next to the old still, the water fell from the sluice and made a clean puddle of water before winding away to feed into a slightly larger creek at the far edge of the clearing.

Distracted, Jackson didn't notice the low earthen wall that almost completely ringed the little meadow until he took a step forward and tripped on it. Trying to break his fall, he reached out and knocked the sluice. It swung noisily over to the still's worm box, generating a shower of rusty flakes that fell to protest the disturbance.

Lightning flashed dully behind the clouds and the entire clearing was engulfed in an eerie blue-white light. Rubbing his eyes, Jax looked closer at the moss. The blue and white flowers glowed briefly in reaction to the lighting, then paled as the lightning dissipated. The flowers echoed each subsequent flash of lightning, holding a residual brightness that intensified with each bolt. Intrigued, he shook the sling from his shoulders and let it puddle on the ground at his feet. Patting the knife in his pocket, he moved his rifle to his left hand before stepping closer to the still. Cautiously, he reached out to touch the flowers.

Lightning flashed again, much closer now, and Jax was almost blinded by the lightning-like response in the flowers. Jax heard the boar snuffle as his eyes tried to adjust to the gray-green darkness after the flash. The boar was hunkered down in the shadows near the base of the still – much closer in the gloom than it should have been, and not across the clearing as Jax initially thought.

The sound of its heavy hooves pounding the earth spurred Jackson to move. With no time to aim or shoot, Jax leapt up onto the rusty still. As soon as his body touched the flowers, the energy within them transferred to him. It gave him goosebumps and raised the hairs all over his body. For a moment, Jackson's adrenaline rush kept him from realizing his hand was cut and his arms scratched by the rusty old metal. The awkward perch made him feel foolish, but he felt safer there. His boots began to slip on the slick moss, so he let go and lunged higher for a better handhold while trying not to drop his rifle. His right hand, now slick with blood, sweat, and dew, only slipped on the curved metal.

Lightning flashed again, even more intensely than before, and this time it struck the still! Searing heat shot through Jackson and lifted him from his perch. His back arched and his mouth flew open as energy flowed through him. His startled cry of pain was completely drowned by thunder. His hat was thrown aside by the force of the spasm, and his head was lit from within, his entire body radiated light. The intense electrical power surging through him made him feel stronger and larger, as though his body was somehow evolving. Jax's hands clenched reflexively into fists as currents of electricity lifted him effortlessly into the air.

Hovering near the still, Jax flailed his arms in panicked wonder. He pushed at currents of energy he couldn't see and the movements threw him into a chaotic spin. He felt like he was going to vomit. Jax swiped at tree branches, twigs, anything and everything nearby in a futile attempt to stop the nauseating merry- go-round. He made a conscious effort to uncurl the vise-like grip of his fingers so he could drop the rifle and use both hands. With growing frustration and fear, he flailed against the air, but that only propelled him into an even faster and wilder spin. Raging spouts of energy flared erratically from his hands and quickened the spin's rotation.

He finally decided to close his eyes and cross his arms over his chest. He took a series of slow, deep breaths, and willed himself to calm down. The few moments it took for the spin to stall and end felt like a lifetime to Jax. As the nausea passed, he opened one eye to peek at his surroundings. Seeing nothing but light, he took another deep breath and cautiously opened the other eye.

Everything was a blur of light and color. Light was pouring into him – through him – out of him! He slowly uncrossed and lowered his arms. Since that didn't send him into another wild spin, he experimented by opening his hands and flexing his fingers, trying to release the tension. He felt a shift in energy as rain began to fall in earnest.

Jax started to shout. The rain interacted with the intensified light pouring out of him, but didn't quench it, only altered the way it looked and increased its power level. The whole thing baffled Jackson – he simply couldn't wrap his head around what was happening to him or why it was happening. His blood felt like it was on fire and made him feel like he was on the verge of boiling. He started to stretch out his arms in a desperate attempt to cool the heat burning within him but stopped short. It felt like he was dragging his hands through water. Still floating, Jax wiggled his fingers, creating water-like ripples in the air that he could see. The entire scene startled him so much that he stopped shouting.

He moved his hands quickly but immediately regretted the swift move because it sent him into another spin. He pulled his arms in and crossed his hands over his chest again and waited, resigned to let the drag of the current slow him and stop the spin. This time he was able to keep his eyes open, and what he saw amazed him!

Everything in the meadow looked like it was burning without being consumed; the whole thing looked like someone's crazy idea of Christmas lights on steroids. Each individual fire was unique- a different size, a new color, a fluid shape. Some of the flames were bright, some were dim, and some even had rivers of light pouring out of them like water from a tap.

Without thinking, Jax reached out to try and touch some of the bright spots. As he reached toward one, the power in his body increased proportionally. He didn't notice at first, but each light shrank in intensity as he "connected" with it. It was as if his body soaked up their power like a dry sponge soaks up liquid.

Reaching further away, Jax experimented by trying to focus on one of the trees beyond the low dirt wall, then waited to see what would happen. Trying to "touch" the tree with his mind, he started to feel sturdier, more solid. As he watched, he thought the tree started to look a little smaller and the bark started to look fuzzy or dull, like all of a sudden, the tree was dying. Jax immediately broke the connection.

Hovering in mid-air above the still, not touching the whiskey-brewing device, Jax felt joined with it. The still itself seemed to be acting like a conductor, channeling energy into him. He felt power magnify and increase in him with every passing second. Eyes now wide open, he strained to see everything more clearly – then squinted to try and sharpen the blurred images. First, he tried to figure out what the smaller bright lights were. Ever so slowly he began to realize the lights were in each living organism. He started to differentiate more and more be-tween the plants around him and the bright hot center of paralyzed fear below him – the boar.

Too many things! his inner voice screamed.

Jax's thoughts circled and threatened to spiral out of control! Taking a deep breath, he tried to concentrate. Deciding "the squeaky wheel gets the grease," he focused on the hottest energy spot – the boar. He watched as the animal's energy pattern seemed to fluctuate and cycle through different intensities of hunger, fear, and what might have been anger. He wondered if he could connect to it without touching it. At first, he kind of "skimmed" the ripples of energy he could see emanat-ing from the boar, like skipping a stone across a pond. He saw the rip-ples bounce back to and around the animal without much effect. That made him feel more at ease, so he moved deeper into the boar's energy source with his mind. A sense of calm enveloped the boar and its energy pattern dampened. Jax tried to intensify the boar's energy and was sur-prised that he could raise and lower how bright the boar glowed just by thinking about it.

The boar squealed uncomfortably as it strained against the unfamil-iar stress. Jax reacted as if he'd been slapped in the face and dropped the boar from his thoughts – like he'd physically taken a step back. By then the animal's energy level had dampened to a pale, thin wash of light, though the connection between them glowed brightly with their merged energy. The boar fell to its knees once the link was severed, its energy completely and instantly snuffed out.

A rush of raw animal power filled Jax! The smells of mud, fresh green plants and rotting muck violently struck him. Their scents filled his nos-trils and made his mouth water with unfamiliar desires. The smell of a man assaulted his senses – hot and oily – making him simultaneously shrink away in fear and bristle with strength and defiance. With a start, he realized the smell of "man" was from himself. He screamed! Light ex-ploded once again in the clearing. It poured from him in all directions, ricocheting off the still before streaking into the atmosphere as a bright, hot bolt of lightning. Thunder filled his head as the lightning streaked skyward.

The heady rush of power dissipated, and the meadow came slowly back into focus. Jackson now stood next to the still in a ring of newly singed grasses. Smoke rose in curls from his body. He didn't realize he was mostly naked until he felt the cool rain falling on his hot skin. His clothing, scorched by the heat, hung from him in shreds.

Jax blinked at the stark negative the brilliant light had imprinted on his rods and cones, waiting for the muted colors of the rainy afternoon to return. He smelled the fragrances of the blue and white flowers and deep green moss before his eyes returned to normal vision. Their musky scent was burned into his brain. Each individual flower lit up as he glanced at it. His eyes narrowed in surprise, and the flowers shot off sparks like sparklers on the 4th of July. He looked down and saw an answering glow in the veins and arteries of his exposed arms. He could see the glowing heat course through his legs and chest and felt it in his face as well. Liquid light dripping from a cut on his forearm caught his attention. He was bleeding. He instinctively held gentle pressure with one finger until it stopped.

Jax sagged with fatigue and the power that enveloped him wavered, muted, and fell. Suddenly, it was just another rainy afternoon. He was just a partially dressed man in a clearing with a dead boar at his feet, standing next to a broken and forgotten old still. He held his arms and hands under the sluice, letting the spring's water clean them before gently prying a patch of moss and flowers from the still. He put it in the only intact pocket left in his overalls.

The smell of ozone hung heavily in the air, and the hairs on Jax's arms were standing up at attention, full of static electricity. He brushed at them and small sparks flew with the contact. They died out as they fell but the feeling of explosive power remained in him just below the surface; a power that threatened to emerge again at any moment. The smell of burned hair made him wrinkle his nose in distaste. He reached up gingerly to touch the hair on his head. Under his normally full, loose curls he felt a jagged emptiness. It started just above his left ear and reached toward the back of his head.

Great, he thought. *Well. . . Mamere has been wanting me to get a haircut.*

He examined each finger and toe and touched his ears and his nose. Jax sighed gratefully as he confirmed that nothing was missing. There were stories about people losing fingers or toes after being struck by lightning. So far so good.

Jax sat down on a rock in the meadow and looked at the dead boar. One sick looking tree and more singed plants ringed the clearing, all nodding under the incessant fall of raindrops. He sat there in the rain for a few moments, trying to collect his scattered thoughts, but didn't wait long before getting up to field dress the boar.

Shaking his head as if he could jostle his thoughts into some semblance of order, he sighed again and stood up. There was no sense in just sitting there letting the meat age. He took the rope out of the sling and hung the boar from a large tree branch as far away from the water as he could get. Muscle memory took over to make his work swift and precise. The meat fell neatly from the carcass into the sling. It was good that he didn't have to concentrate on the work because his mind continued to spin over all that happened.

The hike back to the truck was uneventful. At the truck, Jax removed his tattered overalls and donned the swimming trunks (always packed just in case he needed to go swimming) and the shirt he kept in the truck to use as a rag. Now more fully clothed, he rinsed the meat with fresh water from the 5-gallon jug in the truck bed and packed it in the first cooler. He covered the meat with ice from the second cooler. Jax let his mind wander as he carried out the familiar tasks, relieved that things seemed to be returning to normal.

He thought to himself, *How the heck did I float in the air? There wasn't enough wind or storm to pick me up and keep me floating.* He wasn't burned by the lightning that coursed through him. He didn't lose any fingers or toes. And somehow – *somehow* – he connected with that boar and snuffed out its life with just a thought! Ok, that was an accident, but it still happened!

Jax figured that the strange blooming moss must have had something to do with everything that happened. He took it out now and stared at it in his hand. The flowers looked innocent enough on their bed of green. Curiosity urged him to bring the index finger of his other hand over to poke at the moss and as his two hands neared each other... the flowers brightened! A spark flew off his fingertip and traced the flower petals. It felt like he was drawing power from the foliage, but neither the moss nor the flowers looked drained or weaker. His senses and mind were jumbled, and he jerked his hand back swiftly, stuffing the moss and flowers back into his pocket. A little shower of sparks cascaded onto the ground at his feet as he wiped his hands off on his thighs. They smoked as they landed in the wet soil.

"That's enough!" Jax shouted indiscriminately at the sparks as he used his shoes to quench them.

Jax hopped into his truck, threw the engine into gear, and stomped on the gas pedal. He spun the truck around and headed back to town, mud flying behind him. Time to get the boar back to Mamere and Papere. *Maybe Augie can help me figure this out*, Jax thought to himself before turning his full attention to the muddy road in the waning light.

Jax and August had been friends for what seemed like forever. They grew up in the same part of town and went to school together. Both were smart and good students but Augie, as Jax called his friend, cared more about earning good grades than Jax ever did. Augie was supposed to have accompanied Jax on the hunt today, but he'd been called in to work an extra shift at the hospital. He could hear his best friend's voice in his head now.

"Jax," Augie would say, "what have you gotten yourself into now? Don't you know you shouldn't go hunting alone?"

Jax smiled at the scolding he imagined Augie giving him. He knew that Mamere and Papere would agree if they knew he'd gone hunting without his best friend. Hunting alone was a bad decision. Just look at where that kind of decision making had gotten him today. The imaginary scolding was crowded out of his mind by the thought of delicious boudin.

As he reached the edge of town, Jackson's smile got bigger and bigger. It had been quite a day.

2

Genesis

Mamere sat on the front porch in her old rocking chair. She loved to sit on the porch in that chair, it was her source of renewal. When she needed to rest, she sat there. When she needed to talk, she sat there. When she was angry and needed to calm down, she sat there. When she needed entertainment, she sat there. And in times like these, when she needed to think long and hard about something, well, everyone knew where to find her. The high stone wall surrounding Mamere's front garden shielded her from passersby on her side of the street unless they walked past the arched gate, but she could see the people walking on the opposite side of the street. She watched them as they passed by. Some of them looked pressed for time, some acted friendly, and a very few of them were rude.

Such was the pattern today. Mamere chewed a bit and spat into a cup. It wasn't lady-like to chew tobacco or spit. Not that it particularly concerned her . . . she was her own woman and did what she saw fit. She chewed and spat again. The street had been full earlier, but the storm chased everyone else inside. Now that the clouds were rolling away, a few souls again braved the street. She was waiting for Jax and Augie.

Were she not waiting for the boys to come home, she wouldn't be out on the porch today either. The weather was very peculiar. What started out as a fairly normal rainstorm had twisted on its side and produced some unusually heavy lightning over the Bayou. It wouldn't surprise her if Jax, Augie, and every hog nearby, were waiting out the storm under some sort of protective cover. Mamere wondered if the boys would just come home and try again tomorrow instead of wasting time in this weather.

She rocked slowly in her chair. Quietly pondering everything, she waited to either congratulate the boys on their hunting success or, should they come home empty-handed, offer consolation. As she waited, she chewed her tobacco and spat occasionally into the cup. Jax was her grandson. Her only daughter, Janetta, had given birth to him when she was far too young, and she faltered under the weight of responsibility. Janetta wasn't very strong. She fought for a while to live up to her personal expectations in raising Jax, but the same decision-making habits that got her pregnant before she was "ready" simply continued to haunt her. So Mamere raised him.

Jax was a beautiful baby. He was all rolls and smiles. He cooed, cuddled, and only cried when it was really truly necessary. Everybody loved him. Mamere could sit him down on a blanket and tell him to "wait there." Then she could walk away to cook, clean, or whatever and when she came back, well he would still be sitting there on the blanket playing happily with his toys.

Janetta would visit occasionally. Mamere listened as her daughter cuddled Jax and talked wistfully about being his mama. At first, she tried to believe Janetta was sincere, but time after time she left without him. Mamere just kept on raising her grandson. He was so full of love and such a wonderful baby that she never felt he was a burden. Her heart just grew bigger and their bond just grew stronger. Bishop, Mamere's husband and Janetta's father, knew immediately that Janetta wouldn't stay to raise Jax. He loved his daughter but wanted what was best for everyone. From the day Jax was born, he decided the boy was his own. He was content to wait until Mamere and Janetta came around to see the truth as he did – that Jax belonged with him and Mamere. Whether or not that ever happened, Jax would still flourish in the love from Mamere and Papere.

Mamere just about decided she was done waiting when she heard the familiar grumble of Jax's truck. She saw the truck pass by the front gate and noticed the soiled tarp tossed in the bed of the truck next to the coolers – that told her the hunt was successful! She watched until he turned down the alley at the end of the block to park in the driveway at the back of the house. Though she was anxious to get everything ready and start cooking the boar, she continued to sit patiently on the front porch and wait for Jax.

Jax pulled up and hopped lightly out of the truck. Hoping that Mamere would still be sitting on the porch waiting for him, he vaulted the back stairs and tore through the house. He burst through the front screen door to greet her. Static electricity sizzled as his lips lightly brushed her cheek. Mamere drew back in surprise and almost swallowed her chew. "Ouch! Watch what you're doing Jackson!" She wondered again, like many times before, how anyone as large as he was could move so lightly and quickly.

"Sorry, Mamere. Just a little static. Must be the storm. Have you been waiting long?" Jax asked. He put one big hand on the back of the rocking chair and gave it a little push.

"Nah. But I thought that storm might have spoiled your hunting trip," Mamere said.

"Almost! Had to chase that boar further than expected, but he tuckered out," Jax answered. He was hot and sweaty from the day's exertions and Mamere wrinkled up her nose at him.

"Whew" Mamere exclaimed! "You go unload that meat and get showered. You sure need some freshening up." She paused for a moment, squinted against the sun and reached up to brush his hair away from the side of his head. "And what have you done to your hair?" she asked.

Jax smiled uncomfortably. "Oh, just thought I'd try a new style," he said quickly. "I'll go get showered, but first I need to let Augie know the feast is on!"

"Augie didn't go with you?" she asked, frowning. "That wasn't smart Jax," she stated, using Augie's nickname for Jackson.

Jax ducked his head, knowing he was being scolded. Mamere usually only called him "Jax" if he was in trouble. "Sorry Mamere. Augie got called and had to go in to work at the last second – and I just couldn't disappoint."

She sighed heavily. "You get that meat inside and get yourself cleaned up before Papere gets home," she instructed.

Jax gave her another quick peck on the cheek and did as he was told. Unless he wanted a more detailed and thorough scolding, he wouldn't call Augie until after he was done unloading and cleaning up. Jax smiled while he worked. Mamere could never bring herself to really unleash on him. He was sure he probably deserved it far more often than it ever happened, but she was too tender hearted to do it. *Thank goodness Papere was around to lick some sense into me when it was really necessary,* he thought to himself.

Mamere waited on the porch while Jax unloaded the meat and carried it inside. She rocked and spat a few more times before she got up to sashay into the house. She moved surely and confidently, with the easy grace of a woman comfortable and secure in the knowledge that she was a fantastic cook. There was a wedding feast waiting for her to work some magic.

After unloading, Jax took his shirt off to wash the bed of the truck down, then turned the hose on himself. He rinsed off most of the dirt and was cleaner, but still dripping wet, when he went back inside the house. He snatched a box from Mamere's well-stocked mud room before going upstairs to his bedroom to call Augie. He really wanted to get his best friend's thoughts on everything that happened today, but first he needed to do something with the moss and flowers.

Once safely in his bedroom, he dug the foliage out of his pocket and placed it in the box. Finding a good hiding place in his room might not be easy. Right now, the flowers looked innocent, but he didn't trust them to stay that way. He tried stuffing the box in the back of his dresser drawer under his socks but that seemed too obvious. He toyed briefly with the idea of putting it under his pillow but almost immediately decided against it – *what if Mamere strips the bed*? Scanning the room, he finally decided to hide the box in the space above the blades of the ceiling fan next to the down rod. He stood on the bed and stuffed it up there, spinning the blades to make sure they'd move freely without dislodging the box. He hopped down off the bed and stepped back to look up at the fan and saw that the light effectively hid the box. Nodding his head in approval, he turned to the next task and reached for his discarded shirt to dig in the pocket for his cell phone.

Unexpectedly, as his hand got closer to the device, a small, but intensely powerful spark sprang from his fingers. Without thinking, he jerked his hand back. He could feel energy building up in his fingers and hand so he dropped the phone and shirt onto the bed and curled his hand into a fist, hoping that would control the erratic energy burst. He set his mind on not damaging anything in the room – including himself. He decided not to use his cell phone and went downstairs to use the old phone hanging on the wall in the hallway; if he was going to blow up a phone it needed to be this old one.

He punched in his best friend's phone number. After a few short rings, a recording prompted Jackson to leave a message. Augie was still at work. "Augie, it's Jax. Call on my home phone when you can. We've got to talk." Jax ended the call and went back upstairs to his bedroom.

Back in the privacy of his room, he looked at his arms, expecting to see a small network of scabs and scratches from being cut by the still. His skin glowed with health. He looked all over but couldn't find any evidence of being cut or even scratched. He remembered the blood dripping from his arm and how it glowed with light. His mouth dropped open in surprise. There wasn't a mark on him!

He looked for the scrape on his shin he got last week when he was chucking lumber. That too was gone. He flexed and looked for every recent scratch and bruise . . . all gone. There were no old injuries on his body. He couldn't even find a jagged toenail. Confused about his newfound good health, he scratched himself lightly with a fingernail. No mark. Not so unusual. He dug around in his desk drawer for something sharp. He was sure the needle Mamere gave him years ago when she tried to teach him to sew on a button was still back there somewhere. He found it and poked the tip of his finger. A bright spot of blood welled up immediately and he sighed with relief. He wiped the tip of his finger with a tissue and put the needle back in the drawer. He didn't notice the subtle glow of light above the ceiling fan, didn't notice the tingling in his fingertip as an unknown energy healed the tiny mark.

His major chores done for the day, there was time on his hands. Jax would normally be at work but he'd taken a few days off before and after the wedding. He worked at the local lumber yard and the manager was a friend from high school so getting his schedule free was fairly easy. He paced back and forth in his small bedroom as he mulled over the events of the day in his head.

He remembered brushing his arms off in the clearing and seeing small sparks rain down from the contact of flesh against flesh but when he gutted the boar there was nothing out of the ordinary. When he kissed Mamere there was that small shock of static electricity, but he bathed without incident. Not being able to use the cell phone might prove problematic. None of this made any sense to him. He checked out his hair in the mirror. He kind of liked the jagged accent. He ran a big hand roughly through his hair and noticed a tingle of electricity when his fingers brushed his scalp. It was invigorating and frustrating at the same time.

"Jackson!" Papere called from the bottom of the stairs. "Come here and tell me about this boar."

"Yes sir" he answered. He paused a moment to get his thoughts in order before bounding lightly down the stairs to greet his grandfather. Papere was a hard worker. He loved to see a job completed correctly and done well and instilled those same desires in Jax. He tried to raise Jax to be a gentleman and loved to hear the comments of his buddies when they saw his grandson holding a door open for a lady or carrying something for somebody. They also liked to talk with Jax because he always spoke with respect.

Jax met Papere at the bottom of the stairs with a brief bear hug, drawing back quickly as he sensed surging static electricity.

"Nice haircut, Jax," Papere said. "That's a mighty fine boar in there." Jax could hear the satisfaction in his grandfather's voice. Papere paused.

"But I also heard you went without Augie." Jax heard the edges of disappointment deepen in the older man's voice.

"Yes, sir. Sorry," apologized Jax. "It just sort of . . . happened." He shrugged his shoulders.

"That was foolish. You know better than to hunt alone." Papere grunted. "But looks like you didn't hurt yourself," he admitted.

Jax listened quietly while Papere scolded him. He didn't realize he was holding his breath until the air whistled out between his lips. He was relieved Papere didn't seem very angry with him and vowed to himself not to disappoint his grandfather again. Jax shifted their attention back onto the boar.

"You think it'll do for the wedding?" Jax asked.

"It's sure to be the best feast we've seen in quite some time. And Evie will be the most beautiful bride the city's ever seen," Papere continued. Jax nodded his head vigorously, agreeing wholeheartedly.

Everyone called Evangeline "Evie." Jax loved that girl like a sister. When they were little, Evie's mother dropped by one day and asked Mamere to babysit. From the moment Evie arrived, Jax acted as if she was *his* baby. After that first day, they were mostly inseparable. Mamere offered to watch Evie whenever it was needed, and her mother was keen to take her up on the babysitting offer. Mamere treated Jax and Evie as if they were true brother and sister.

Summer after summer, Evie and Jax spent their time racing down sidewalks, swimming in every body of water they could find, and climbing trees. As might be expected, everything evolved into playful competitions. Over time, both grew up lean and strong. In contrast, their appearances were quite different: Jax's skin always darkened under the summer sun to a smooth, rich chocolate hue, while Evie's remained the color of a delicious, lightly colored mocha latte. Both of their heads were covered with curls but Jax's hair hung in both tight and loose coils, while Evie's cascaded around her face in irresistibly soft ringlets.

During high school, Jax and Evie took different paths when it came to dating members of the opposite sex. Jax only dated a few girls, while Evie lost count of her many boyfriends. Whenever they felt they really liked this one or the other one, they would bring the prospective sweetheart for approval. No boyfriend or girlfriend continued in a relationship if they didn't pass muster. Once Evie started dating Franklin, though, she made sure that Jax met him.

Franklin was the only one that Jax liked immediately. At every turn, Franklin treated Evie with respect, and Jax thought that the way he spoke to her was like listening to an accomplished musician play beautiful music. Franklin chose his words carefully, and the word "love" frequently seemed to find its way into the conversation. Jax could clearly see why Evie chose to love Franklin. At first though, neither Jax nor Evie imagined she and Franklin would become man and wife in the near future.

His thoughts were interrupted by the slamming of the screen door. "Jax!" Evie's familiar voice rang out as she came through the kitchen. She stopped only long enough to plant a kiss on Mamere's cheek. "Is this my wedding feast or just a little something Mamere's whipping up for you?" asked Evie.

"Rehearsal done already, Cher'"?" asked Mamere. "Yes ma'am," she replied. "And I'm starved."

"Evie, whatever Mamere's cooking is yours! It could be escargot, etouffee, or fried worms. As long as Mamere's fixing it, it's *your* feast" he replied.

Evie continued through the kitchen and greeted Papere in the hallway with a hug. "There you are old man! I've been waiting for my hug all day!" Papere's arms went around her slim figure and held her tightly.

"Young lady, my arms have been empty until this very moment, just waiting. Thank goodness you came when you did so I wouldn't have to keep reaching for the ceiling to hug Jax," Papere said with a smile as she buried her face in his shoulder.

Evie released him and turned to Jax with a smile. "Thank you for my wedding feast!" Then she noticed his hair. "Wow! Nice, uh . . . haircut! You trying something new?" Though she tried to hide it, Evie struggled for the right words to describe Jax's "new" hair.

"Yup. You like it?" he asked. He watched her squirm politely, knowing full well she didn't really like it. But it wasn't as if he'd *paid* for the cut.

Hesitating, Evie tilted her head to the side and looked at him for a moment before nodding and saying, "it's different. I would have never taken you for a guy who wanted to have designs cut into his hair. But hey . . . it suits you!" As Evie's voice trailed off, Jax sensed something curious in her polite but stunned tone.

"As for the boar, it's my pleasure," he grinned. "I get to eat it too, you know." Jax opened his mouth, then shut it before he could blurt out anything else. He was dying to confide in her about the unusual events of the day, but he clearly saw that now was not the time. And he didn't want to worry his grandparents about something he couldn't yet explain. As occasionally happened, Evie and Papere had already tuned Jax out completely. They were deep in conversation about the barbeque bachelor dinner Franklin's family would serve tonight. When it came to barbeque, they were local legends.

Jax's focus and attention wandered as the conversation shifted and was now about ceremony details, the wedding dress, and the current bridesmaid drama – not his favorite topics of discussion. Besides, he suspected that Evie was trying to play Cupid between him and one of the bridesmaids – *any* one of the bridesmaids. It didn't seem to matter to Evie which one of the girls it was, just so long as he was romantically entwined with one of her friends. He wasn't interested in any of them. Nevertheless, he let the young bride have her little intrigue as sort of a wedding present. He would be a perfect gentleman, but he would be sure not to let any of the girls think he was serious about them. That kind of drama almost always seemed to end with someone's feelings getting hurt.

In the bigger picture, Jax wasn't ready for a serious relationship with anyone right now. He'd graduated from high school last year, was working in the lumber yard, and was trying to figure out what he wanted to do about college. His plate was already full.

"Jax!" exclaimed Evie, giving him a nudge and jolting him back to the present company. "Are you even listening?"

"Sorry, Evie, I was thinking about something else," he apologized.

"Umhumm. I need you to be all smiles and good manners tonight at Franklin's," Evie cooed.

"Of course! Is there anything else, your highness?" he asked, sketching a quick bow toward her.

"Not yet, but when there is, I'll be SURE to let you know," she replied, holding out her left hand for him to kiss.

He grabbed her hand and brushed his lips on her fingertips, the static shock at the touch caused her engagement band to glow and she pulled her hand back with a small gasp of surprise. "Jax! That hurt!" she exclaimed. "Are you rubbing your shoes on the carpet or something?"

"No. But it seems like I've been getting shocked all day," he replied.

Evie hesitated at first but overcame her small fear to give him a hug, kissed Papere, and then headed toward the kitchen. "Well," she called over her shoulder to Jax, "I always knew you had an electric personality."

"Ouch! Couldn't be any cheesier!" replied Jax.

In the kitchen, the two women consulted briefly before Evie left to prepare for the bachelor dinner. Jax and Papere watched her leave. Papere shook his head and smiled while Jax seemed unusually absorbed in his own thoughts. Papere headed into the kitchen to help Mamere and Jax retreated to sit down on the bench in the hallway by the phone. He picked up the newspaper nonchalantly and pretended to read while he waited for Augie to return his call.

3

Growing Pains

As the day wore on the phone remained silent. Jax decided he couldn't wait in the hallway any longer for Augie to call back. He'd stared at the newspaper headlines without even reading them. As the last flicker of sunlight faded, he turned on the nearby lamp. It was almost time for him to get ready for the bachelor dinner. Before climbing the stairs to his room to put on a nice shirt, he popped his head into the kitchen to be sure Mamere didn't need any help. As always, she had everything under control.

Upstairs, buttoning up his dinner shirt, he checked his look in the mirror. *Perfect*, he thought. Satisfied with what he saw, Jax turned to the next task. As a precautionary measure, he fished a bandana out of his dresser drawer, wrapped it around the cell phone, and gingerly picked it up. Jax was relieved that there wasn't any kind of shock between his body and the cell phone. He figured a layer of anything, even that flimsy cloth, couldn't hurt.

No shock, he thought again with a sense of relief.

In the back of his mind, he was hoping that Augie'd get out of work early enough to meet him at Franklin's for a short chat before most of the guests arrived. Since they were both ushers at the wedding, they were both invited to the bachelor dinner.

Ready, Jax headed down the stairs again and toward the kitchen. He and Mamere almost bumped into each other in the hallway as she left the kitchen.

"My, my, my, Cher"; you're sure gonna turn some heads tonight! Which girl does Evie want you to court?" Mamere asked playfully.

Jax blushed in response. "I don't know, but it doesn't really matter. Tonight, I'll be a gentleman, not a suitor. This week is all about Evie and Franklin. I'm just window dressing."

"You'll just make those girls hungrier!" said Mamere as she smoothed the nonexistent wrinkles from his shirt and gave him a small push. "You go on ahead; Papere and I will be along shortly."

Jax noticed that he wasn't shocked when she touched his shirt; that was good. Maybe he'd imagined it. Maybe he'd imagined *everything*. Maybe the world hadn't taken an odd, supernatural type slant and everything was just fine. He took a deep breath and smiled. Despite Evie's attempt to link him romantically with someone – anyone – he was still looking forward to the evening's dinner. He headed out the door and climbed into his truck.

Living in a small town meant everything was in close proximity, people included, and it only took a few minutes to make the short trip to Franklin's. Franklin was older than Evie, Jax, and Augie, but they'd all known each other since elementary school. They didn't share the same groups of friends but that hadn't mattered much. It was an easy choice for Franklin to ask Jax and Augie to be ushers at his wedding. Long before the final turn to Franklin's parents' house, Jax caught whiffs of the barbeque; it was almost enough to push him over the edge from "hungry" to "famished." Jax was glad that as members of the bride's entourage, he and Augie would be free to mingle and enjoy the party without having to do much work. Jax spotted Franklin by the barbeque pit right away, picking up wood to build up the fire.

"Something smells fantastic!" hollered Jax as he walked up the driveway.

A big grin spilled over Franklin's face as he turned from the smoker and unexpectedly wrapped Jax in a bear hug. Jax held back at first, afraid of another shock. Only when everything felt normal did he wholeheartedly return Franklin's hug and pat him on the back.

The smell of smoked meat hung heavily in the air and Jax's stomach grumbled. Franklin heard the hungry muttering and said, "Buddy, we'd better get you a snack before dinner!" Franklin pointed over his shoulder to a table that was littered with burnt ends from already carved meat. "Help yourself!"

Jax nudged past the dog sleepily "guarding" the table, picked up a piece of juicy brisket, and popped it into his mouth. The meat was so tender it almost melted in his mouth before he could chew it. Savoring the smoky flavors, he marveled at Franklin's skill. *He sure knows how to barbeque!* thought Jax. The family reputation for phenomenal barbeque would be upheld tonight. Jax grabbed another piece of meat and toyed briefly with the idea of confiding in Franklin about his unusual morning, but before he could utter a single word Jax was surprised by a slap on the back. He tightened his hold on the slippery piece of moist brisket and turned to see Augie grinning at him. "Augie! I've been trying to reach you." Jax said.

"Jax, man. Good to see you. By the time I got a minute to call you, Mamere said you'd already left" he replied. "How'd the hunt go?"

"Success!" beamed Jax. "But did I get in trouble for hunting alone." The two of them turned their attention back to Franklin. "How're you holding up?" Jax asked Franklin.

"Man. I'm glad all I have to do is show up dressed nice and carrying a ring! Getting married is one thing, having a wedding adds an exquisite layer of stress that I never suspected," confided Franklin. "All I know is, at the other end of the wedding I'll have the smartest, most beautiful woman as my bride!"

Jax and Augie nodded in agreement as Franklin pardoned himself from the conversation to greet and shake hands with other friends and family members who were just arriving. Grinning at each other and gazing around at nearby guests, Jax and Augie picked up a couple more pieces of brisket and took seats near a fan at one of the outer tables. The entire yard was magnificently decorated. A large tent was erected to protect guests against the threat of rain; small tables – laden with barbeque meats and all the fixings – were casually arranged around a larger table. A bridal party table reigned over the scene at one end of the tent, easily identified by an elegantly draped, wine-colored tablecloth that surely brought a smile to Evie's eyes (wine was one of her favorite colors). As the two of them took it all in, a refreshing breeze stirred and caused the cloth to flutter slightly as it pushed aside some of the humidity.

Jax leaned in, eager to tell his friend what happened that morning, but before he could say anything, they were interrupted by three of Evie's bridesmaids. They stood up to greet the young women and invited them to sit down.

Nearby, one of Franklin's sisters was flitting from table to table with a box of matches, she was lighting candles and putting the final touches on decorations. Evie called her away before she made it over to light the candle in the middle of their table.

While the girls made casual conversation with Augie, Jax let his mind wander. He became acutely aware of the storm building behind the ominous threat of rain. The escalating turbulence caused his skin to tingle. Trying to relax, he leaned back in his chair and focused on Augie as he entertained the girls with some kind of story. He raised his arms, unbalancing himself on the flimsy chair's unstable footing in the grass lawn. Quickly, Jax reached over and grabbed Augie's shoulder to keep him from falling. They heard a loud "snap" as static electricity flared and shocked them both.

"Ouch!" Augie yelped. "Why did you pinch me?" "Sorry. Your chair almost toppled over," Jax replied.

Augie blushed as the girls watched and giggled. Jax could understand why the girls wanted to chat with his friend. Per Evie, Augie wasn't just fun to talk to, he was also "easy on the eyes." Augie's blonde hair and blue eyes stood in stark contrast to Jax's dark hair and eyes. Though equally matched in height and speed, Augie was more lithe. Both displayed good manners, but when it came to competing athletically, they enjoyed a friendly, ruthless passion for winning.

Augie said, "Well then. Thank you," and turned back to finish his conversation, unfazed by the interruption.

Jax coughed nervously as he fiddled with the unlit candle on the table. The energy he felt building in his body made him very uneasy. Augie glanced over at Jax when he coughed and clearly saw a spark leap from Jax's finger and light the candle wick. He gasped, and Jax met his gaze as thunder rumbled in the distance. Augie whistled softly.

Hoping to rescue the moment, Jax whispered, "I've been meaning to tell you about my hunting trip this morning."

Augie raised his eyebrows and tilted his head, "Not your average, every day, hunting trip?" he asked.

"You could say that," replied Jax. He stood and said, "Excuse me, ladies." Augie also stood and excused himself. The girls responded in light-hearted tones but couldn't hide the disappointment in their faces as the two young men moved off.

The guests gathered in the tent started finding their places in anticipation of the coming feast and toasting festivities. In the midst of it all, Jax felt chaotic energy pressing in on him; the increasing pressure seemed to be in direct correlation to the building storm. Augie noticed his friend was acting nervously; a very unusual thing for Jax. Hoping to give Jax a moment to recover, he steered him behind the now vacant barbeque pit. They stood in silence and listened to the muted noises of people chatting in the tent and the tantalizing sizzle of fat as it dripped onto hot embers in the pit.

Then, without warning, Jax blurted out the beginnings of his incredible day. "I chased the hog into a clearing that held an old still," Jax began without preamble. Once he started talking, he couldn't stop the whole story from spilling out of him. Though completely flummoxed by Jax's words, Augie listened without interrupting. Augie snorted in disbelief when Jax mentioned his blood looking like liquid light. Unfazed by any of Augie's reactions, Jax kept right on talking, his words tumbling over each other. Jax held nothing back as he unloaded the story, one incredible detail at a time.

As he talked, rain started to fall gently. Both sought shelter by moving closer to the barbeque pit and under the small eave that extended past the covered patio.

"I just don't know what to make of it," Jax concluded, catching his breath from speaking so fast for several minutes.

For a few moments, Augie stood in silence. Then, shaking his head with a puzzled look on his face, he drew a breath as if preparing to speak.

Before he could utter a single word, Jax started to glow! The storm's energy awakened the latent energy within him, and it could no longer remain dormant. Rivers of light coursed through every artery and vein in Jax's body. Each flash of distant lightning made Jax's body glow more intensely. Unexpectedly, his body lifted off the ground; he was floating in air! A shimmering sphere of energy, limned with a hyper opacity, enveloped Jax. His senses became acutely aware of different energy sources and levels of power around him.

Augie was knocked over by the surging powers and started to fall; Jax immediately reached out to catch him, but the power emanating from him pushed his friend further away. Jax was stunned! He instinctively reached out with his mind and "touched" Augie's energy source. Jax's efforts allowed him to cradle his friend with his thoughts and cushion him from impact with the ground.

Now fully connected to Augie, Jax felt the power between them strengthening. Energy drained out of Augie and into Jax. Intuitively fearing that the boar's fate would befall his friend, Jax yanked his thoughts away from Augie with a flinch, as if he'd been slapped. Augie was tossed gently to the ground without ceremony; knees wobbling, eyes wide, and mouth hanging completely open.

Although Jax's body no longer siphoned energy from Augie, the power within him continued to expand. Smoke rose from his skin as his body temperature increased. Instinctively, he raised his arm, and a vivid bolt of lightning sprang from his hand and was thrown high into the sky. It bounced in the atmosphere above him before skittering across the horizon with explosive force. Shaken and drained after the release of energy, the shimmering border disappeared and Jax, too, dropped to the ground. Augie, in a state of shock from all he'd seen and felt, simply stared. Inexplicably, Jax could "read" the energy levels within Augie's body though swirls of energy hid the expression on his face.

The crowd in the tent peeked timidly out at the storm. With the simultaneous flash of lightning and roll of thunder they knew the bolt had struck close- by. From the relative safety of the tent the partygoers couldn't see Jax and Augie under the overhang. The carving table next to the barbeque pit had been caught in the energy bubble alongside Jax. Now, it was little more than a smoking, twisted, unusable pretzel of plastic and metal. The carving knife that was previously on the table was white hot and curiously driven into the side of the barbeque pit. Fumes from the burnt plastic stung Jax's and Augie's eyes, forcing them to move away.

"Wow," was all Augie could manage to say for a moment. "Are you ok?"

"I'm not sure," Jax replied as he brushed at the rain dappling his arms and sparks sprinkled the earth at his feet. Augie sucked in his breath at the sight. He reached out to touch Jax's shoulder and heard a loud "snap!" as he was rewarded with a shock.

"Ouch!" yelped Augie. "You're smoking."

"Oh yeah. And you've got to watch out for shocks for a while" Jax cautioned.

"What are you going to do?" asked Augie.

Jax gave him a half-smile. "Haven't figured that out yet, but maybe I'll have to avoid thunderstorms."

Still acutely aware of the energy around him he said, "I think this little squall is weakening." He stomped his foot on the ground and a surge of energy lit the ground under his foot, singeing the grass. "It should be safe to rejoin the party now." They tried to walk nonchalantly back to the tent and were rewarded by remaining largely unnoticed by everyone; everyone, that is, except Evie, who openly frowned at them when the two disheveled men sat down. She whispered in Franklin's ear before casually moving among the guests, making small talk and greeting friends at various tables as she sashayed across the tent.

By the time she reached them, disappointment was a distant memory and her eyes once again sparkled with happiness. "This storm is a little bit of excitement!" she exclaimed. "You know, I love a storm, but this needs to end tonight so everything isn't ruined tomorrow."

"It wouldn't dare rain on your wedding," Jax replied as he stood to plant a kiss gingerly on her cheek. He stopped short of actually touching her to avoid a spark. Augie stood up quickly and mimed brushing Jax aside, planting a kiss firmly on Evie's cheek. "Hello beautiful," he greeted her, "nice party. Your fiancé sure knows how to barbeque. I hear his Asian-style barbeque is just as good."

"Better," she replied as she glanced over her shoulder at Franklin, appreciating the way his father's American features blended with his mother's classic Chinese traits. "I'm not just marrying him for his good looks, the man can cook! Looks like you two aren't mingling very much," she prompted, giving them both a little pout. "The girls will be disappointed."

"I thought that was all about Jax," replied Augie with a grin.

"No way, man!" interjected Jax. "We are in this thing together. "

Jax paused dramatically for effect and captured Evie's eyes with his own before continuing. "Everyone gets a dancing partner, and everyone goes home happy . . . and alone."

4

Nightmare

Augie and Jax got through the rest of the evening without further incident. They asked each other questions neither one could answer. Their conversation lagged when Jax realized Augie wouldn't be able to give him any insight or reassurance that the world wasn't just suddenly wilder and more twisted. Girls wandered in and out of their little huddle all evening long. Some of the braver girls sat with them at the table to chat; others just smiled shyly at them from across the tent. The stereo system, wrapped in plastic to protect it from the storm, gave Jax a reprieve from dancing. The last two women who stopped to visit were bridesmaids that left abruptly when the maid of honor swept by and whispered conspiratorially to them. Soon after, Evie said her good-byes and left with a gaggle of giggling women. Rumors were whispered about a bachelorette party that featured late night spa treatments.

When the rest of the guests started leaving, Augie and Jax got up to help clear the tables and stack the chairs. They walked toward the kitchen to pitch in, but Franklin's mother just stood in front of the door and thanked them politely for the work already done. She said the women would do the washing up but asked if they would help Franklin tidy up the barbeque pit. Not really wanting to get involved with the whole soap suds and dishes thing they quickly agreed and left the kitchen clean-up in her capable hands. They wandered across the yard to the barbeque pit.

"Do you see this?" Franklin queried, pointing to the table when he noticed them. He was standing with his hands on his hips, staring incredulously at the carving table.

Jax and Augie stood awkwardly and stared at the misshapen table. Augie pointed to the knife still sticking out of the barbeque pit and said, "I'm more interested in that!"

Franklin turned and saw the knife for the first time. He whistled long and slow. "I guess we know what the lightning hit. Thank goodness no one got hurt." He shook his head and tried to pull the knife out, but it was stuck fast. "Guess I'm no King Arthur!" he said, giving up. "The table is a total loss."

Jax motioned Franklin to step back, then took a step toward the knife and kicked the flat of it with the bottom of his foot. The motion snapped the knife off cleanly, sending the hilt skittering harmlessly across the patio. Then he grabbed a log from the pile of wood and rammed it down against the blade on the inside of the pit. Watching the blade fall into the red-hot embers distracted both Augie and Franklin; they didn't notice the faint glow starting to build in the log as Jax held it. Jax drained as much excess energy into the log as he dared before dropping it into the embers to burn in the pit.

"Nice," said Franklin. "Guess I'll need to take the table to the dump when we get back from the honeymoon. You get enough to eat? Did either of you make a *love* connection?" he asked jokingly, rolling his eyes and drawing quotes in the air as he asked.

Augie snorted and Jax coughed. "No," replied Jax. "But Evie sure is enjoying this little intrigue she's whipped up."

"Maybe it's her way of not going bananas with the stress of the wedding," suggested Franklin. "I'm glad you know her well enough not to be offended."

"Did you really cancel your bachelor party?" Augie asked."

More like I told my best man not to organize one. Throwing the wedding party is stressful enough without the prospect of attending the wedding at less than my best. I want to remember what happens," laughed Franklin.

Augie and Jax exchanged questioning glances. "So, how will you spend your last night as an unmarried man?" asked Jax.

"I'm going to bed early to try to get some rest," he answered. "I've got one gorgeous bride to wake up for in the morning and big honeymoon travel plans!" Franklin clapped Augie on the back and smiled over at Jax. "Don't be late tomorrow," he finished. They watched Franklin walk back to the house. By now, they were the last ones standing in the yard. All that remained of the party was the deliciously smoky, heavy fragrance of barbeque clinging to the tent flaps.

"He's probably a better man than I'll ever be," Augie observed. He started to say something else, then stopped. "Jax, there's too much to digest all at once. See you tomorrow, buddy."

They shook hands and both were glad when neither received a shock. Augie jogged off to his car and Jax walked back to his truck. A few hours earlier at dinner, Jax spoke briefly with Mamere and Papere, but even they were already gone. When Jax got home he got out of the truck and stood quietly outside the house. He watched his grandparents' shadows as they moved together in the kitchen, as if they were doing some sort of culinary dance. They worked seamlessly to finish preparing for the wedding feast. He grew up watching them, and could see in the ways they spoke to each other and treated one another that love, tenderness, and respect permeated their relationship. It was the same way Franklin and Evie treated each other. He hoped that someday he would find that kind of partner for himself.

He wasn't standing there long before they turned out the lights and walked through the house to their bedroom. Jax entered the kitchen and crept to his own bedroom without disturbing them. He closed the door and took the box down from its hiding place. He was surprised to feel it vibrating slightly. Opening the box, he touched the petals with one finger. The flowers glowed brightly in response to his touch, emitting more light than a night light. He closed the box quickly and tucked it back into its hiding place. All day long he'd unsuccessfully tried to make sense of what happened. Now there were even more things to figure out. He sighed and sat down on the bed.

Fatigue, coupled with the events of the day, quickly overwhelmed him. He laid down, put his head on the pillow, and closed his eyes, falling into a deep sleep almost without transition. But suddenly he was up and running! The grass under his feet was wet with rain and burdened with patches of slick moss. Terrified, he ran faster and slipped in the runoff from the spring by the old still. Jax couldn't see an animal, but he could smell its pungent fear smearing the landscape.

Jax felt like he was choking! He clawed at the base of his neck as he struggled to breathe and gasped for air in the humid bayou. Desperate to survive, he dropped to his knees in the soggy grass and thrust his hands in the little spring to splash water on his face. The cool shock of water helped, but unsteadied him, and he reached out to brace himself on the still. Jagged metal sliced his hand and liquid light pulsed in his blood, pouring out of the cut. His otherworldly blood lit up the flowers and trickled down into the spring. In a flash, the gurgling water quickly doused the glow.

Suddenly, out of nowhere, Evie was there in the nightmare with him. She reached out to grab his hand, but an energy pulse surged from him and tossed her aside like a rag doll! Jax heard a sickening thud as her head struck the ground. He stood, dumbfounded, and stared wide eyed. Paralyzed with fear, he waited for her to stir. He prayed for her to breathe, but she just laid there quietly, deathly still.

He took a step toward her and bridesmaids appeared between them, smiling coyly at him and trying to flirt! Angry that they were in his way, Jax yelled at them to move aside, but they just crowded closer together. Inexplicably, the maids kept multiplying in number until they completely clogged the little meadow, making it impossible for him to reach Evie.

He was afraid to touch them, so he tried to shoo them away with his hands. As he waved his arms, an unexpected brisk breeze filled the small clearing. Magically, the girls turned into butterflies, tossed aside in all directions by the new currents of churning air.

Slightly relieved, Jax took another step toward Evie, but now Augie was there to block his path! Augie was yelling at Jax, but the breeze stiffened and tore the words away before Jax could hear them. Augie stood resolutely blocking the path, not allowing him to reach Evie.

Frustrated and growing increasingly concerned for Evie, Jax held his hands together at chest-level, concentrated, and created a power surge between them. Jax felt energy swirl and build before it became visible. Once visible, the energy started spinning between his hands. He wrestled with the mass. Without explanation, a growing desire to throw the mass of energy at Augie surged deep within him. Tears coursed unchecked down his cheeks as his emotions reigned supreme. Uncertainty and fear blanketed Jax, afraid of what he might do to his friend in his haste to get to Evie.

Now completely torn between the twin prospects of hurting Augie while trying to help Evie, Jax shouted in frustration! Desperate, he launched the ball of energy forcefully into the sky. The violent release spun and whipped the clouds into a dizzying gyration before dancing harmlessly away into the upper atmosphere.

He woke from the nightmare abruptly, sweat soaked and chilled. He was still on top of the covers, fully clothed, in the same spot he'd been when he laid down. His room was eerily lit by pulses of energy emanating through his skin that grew less intense with every passing beat of his heart. Faint plumes of smoke circled the ceiling fan crazily spinning above him. Afraid to move, Jax just laid there, motionless, until the light in him blinked out and the fan slowed. Despite the pleasant breeze created by the fan, Louisiana's familiar humidity pressed down on him, eventually making him so uncomfortable that he got up to bathe.

Jax wanted to linger in the cool shower, hoping the fresh soapy scents would burn off the foggy memory of the nightmare. Now fully awake, he struggled to remember exact details of his bizarre dream. Fractured images and glimpses of uncontrolled power and danger flew at him intermittently, frightening him with their intensity and his inability to command them. Fearing the running water would be heard by Mamere and Papere and wake them, he finished showering hastily.

As Jax dried himself off, the hairs on his arms rose and a nauseating buzzing noise filled his ears that was so intense it made him dizzy. In a frantic attempt to lay his arm hairs back down, Jax rubbed his forearm with a towel. The motion caused sparks to rain down onto the tile floor. Wrapping the towel around his waist, he tried to wait out the power surge. This time, the unrestrained power built in him so quickly that it threatened to throw him to the floor. Grabbing the side of the ceramic sink to keep from falling, the heat coursed through him to the sink and sent tendrils of lightning into the wall. The bathroom lights brightened precipitously, protesting the rapid transfer of energy.

Concerned he might blow the house fuse box, Jax jerked his hand back, then popped open the bathroom window, hoping for a clear path to fire the excess energy at the atmosphere. Lightning flew from his hand and sizzled gloriously across the dark Louisiana sky. Feeling relief as the energy drained, it was possible for Jax to safely touch things again. Still a little wary of the amped up power level within him, he finished drying gingerly and dressed lightly for bed.

With only about an hour left before sunrise, Jax flopped back down, hoping to get a little more rest before getting ready for the wedding festivities. Fortunately, he dozed lightly . . . and dreamlessly.

5

The Wedding

The blaring alarm signaled the start of Franklin and Evie's wedding day. Jax got out of bed and actually felt somewhat, if not completely, rested. Thinking he might be of assistance to Mamere and Papere, Jax went to the kitchen. As usual, his grandparents were way ahead of him. The final touches on the food were done and his grandparents already had most of it packed and ready. There was nothing for him to do here.

"Sit out of the way and eat, Jackson," chirped Mamere as she greeted him halfway across the kitchen. Jax noticed an undeniable cheerfulness in her voice. As she approached Jax, she offered him a plate of food – poached eggs, beignet, and grits – and instructions, "You can help when it's time to load everything and bring it to the reception."

Jax nodded, pausing only long enough to pour himself a large cup of coffee before carrying his breakfast out to the front porch.

"Good morning!" called out Augie, walking jauntily up the side-walk. Augie jealously surveyed Jax's breakfast. "I should have eaten before I came," commented Augie as his stomach growled loudly.

"Nonsense," replied Jax. "You know Mamere would feed you whether you've already eaten or not."

"True," said Augie with a smile. "I was counting on that, and yours looks and smells divine."

"Augie?" Mamere's voice called from the depths of the house. "You already here? Come on and get you a plate of breakfast."

"See?" piped Jax, barely looking up from his breakfast plate.

"Music to my ears!" exclaimed Augie. He took off his suit coat and laid it on the arm of the rocking chair before letting himself into the house. He returned shortly with an identical plate of food and mug of coffee. "This is how mornings should be," sighed Augie as he sat down next to Jax on the top step of the porch.

The boys ate, appreciating the sights and sounds of a Louisiana morning. Last night's storm washed away some of the oppressive humidity, making a glorious morning. Jax sipped his coffee and poked his egg to let the yolk soak into the beignet. The easy companionship of his best friend, the good food, and the familiar sights and sounds of an ordinary morning did more to refresh him than his attempt at sleep last night.

"Are you pregnant?" queried Augie.

"What?!" exclaimed Jax.

"You've got that healthy 'glow' that they say pregnant women have," he replied.

"That's not even funny!" Jax moaned. "You wouldn't believe the night I had," he said as he started explaining last night's dream to Augie. The whole nightmare, waking up to the spinning ceiling fan and glowing room, touching the sink, and even causing lightning to fly from his hand; Jax spilled it all.

As usual, Augie listened intently. They finished their breakfast in silence after Jax stopped talking.

Augie was first to break the silence. "Can I see the flowers?" Augie asked.

Jax nodded yes as they both stood up and took their dirty dishes to the kitchen before heading up the stairs to the now infamous bedroom.

Carefully, Jax removed the box from its elevated hiding place and handed it to Augie. Gingerly, Augie opened the box and peered at the patch of browning moss and flowers that were now wilted.

"These don't look very special," commented Augie as a whiff of rotting flora rose from the box, causing him to wrinkle his nose in disgust.

Jax reached toward the box. A quick jolt of energy leapt from his finger before he could touch them and caused the flowers to change. They became fresh and vital! Some flowers glowed white, some burned an iridescent blue, and the moss became a vibrantly healthy green.

"Now *that* is special!" Augie whistled. He touched them, making the tip of his finger tingle. The bioluminescence faded and the flowers became ordinary white and blue flowers on a bed of green moss. "Wicked cool," he whispered. "When can you take me to see that still?"

"Maybe tomorrow," replied Jax. "Today is too busy. In fact, I need to get dressed."

"Yikes," exclaimed Augie. "I left my suit coat outside. See ya' downstairs." He left to retrieve his coat, stopping by the kitchen to grab a second cup of coffee to drink while he waited on the porch.

Once dressed, Jax met him outside and the two left for the wedding in Augie's convertible. The ceremony would be in a chapel behind the church that they attended all their lives. The pastor that baptized them would be officiating and was known for his brief, but insightful sermons. Jax was looking forward to hearing him preach. Augie parked the car and they sauntered past the main body of the church to the chapel. The path around the church was made of large flat stones that meandered past hundred-year-old trees draped with Spanish moss. The lavender petals of cardinal flowers graced the shady spots and bright orange poppies crept from the shade to stand in full sun. The air was dominated by the heady scent of Sweetbay Magnolia wafting on the small breeze. It was a magical setting for a wedding.

As they entered the chapel, Franklin and his best man were deep in conversation near a bank of candles. The relief and silent plea for help on Franklin's face when he saw his two friends was painfully palpable.

"What's up?" asked Jax as they walked down the aisle toward the huddled men.

"Just in the nick of time!" Franklin greeted them. "Seems my groomsmen decided to celebrate a little too heavily last night and they are prostrating themselves before the porcelain god as we speak. They can't seem to pull themselves away. Would you stand in for them?" he asked, almost pleaded.

"No worries," said Augie. "We'd be happy to help out."

"Sure thing," said Jax. "But their tuxedos won't fit us."

"What you're wearing looks great!" said Franklin. "Here," he said as he handed them each man a pair of dove gray gloves with wine colored stitching and an orange and white boutonniere tied with wine colored ribbon. "Thanks guys. This means the world to me." Suitably accessorized, Jax and Augie busied themselves with their first job, ushering guests to their seats on either the bride's or groom's side of the chapel. Jax was grateful for the gloves as they seemed to provide just enough insulation to keep him from shocking the guests. As they went about their duties, Jax overheard Augie making polite conversation, but his own inner turmoil prevented him from saying anything except to ask, "bride or groom?" to confirm the seating. A deferential nod after leading the guests to their seats completed the conversation. He got a warm hug from Mamere, and Papere clapped him on the back as he seated them.

With a full chapel and only fifteen minutes before "go time," Jax and Augie excused themselves and slipped into a little room off the east side of the chapel where they joined Franklin and his best man. The two original groomsmen were there as well. They looked pathetically wan and reeked of stale booze. The group of young men made small talk and tried to take the edge off Franklin's nervousness by telling each other bad jokes. All were relieved when they finally got the nod from the preacher to enter the chapel and take their positions for the ceremony.

The next hour was a happy blur for Jax. Evie walked down the aisle and accepted Franklin's arm after giving her father a kiss on the cheek. She was the most beautiful bride he'd ever seen. Her brows raised in silent question when she noted the groomsmen substitution, but she quickly forgot about them as she approached the altar with Franklin. The solemn atmosphere of the ceremony was lifted by the pastor's sermon. He caught the congregation off guard, making them chuckle at his humorous insight. Once vows and rings were exchanged, the happy couple faced the audience, full of friends and family, and greeted them as husband and wife for the very first time. Now more than ever before, Jax thought they looked like the perfect couple.

Fortunately, Jax's gloved hands prevented him from shocking the bridesmaid paired with him for the recessional. Once outside the church, the wedding party lined the path and exchanged hugs, handshakes, kisses, and polite conversation with the guests as they exited. Shortly thereafter, the wedding party retired to the well-groomed lawn for pictures. As soon as they could slip away without being missed, Jax and Augie excused themselves from the wedding party to find Mamere and Papere.

Jax gave Mamere another quick hug and brushed the tears from her cheeks with his gloved hand. Before he could turn away from her, he felt Papere's warm embrace. As they visited, Jax's joy for the happy couple was tempered with a vague sense of loss. All things "Evie and Franklin" were forever, instantly and dramatically changed – for the good.

"Ready?" he asked Mamere.

"I was born ready, Cher'" she replied, dabbing at the new tears on her cheeks with a delicate handkerchief. "You boys get yourselves over to the house and load the food. We're gonna have ourselves a feast!"

Dutifully, Augie and Jax hopped into the convertible and made the short trip back to pick up the food. Both thought they couldn't have been hungrier last night when they'd first smelled Franklin's barbeque; but the smell of Mamere's cooking dulled that memory. Augie slapped Jax's hand to keep him from stealing a bite before loading and transport. Jax's stomach grumbled in protest, making him work even faster at getting the feast delivered to the reception.

6

The Reception

Mamere and Papere lingered with Franklin's parents and Evie's mother at the chapel, happily chatting with the wedding party. Mamere liked to visit and was in no hurry to leave. Jax helped her with many parties over the years so he knew exactly what to do. She was confident that, in no time at all, he and Augie would have the buffet table looking as good as any professional caterer could.

Jax and Augie, with Franklin's sisters helping them, wasted no time setting up the reception hall. The empty room was soon redolent with an array of mouth- watering lures. Hovering over Mamere's table of traditional Louisiana dishes, the aromas of crab bisque, green beans covered in garlic sauce, spicy boudin, and pork tenderloin beckoned like siren's songs. Soft white tablecloths and bouquets of white magnolia dotted with orange poppies and tied with wine-colored ribbons completed the elegantly simple details. Everything looked perfect when the guests started filing in to claim their seats.

Mamere and Papere arrived and surreptitiously checked every detail. Pleased with what she saw in the room, Mamere gave each man a kiss on the cheek and took her place with Papere at a small table next to the bridal table. The reception was a happy blur of toasts, impromptu speeches, feasting, and dancing. Augie and Jax were pressed into dancing several times, and by the end of the evening they were worn out. A few of the women had taken their shoes off to dance so they had to be extra attentive to avoid stepping on bare toes. One of them confided to Jax that though the driveway was pretty, the flint and quartz gravel was awful on ankles in high heels. Jax was grateful time and time again for the gloves Franklin had given him. No matter how many women danced with him, his hands were handsomely protected, and no shocks were exchanged.

Once or twice during the party, Jax felt energy start to build, announcing itself with goosebumps that raised the remaining hair on his arms and a cool tingling sensation along his spine. Fortunately, by removing a glove and touching the ground, he was able to effectively drain each power surge. He noticed that the more time he spent on the dance floor, the more frequently he had to "ground" himself. Once, during one of the more powerful surges, Jax intentionally dropped his fork so he could duck down under the table to retrieve it, his primary purpose – to make contact with the ground and drain the power.

Jax's peculiar motion caught Augie's eye. Hoping to understand what was going on, Augie took a much- needed break from dancing and plopped down in the chair next to Jax.

"Don't mean to pry, but what exactly are you doing down there?" Augie asked in a slightly sarcastic tone.

"Simple; draining off some energy," quipped Jax, in a voice so soft and low that only his friend heard.

"Well, you need to be sneakier about it. From over there it looked like you were just avoiding a dance with a pretty girl. That 'fork drop' looked totally contrived," he said.

"It was," Jax agreed. Then he sighed and said, "Man! These women are relentless. I think I've danced more today than I have my whole life. At least they seem to have figured out that I'm not relationship shopping. Have you danced with Evie yet?"

"Yes, and may I say, she is an excellent dancer," replied Augie.

"If you'll excuse me, I need to dance with the bride."

Jax got up and approached the bandleader. He whispered in the musician's ear and handed him a manila envelope decked out with ribbons and a wine- colored bow. The bandleader walked over to Evie and bowed as he handed her the envelope. A puzzled look crossed her face. She recognized Jax's handwriting and looked around the room, her eyes resting briefly on the empty chair next to Augie. Augie raised both hands up in the air and shrugged his shoulders, indicating he knew nothing about the envelope and pointed across the hall toward Jax.

Evie opened the envelope and withdrew the contents; beautifully scored musical notes danced across manuscript paper. She didn't know how to read the music, but she recognized the lyrics immediately and smiled. The bandleader raised his hand and the simple notes of their familiar waltz floated across the hall as Jax crossed the dancefloor to ask the bride for a dance. Evie kissed Franklin on the cheek and accepted Jax's outstretched hand as he led her out onto the dance floor.

Mamere and Papere paused mid-conversation to watch Jax and Evie dancing to the special musical arrangement; they danced perfectly. Mamere remembered the day that song first tumbled out of her. The usually happy Jax was crying brokenly during a thunderstorm. Nothing she tried worked to console him. Exhausted from pacing back and forth with the big toddler, she finally sat down in the rocker with him. She rocked him quietly for a while, just patting him on the back and letting him cry. Still trying to console him, she talked about Jasper, a beautiful place she'd heard about in Canada. Eventually, after she'd run out of things to say, a new, improvised song tumbled out of her. The calming effect of the song was magical, and ever since, both Jax and Evie begged Mamere to sing that song. Over time, the song was dubbed "Jasper's Rain Song," their own, personal lullaby.

Unknown to many, Jax rehearsed with the band in advance, hoping to surprise Evie on her wedding day. "Oohs" and "ahhs" erupted around the tent as, one by one, guests learned the story behind the waltz. Looking at each other with "forever family love," Jax and Evie sang along softly:

Do you think that it's going to
rain?
Is it going to rain
today

Do you think that it's going to rain
today?

—

I don't think that it's going to rain,
Oh no it won't rain
today.
I don't think that it's going to rain today.

—

I don't know why you're crying
When the sky's so
blue.
Could it be that you're trying
To make the clouds cry with you?

—

Oh, stop your
crying!
You can't make it
rain.
You won't make it rain
today.
Stop your crying,
it simply won't rain
today.
I said stop your crying, you
can't make it rain today!

A thunderous flare of cymbals by the drummer concluded the song. As the crowd applauded, Jax lifted Evie up, spun her around, and hugged her closely. Unshed tears of joy filled her eyes as she returned his hug and said, "That is the best present I've ever gotten, Jax, thank you."

Franklin joined them immediately on the dance floor, shook Jax's hand, and reclaimed his bride. As the band played their signature song, the bride and groom danced as if they were the only two in the room.

After the first verse, their parents, Mamere and Papere, and then more couples joined them on the dance floor. Jax meandered back over to Augie, skillfully dodging women who were obviously waiting to be asked to dance.

Augie yawned largely as Jax got to the table, sat down, and "accidentally" swept a fork off the table. As Jax had done several times that evening, he pulled a glove off one hand, and touched the ground to discharge energy as he picked up the fork.

"Tired?" he asked Augie.

"Nope," his friend grinned. "Just trying to deflect another chatty woman. If they *think* I'm tired, they might just pass me by." Augie paused, then continued, "You're making this whole thing a little harder, you know. That present just made you even more eligible to these hopeful young ladies."

"Seriously? Whatever!" Jax shrugged. "Let me know if that 'fatigue' ploy works. I don't know what Evie said to them, but they sure have been persistent. I'm already tired, and we still need to clean up!" sighed Jax with a resigned tone.

"Be sure not to 'invite' any of these women to help! Who knows what they'd read into that!" Augie shuddered.

"Done," replied Jax.

The current song ended, and the best man took the microphone to ask the single men and women to stand on opposite sides of the room. As expected, Evie and Franklin collaborated on tossing the bridal bouquet to the women and the garter to the men. Franklin put on a big show pretending to be jealous when their friends and family whistled at Evie's exposed legs. Then, unplanned, Franklin scooped up Evie and spun her around with her dress hiked up to her knees, giving everyone a better look at his bride's lovely legs. It was impossible for every, young single man in the room to not be jealous of Franklin. Evie was a magnificent catch. Already exhausted from the long day's festivities, Jax and Augie didn't get up to join the men hoping to catch the garter. They just sat quietly, thrilled to not be the center of attention or even part of the happy commotion. Once the bouquet and the garter had been tossed, Franklin and Evie circled the room and spoke with every guest. They thanked everyone for coming and blessing their wedding with their friendship.

Bride and groom then cut their cake, ate the first slice without smearing it on each other's faces, and excused themselves to change into traveling clothes. Just like any other newlywed couple, they were eager to make their escape and start their honeymoon.

It wasn't long before the DJ asked the guests to file out onto the driveway and wave goodbye. Evie and Franklin ran to the car amidst happy cheers and words of encouragement. The best man and the original groomsmen tied cans with twine wrapped in streamers to the rear bumper of Franklin's car and wrote "best honeymoon ever" in shaving cream across the rear window. Jax watched the cans scrape the driveway as the happy couple drove off.

Suddenly he felt like the world switched into "slow motion!" As he watched the car speed away, sparks began to fly from the cans bouncing wildly on the quartz and flint stones. The crowd's enjoyment turned to horror as they watched the streamers catch fire from the flying sparks. Fire crept hungrily up the crepe paper streamers toward the trunk and the tailpipe.

"Evie!" Jax yelled, sprinting toward the car, ripping his gloves off and throwing them to the ground. "Someone call 911!" he shouted to everyone staring in disbelief and shock, hoping someone would make the call. The bride and groom, still unaware of the situation due to their vantage point, smiled and waved back at the crowd as they continued down the drive. The streamers burned madly. Before Jax could reach them, the flames licked the car's newly waxed finish and the melting wax dripped precariously onto the white- hot exhaust pipe.

Jax's perception shifted and energy flows blossomed into rich detail. Instead of burning paper, he saw energy and fire leaping from one fuel-rich pocket to another, like a hound dog following a scent. The burning paper was a lit wick getting closer and closer to a river of unburnt fuel that Jax saw trickling from a pinprick of a hole in the corroded gasoline line above the exhaust pipe. The fuel beckoned to the fire, and he calculated that the flames would reach their destination before he could reach them to turn the car off.

Wild energy rose within Jax, triggered by the danger. He stretched his hand out instinctively toward the car. Pinpricks of energy stung his hand and coalesced into a bright blue ball that danced on his palm before leaping toward the vehicle and exploding on the trunk! The explosion's shock waves extinguished the flames and propelled the car into a frantic spin. Gravel sprayed wildly as Franklin turned out of the spin and brought the car to a skidding halt.

Smoke eddied around the back of the vehicle and curled up from Jax's hand as the shaky passengers climbed out and were surrounded by a concerned and loving crowd. Somewhat traumatized, Franklin and Evie clung to each other. As they hugged, Franklin joked, trying to diffuse the situation, "Our marriage is starting out with a bang! What will we do for an encore?" Everyone in earshot groaned at Franklin's bad joke. Shaking, Evie just rested her head on Franklin's shoulder and smiled weakly.

Fortunately, Jax thought no one saw the energy that sprang from his hand. Everyone's attention was fixed on flames and the car. Trying to protect the curious, Augie shooed people back from the smoking car. But Augie had been running next to Jax, and saw the blue ball of light that leapt from Jax's body.

Without thinking, Augie stepped closer to Jax and moved to grab his arm. Augie didn't notice that Jax was smoking slightly and trying to deal with the energy that still coursed through his body. Jax immediately drew back in an attempt to protect Augie. He didn't want to risk creating a shower of sparks.

"Wait," he said to Augie. "Touch me now and we'll ignite that heavy vapor trail."

"You're smoking," Augie said, noticing for the first time, then asked, "what *was* that?"

"Heck if I know," Jax answered, shrugging his shoulders. "All I could see was energy waves and I knew I had to stop the flames before they reached the gas leak."

"Gas leak?" asked Augie, raising his eyebrows. "You saw a gas leak?"

"Plain as the nose on your face. It looked like a river," answered Jax

"How come you didn't see that before?" Augie asked. "I don't know!" Jax replied, perplexed. "Everything was normal and then, BAM!" Jax exclaimed, throwing his hands in the air for emphasis. "I saw hundreds of colors and felt energy flowing and changing. Everything smelled 'charged' and it was all. . . just. . different. I can't explain it. I think I'm losing my mind!" he groaned.

"It doesn't look like you're losing anything!" said Augie. "You just saved their lives! How did you do that . . ." he searched for words, "make that thing?!"

"You saw. . .umm. . ." he paused, "it?" Jax asked as he knelt to drain energy from his hand into the ground.

"Yup. I don't think anyone else did. I was only a few steps behind you. Everyone else was clumped back by the edge of the drive, so I'm pretty sure they didn't see anything," replied Augie. They hung back from the crowd as everyone followed the bride and groom back into the venue.

"Give me a hug, Evie!" Augie demanded as he jogged up to her and pulled her in close, but Jax cut his embrace short.

"My turn," Jax said, folding her into his arms. She gasped and heard a loud "snap" as her arms closed reflexively around him, sharing an unpleasant jolt of energy. "Sorry," mumbled Jax as he released Evie from his grasp.

"Ouch!" she cried as she stumbled into Franklin.

Baffled by what just happened, Evie arched her eyebrows questioningly at Jax.

"We all need to sit down and talk, but it can wait until you get back from your honeymoon," Augie said, answering the unspoken question in her eyes. "Franklin, would you like to take my car?"

"Thanks," answered Franklin. "But I'm a bit shaken up. Would you mind just driving us to the airport?"

"It would be my pleasure!" grinned Augie. The bags were quickly transferred to Augie's convertible, and after another round of hugs, well wishes, and goodbyes, Franklin and Evie were off again. As Augie drove away on the far side of the venue, Papere flagged down the approaching fire truck and directed the firemen to the smoking vehicle. Franklin would be available to sort that mess out when the newlyweds returned. Jax escaped the scene by ducking into the venue and busying himself helping Mamere clear up the debris from the party; he was glad for the distraction.

"Well," Mamere said with a sigh and a large grin, "that was something of an adventure! One down, one to go!" Jax ducked his head and kept working. "Don't you worry none, Cher.' I don't have any plans to marry you off quite yet," she chuckled. "Do you?"

"No ma'am," he replied with a smile. "It was easy enough staying single tonight. All of the attention from Evie's friends had me feeling pretty adorable."

"You *are* adorable, 'Te Cher'," she agreed. "I bet they didn't realize they were pushing you away."

"It was the air of quiet desperation and pleading that made it easy," said Jax.

"Whatever it was," Mamere sighed, "I'm glad to have you in your own bedroom for as long as you'll want it." She reached over and patted him on the arm, then continued cleaning.

Jax stopped to look out at the thinning crowd. There were two women lagging behind the group and the prettier one caught his eye as they saw him looking their way. She smiled and walked toward Jax, but her friend tapped her on the arm and whispered in her ear. By the time she looked back toward Jax, he managed to grab an armful of dishes and was following Mamere to the kitchen. Sighing and letting her shoulders drop dramatically, the young woman turned and followed her friend to the parking lot. The ploy was not lost on Mamere, and her shoulders shook with silent laughter by the time the girl's back was turned. "Son," she chuckled, "you can't just avoid the ladies! Eventually you will want to meet them."

Jax blushed. "Yes ma'am, just not tonight."

7

White Lightning

Jax walked home slowly after the reception, allowing time for night to fall. Physically, he was "pumped" and felt like he could run a marathon; but he was mentally and emotionally exhausted. It was hard for him to wrap his mind around what happened over the past forty-eight hours.

"Two days!" groaned Jax out loud, not worrying it anyone heard his outburst.

It seemed like just when he convinced himself it had all been a dream, something else happened. First – he found the still. Second – he realized that something actually happened to him and it had something to do with lightning. Third – he killed the boar, etcetera.

"The lightning came so close to me; maybe I have a concussion," Jax debated aloud with himself. "Or maybe I imagined the whole thing."

Jax continued his mental regurgitation. He mulled over the unusual events that kept happening. Unless he was careful, he shocked everyone and everything he touched. He was able to light candles in some strange way. And he could put out the fire with an odd, unexplainable explosion of energy. "What next?" Jax sighed, asking himself one of the many questions he couldn't answer.

Jax quietly entered the house and crept up the stairs to his room. As always, Mamere already turned down the bed and had the ceiling fan on low so he'd be able to sleep in cool sheets. Geez he loved that lady. He peeled off his damp clothes and popped into a cool shower. He couldn't remember the last time he'd taken so many showers in such a short amount of time. Wrapped in a loose towel and feeling refreshed, he reached up above the bed to hold the fan blades still and take the box out of its hiding place. He peeked cautiously at the flowers. He didn't even have to touch them this time; the flowers just started to glow when he breathed on them.

A fine shudder ran along his spine. He snapped the lid shut and tucked the box back into its hiding place. The room, briefly but brilliantly lit by the glowing flowers, seemed unusually dark with the lid shut. It took a few seconds for his night vision to return but he kept the lights off. He just sat quietly on the edge of his bed for a moment, not wanting to attract his grandparents' attention.

As he sat there, motionless, Jax realized that since Augie had taken Evie and Franklin to the airport, they didn't get a chance to talk. Jax toyed with the idea of calling him. After considering everything, he hesitated to make the call. Jax realized he was concerned about damaging his phone in the process. Earlier, he'd plugged some earbuds with a microphone into the cell phone, hoping to protect it. But thinking about it now, he wondered if talking on speaker would be safer. Bottom line – he wasn't interested in having to replace a cell phone.

Better to wait until morning, Jax thought. *Besides, Augie probably wouldn't be able to help me find any answers tonight*, Jax rationalized as he thought through all the options.

With that settled, Jax got into bed and closed his eyes. He fell asleep quickly. Sleeping soundly and dreamlessly, it felt as if only moments had passed when he woke, but the sun was already starting to clear the eastern horizon. He rolled out of bed and crept quietly downstairs to make a pot of coffee. Soon, the aroma of thick, hearty coffee wafted through the kitchen. He poured himself a large cup of coffee, sweetened with a generous helping of molasses, and headed out to the front porch.

Jax sank into the rocking chair and set it in motion, his mind on the enchantingly quiet beauty of the sunrise. One rising ray after another gently nudged his hometown awake. Then, as if the world were hard at work trying to make his life better, the most delicious breakfast smells wafted through the house, onto the porch, and beyond; Mamere was at it again!

Jax caught a glimpse of Augie and his dog, Justice, as they paused at the garden gate. Augie opened the gate and, together, they sauntered down the walk. They came straight down the path to the porch where Jax rocked; entering right on cue, no invitation needed, welcome more as family than as guests.

"Morning, boys!" Jax called out. "Just in time for breakfast!"

"Howdy, sunshine!" Augie called back. "Coffee ready?" He jogged lightly up the steps and Justice settled down at the base of the stairs to scratch.

"I thought you had to work today," probed Jax. "Called in sick, a 'mental health day,'" replied Augie with a smile. "I love the perks of this job!" While in school full time for his nursing degree, Augie paid his bills by working as a patient care technician at the local, in-patient psychiatric hospital. Fortunately for Augie, his boss understood that people occasionally needed time off when they weren't sick or under pressure to take care of urgent personal business.

Sometime early that morning, Augie decided that today was definitely one of those days.

"Thought we might go hunting and . . . maybe check out the . . . you know what," whispered Augie so Mamere couldn't hear what he said.

Jax thought about it for a moment before nodding in agreement. "We'd better start with breakfast," he said, without even acknowledging Augie's interest in seeing the clearing, and the mystical still.

"I never could turn down one of Mamere's breakfasts," responded Augie as he headed for the kitchen.

"Here, buddy," Jax said, holding his hand out to Justice. But the dog just stared warily at him before dropping his eyes and lying down on the ground to wait for his master's return. "Don't be afraid, Justice," Jax said as he stood up and walked down the stairs to pet the dog. The hairs on his arms rose and he felt energy building up in this body. To Jax's surprise, Justice hunched his back, raised his hackles, and growled low in his throat. He knelt down and placed his hand on the ground, willing the charge to dissipate, and saw Justice relax. The dog then wagged his tail and got up to nuzzle Jax, coming as close as a dog could to purring when Jax scratched him behind the ears.

"My two best friends," Augie said as he came back, balancing two plates on one arm and a mug of coffee for himself in his other hand. In typical Mamere serving style, both were heaped high with eggs, boudin, and grits. Jax climbed back up the stairs to take one of the plates from Augie. Much to Justice's pleasure, Jax tossed a sausage in his direction. Then both boys shut down all conversation as they dove into their breakfast delights. The only sound heard was that of Justice licking the sidewalk where the boudin had been moments before.

After a few minutes, Augie sighed contentedly, wiped egg yolk off the side of his face and said, "So. I figure we go hunting and you show me that clearing. Maybe we can find something to help wrap our brains around what's going on."

"Sounds good," Jax said around a sip of coffee. "I can probably find it again."

With that comment hanging in the air, both boys finished breakfast and brought their dishes to the kitchen. Jax dutifully kissed Mamere on the cheek and gently nudged her aside so he could wash their dishes.

Papere was now awake and already seated at the kitchen table eating his own breakfast. Politely, Augie shook Papere's hand and clapped him on the back as they exchanged greetings.

"We're going hunting today," Jax announced. "Sounds good," replied Papere. "But please don't hunt for anything big. We've still got a lot of meat in the freezer. But if you see a turkey . . ." sighed Papere with a gentle smile on his face, "well, there's always room for wild turkey."

"Your wish is our command," said Jax as both boys smiled at Papere. They liked wild turkey too.

Jax told Augie to grab some water bottles and a couple of bags of trail mix out of the pantry as he headed to the gun cabinet. Jax knew that a hungry hunter was a distracted hunter, as Papere had taught him long ago. Everyone in town knew that both Augie and Jax were skilled marksmen; all because of Papere's hunting and shooting range instructions over the years. Both boys honed their shooting skills on the range under Papere's supervision at least once or twice a year. On one trip to the range, the police chief, after watching them shoot for a while, offered both boys jobs as deputies. Having already made up his mind to become a nurse, Augie immediately declined the offer. Jax never committed one way or the other. Once the boys gathered all the necessary items for the hunt, they piled into Jax's truck with Justice in tow. Their destination – the infamous scrub. Oblivious to all but the excitement of riding in the truck, Justice stuck his head out the window and licked the breeze.

Jax loved driving; it relaxed him. Lost in the moment with his best friend and the big Catahoula, the whole situation made him feel almost normal again. For Jax, the drive was over too quickly, and he was parking in almost the exact spot that he'd used a few days ago. Despite the recent rain, there were still impressions in the mud from his previous visit.

"Which way?" asked Augie, as they got out and stood by the truck, their shoes sinking slightly into the damp soil.

Jax kicked at the soft dirt as he spun around to point at a small path.

"I started off that way, tracking the boar from that little deer run to the brook. We ought to be able to pick up my trail there." Justice sniffed around the impressions left by the coolers, barked once, and looked at Augie for permission to track. Augie nodded, pointed, and Justice was off like a shot, easily tracing the path made by Jax and the boar.

Following Justice, Jax recalled the headlong chase that made the broken and twisted path. Initially, Jax was delighted at the sight of the lingering, heavy tracks left in the ground from carrying the boar out of the scrub. Yet were it not for Justice's expert scent chasing skills, Jax and Augie would have lost the trail when it crossed a little meadow. Justice simply led them without error, never losing the scent. Moments after crossing the meadow, they clearly heard the spring gaily bubbling.

Ducking through a tunnel of dense vegetation, they followed its watery song.

Augie gasped as he caught sight of the still.

"What now?" he whispered to Jax, but it was more of a statement than a question.

"Rifles against the stone wall and let's check out the still," suggested Jax.

Closer in, Augie could see that the still was covered with shriveled blue and white flowers jammed in a dirty brown mess that reminded him of old tissues used to stop a nosebleed. Like a child who couldn't keep his hands off the toys in a store, Jax walked up to the sluice and pushed it. Protesting the disturbance, the sluice sent a tiny shower of rusty flakes whispering in all directions as the redirected spring ran noisily down the track to the still's broken belly. A bolt of electricity leapt from Jax, and the foliage on the still sprang back into vivid life. Once again, the flowers glowed like little stars on a field of almost violently green moss.

Augie unconsciously sucked in his breath and held it in awe of the sight. Releasing his breath in a long, low whistle he whispered, "White lightning." The long- forgotten charm of the still made him smile. Its copper coils were old and moldy and there was rust on the boiler, but the form was pristine; there was no mistaking the original function of the machinery. Justice, at first eagerly leading them on, now hunkered down next to Augie, his hackles raised. Augie took everything in with a glance, then redirected his attention to Jax.

Energy bubbled within Jax. He stretched out his hand toward the flowers and his body rose mystically off the ground. Only a few feet separated Jax from the Earth as he bobbled on throbbing cushions of energy. Energy patterns coalesced in the sky above him, their pulsations rapidly increasing in strength and speed.

Entranced by what he witnessed, Augie took a step backwards; the glowing flowers and still all but forgotten. In utter disbelief, Augie watched Jax floating in the air; Jax was surrounded completely by a faint, shimmering, "bubble" form.

Generated by the new interplay of energies, storm clouds gathered in the atmosphere high above them. The ominous, gaseous blanket trapped ozone and propelled its sharp smell into their presence. Scared out of his wits, Justice cowered in fear as close as possible to Augie's feet: he wasn't about to leave the protection of his master.

Jax toyed playfully with the energy patterns; first by moving his arms, then by simply thinking about what he wanted them to look like. Strangely, Jax joined Augie's bright energy with that of a nearby, healthy old tree. The union created an unexpected power surge in Augie – something he couldn't even begin to comprehend. Meanwhile, Jax extracted the tree's essential energy and wrapped it completely around Augie until he pulsed brighter and stronger.

"Jax!" yelled Augie. In response, Jax severed the connection between Augie and the tree. The entire event left Augie confused and reeling from the experience of having so much raw natural energy poured into him. Sensationally, Augie felt "green," whole, and impossibly healthy. Augie – mesmerized by his own experience – momentarily lost his focus on Jax still floating in the air.

A cool gust of wind caught Augie in the face and drew his attention skyward. He saw the same storm clouds that Jax saw, but to Jax they were electrical extensions of the power all around him. Without thinking, Jax raised one arm and curled his hand into a tight fist, drawing in and holding the energy. Jax circled his fist above his head, then stopped and pointed at the far horizon. A dazzling bolt of light flew from his hand and caused a cascade of lightning that danced away further than he could see. Jax felt instantly lighter, as if his body actually lost mass with the release of energy – like his very being was becoming energy.

In the wake of the lightning bolt, waves of energy increased around Jax and shoved at Augie and knocked him to the ground, putting Jax at the center of Augie's attention again. The waves grew stronger around them, and Jax's veins and arteries began to stand out like rivers of white light on his dark skin. Steam rose from him and he was completely engulfed in light. His nostrils hungered for the air above the clouds. An undeniable urge to touch, see, smell, and taste the air above the clouds filled Jax. Instinctively, he raised both arms up and tried to embrace the entire sky.

Suddenly, lightning filled the clearing and Jax disappeared! A gently smoking pile of clothing was all he left behind. Thunder reverberated in the tiny clearing and saturated Augie's senses. At first, Augie couldn't even open his eyes. His ears reeled in response to the deafening thunderclap. The normal sounds of the scrub slowly resumed and filtered through his overwhelmed senses. Now, Justice and Augie were completely alone, except for Jax's discarded clothes. Augie thought the sky had opened and ripped Jax away. Confounded by all that took place, Augie plopped down on the ground, not caring as rain started to fall; he tried to comfort Justice, who was clearly rattled by the mayhem. As they sat motionless, the eerily bright white and blue lights faded from the flowers and muted shadows slowly dappled the clearing once again.

Above Augie, lightning tore jaggedly across the sky in a myriad of patterns and colors; sometimes above the massive clouds, sometimes below, and sometimes it disappeared completely. The electrical discharges threaded intricately but haphazardly across the sky so fast and so frequently that the thunderclaps overlapped each other in a frenzied cacophony. The clouds were whipped into puddles that ebbed and flowed with the disturbance. Augie thought it looked like Zeus had dragged his lightning bolt like a loaded paintbrush through watercolor clouds on the overcast sky. The multi-colored clouds swirled together and dropped rain at unpredictable intervals. Augie was glad he was sitting down because watching the spectacle made him dizzy.

It began to rain in earnest and Augie lost track of time. He laid there in the meadow next to Justice, grateful for the cool rain. He didn't know how long it was before lightning flashed down from the clouds and struck Jax's pile of clothes on the ground. His first action was to raise his arm reflexively and shield himself, his senses immersed in the blinding light and thunderous sound. When Augie was finally able to open his eyes, Jax was in the clearing in front of him, standing on the crumpled pile of clothing. Steam dramatically rose in thick curls from Jax's skin. His veins and arteries flowed with a brilliant light that faded with each passing heartbeat. Jax just stood there, wearing nothing but the biggest grin Augie had ever seen.

"What. . .?!" Augie gasped.

"Oops!" Jax said as he scooped up his clothes and put them on. "Guess I'll have to work on that."

"Where? How?" Augie stuttered, "What?!" he said again.

"Dude," was the only word Jax uttered in response to Augie. With a broad smile across his face, Jax continued, "That's one of the things I've always admired about you – you are a brilliant conversationalist. But seriously, ya gotta give me a second." To calm his nerves, Jax paced around the clearing and tried to gather his thoughts.

"It was amazing!" Jax exclaimed without preamble. "Everything around me looked like it was happening in slow motion, and I had **all** this power and an urge to taste the sky. So, I just raised my arms up and bam!" Jax punched his fist into his open hand for emphasis. "I was *tasting* the sky." Words spilled out on top of each other as Jax shrugged his shoulders in disbelief. Jax gestured to vent some of his passion and sparks fell from his hands. "I just wanted to see the other side of the clouds and again. . . bam! I was on the other side of the clouds." Jax's every emotional and physical gesture was accompanied by another shower of sparks that rained down on the grass. His hands pulsed constantly with a seemingly never-ending light source. Jumping in, Augie barked, "And you were floating in the air! You glowed after being struck by lightning!" Augie's excitement could hardly be contained as he continued. "It popped you right out of your clothes. I thought you were dead!"

Suddenly, Augie stopped talking, stood up, then sat right back down again to pat Justice, both of them still pretty shaken up.

Certain that his body teemed with residual energy, Jax stepped as close to Augie as he deemed safe and took a deep breath before speaking. Justice, understandably leery of allowing Jax to get any closer, abandoned Augie's side to quickly scoot under the old boiler for protection. In a hushed, but firm tone, Jax looked Augie square in the eye and said, "Not dead. Not anywhere near dead; in fact, *very much alive!*"

They both noted the dog's reaction without speaking. Unnerved by his friend's declarations, Augie stood up and paced around the clearing to think things through and survey the entire scene. Jax walked across the clearing to sit down on the low wall, giving both Augie and Justice some breathing room. Silence hung in the clearing as the trio tried to come to grips with this new reality. As if now a normal part of his life, Jax sought relief from the enormous energy lingering in his body by resting one hand on the wall, allowing the harmless transfer of energy into the stones.

"How. . ." Augie tried to form a question.

"I have no idea," Jax said, cutting his friend's question short.

"It looked like you were struck by lightning," said Augie.

Jax paused in thought before responding. "I think I became energy. I think I *was* lightning . . . or something like it. Everything happened so fast!"

The rain that had fallen in earnest slowed to a gentle mist. Augie decided to stop pacing and sat down on the low wall a few feet away from Jax, but close enough to speak without raising his voice. Seeming to sense that Jax was no longer a physical threat, Justice crawled out from under the boiler. Augie just looked at Justice and shook his head as the dog slunk over to him while attempting to remain a safe distance from Jax. Looking down at himself, Augie realized his own clothing was full of holes where lightning burned through without harming him in any way.

Jax stood up, walked over to the spring, and splashed refreshing water on his face. When he finished, he sat down next to Augie and punched him gently on the arm.

"Look at that!" Augie exclaimed, pointing toward Justice as he circled the clearing again and came back to where the boys sat. Justice sniffed suspiciously at Jax, then barked softly in approval and laid down at his feet. "Wow," observed Jax. "As if we didn't already have enough to figure out," Jax said as he patted Justice on the head.

"I'm at a total loss," Augie admitted, shaking his head back and forth. "And look, those flowers are all dead now!" he exclaimed as he pointed at the still. Both men saw a lacy pattern of moss and petals singed on the metal of the old still, but all the vegetation was gone; the moss and flowers were now nothing but ash. Augie stood and walked over to the still; no signs of life could be found. He pushed the sluice back and forth before ducking his head under the cool stream to let the water flow over him and rinse his face. Without even thinking, he slurped down a healthy swig of water. "Hmm," he said, "the water tastes curiously refreshing, but a little weird. . . it actually tastes almost like it's green and metallic all at the same time." Augie struggled, trying to describe the water's taste and composition.

Jax nodded in understanding, then changed the subject. "Must have been a sweet little still in its day. Have you ever heard of this one?"

"Nope," answered Augie. "And you know how much I like to keep abreast of the moonshine operations here." He puffed out his chest and rocked back and forth on his heels, tapping at an imaginary pistol on his hip. Jax laughed. Augie never touched alcohol. "Hey!" Augie yelled, "I think I'm going to call you 'White Lightning!'" Jax frowned. "I like 'Jax,' it suits me just fine," he said, hoping to shake free of the "White Lightning" label Augie was trying to pin on him.

"Well, yeah. . . 'Jax'" is a great name. . . but hey, it's not a superhero name! 'White Lightning' is a superhero name!" said Augie insistently and with unbridled excitement.

"Superhero?" Jax questioned. "I think that's going a bit far. 'White lightning?' Right now, I feel more like a freak of nature."

"A freak? No way! I'm not sure if you ride lightning like it's a horse or if, or if you **become** lightning. Whatever! You manipulate energy.

And look at me! There's not a scratch on me. I feel healthier than ever! By the way – how did you *do* that?" Augie asked.

Jax looked across the clearing at the now withered tree. He pointed to it and said, "I, umm," he paused, searching around for the right word. "Connected your energy pattern with the energy from that tree."

"Wild!" exclaimed Augie.

"It's not like riding lightning . . ." Jax started.

"You see? 'White Lightning!'" demanded Augie.

"You're crazy!" replied Jax. "I don't need a superhero nickname."

"Whatever," sighed Augie. "It'll stick whether you like it or not. And wait 'til we tell Evie!" raved Augie, excitement overflowing.

Jax sat quietly. He said, "I saw her on the beach."

Augie looked at his friend, "What? She's on her honeymoon, Jax. Remember? When did you see her?" he asked.

"Just now, when I was up there," Jax said, pointing skyward.

"Can you see her. . . now?" Augie asked cautiously.

"No! I'm not imagining this, Augie," Jax replied, sounding slightly offended. "It's just, when I was, oh I don't know, 'flying,' I guess you'd call it. All I did was wonder if Evie and Franklin were at the beach and – bam! I was at the beach!" reported Jax. "I couldn't believe it! I knew that I needed to get out of there quick, so I came back here. Fortunately, I don't think she saw me," concluded Jax.

"Wow!" Augie exclaimed.

"Yeah. I landed about 30 feet behind her and I guess knocked her off her feet. Or maybe she just tripped. Either way, she fell forward. I caught her before she hit the ground with one of those, umm, 'energy band' type things and got out of there before she could even turn her head," clarified Jax.

"Thirty feet behind her and you caught her? I am not even going to pretend I understand that statement." Augie paused and nervously chewed on his lip before asking, "Do you think you can take me with you? You know, hold my hand or something?"

"I couldn't even take my own clothes!" Jax exclaimed.

"Yeah, that would be interesting if it happens in front of a bunch of people," Augie replied as he sat back down next to Jax.

"I think . . . if I land on or near my clothes maybe I can put them on before anyone can see me," Jax said. "Everything else looks like it's moving in slow motion when I'm all 'juiced' up. Actually, I stood here staring at you for a few moments before you realized I was back. Man, I was flyin'!"

Augie made a face like he'd tasted something bad. "Thanks, buddy. Maybe next time you should try putting your clothes on faster to spare me the display. Now," he paused and smiled, "if you were some hot chick, I might not mind as much," he confessed without blushing.

Jax punched Augie again, harder this time. He asked, "Have you picked out one of the bridesmaids? Do I need to find a new roommate?" They had been planning to rent an apartment together but neither one had moved away from home yet.

"Oh, *no!*" said Augie, waving his hands in front of him for emphasis. "We'd better not start talking like that. Evie as gloating matchmaker might not be as much fun as the Evie we currently know and love."

Jax laughed warmly and the light in the clearing brightened. Augie looked up to see the clouds clearing away and the sun shining with renewed vengeance. "Looks like we haven't even scratched the surface of what's happened to you and what you can do. I wish there were someone we could ask," said Augie.

"Me, too," replied Jax. "Too bad we can't just go to 'superhero.com' and ask for a mentor."

Augie laughed. "That would work!"

"Wow," replied Jax, "this sure puts a wrinkle in the girlfriend hunt. What if I hurt someone?"

Per Mamere, Jax flirted with some "really wonderful girls" in high school, but none of those girls succeeded in maintaining his interest. Lately he'd been too busy. Working, graduating from high school and making himself useful to his grandparents by helping more around the house made him too busy to bother himself about dating.

"Hey, you didn't hurt me," Augie replied, trying to comfort him. "In fact, I think I'm healthier than ever. Maybe you should be a nurse!"

"Ugh! No!" Jax exclaimed, a disgusted look on his face. "Blood . . . guts . . . poop . . . people crying about pain and sickness. You can keep all that wonderfulness to yourself! I don't know how you do it. It's a calling, that's for sure."

"It's not all like that," Augie protested. "Helping people back to health is very rewarding!"

"Ok. I hear that," Jax nodded. "It's just," he paused, "that journey back would wear me out," he finished.

Allowing some dust to settle on the conversation, the boys stood quietly for a few moments. Both were still overwhelmed with Jax's new reality and the infusion of superpowers. Undaunted by the discussion about Jax's energy fluctuations and the like, Justice finally let go of fear and fell soundly asleep. His snoring reverberated loudly through the otherwise stone-silent clearing.

"All right!" Augie said as he stood and raised his hands in mock defeat. "I'll try to stop recruiting you for nursing," he sighed. "But I wonder if you can heal people by doing . . ." he hesitated as he searched for the right words. "Whatever it is you did to me," he said, waving his hands aimlessly in front of him.

"I don't know," replied Jax. When it was happening, it was like I could read you. It looks like what I imagine an aura would look like, but that almost seems too simple of an explanation. I could see places where you were weak or just didn't seem to 'glow right,' so I just tried to fix it. I reached out to the tree and took what looked good over there and used it to patch up what I thought you needed. Thank God I didn't hurt you!"

Augie paced silently in the clearing. "Practicing medicine without a license – or even any training – could get tricky. Do you think you could make the tree strong again?"

"I don't know. I wouldn't want to take what I gave you and give it back to the tree," Jax replied.

"No, that's not what I meant," responded Augie, wrapping his arms around his chest possessively, as if to prevent Jax from taking it away. "I like the way I feel now. I mean – could you give it energy from something else." He looked around the edges of the clearing and after a quick search gestured toward the far side where a stand of glossy leaves peeked up behind the low wall. "Like that poison oak over there."

Without speaking, Jax stood up and raised one hand in front of him, toward the tree. Then, Jax seemed to blur out of focus. Augie rubbed his eyes and Justice woke with a start. Justice backed away from Jax, growling low in his throat. Augie saw the stand of poison oak wither as the tree grew visibly stronger and started to emanate health. Jax's outline solidified again as he dropped his hand to his side.

"Wow," Augie said, mouth dropped open, gaping at the now healthy tree.

"I just thought about what you said," replied Jax. "I thought about moving energy and I saw things shift. It was easy to see the places where the tree needed fixin' so I took from one and gave to the other."

"Does it wear you out?" asked Augie. "In the comics the hero is always drained when he uses his power."

"Augie STOP with the superhero references!" exclaimed Jax. "But, no, I'm not drained right now. So far, I've felt fantastic every time I've moved energy around. It's like waking up from the best night's sleep ever. Thank goodness for that! Although, lately, I haven't slept well at all. I keep having nightmares where I put people I love in dangerous situations but can't help them. It sucks."

"Sorry. Wish I could help you with that," Augie commiserated.

"You are helping," replied Jax. "Just being here, being my friend, listening to me. It helps."

"You're welcome," he replied, bowing with a flourish. Justice once again sat down by Augie's feet, and Augie almost fell over, tripping on the dog. "Sorry, boy," he said as he reached down to pat Justice's head. The faithful dog licked his hand. "Maybe I should change my email to sidekick@superhero.com," he joked.

Ignoring the millionth superhero reference, Jax moved on in a completely different direction and commented about Justice's apparent ability to notice rising energy levels within Jax's body. "Haven't you noticed that your brilliant Justice senses my energy levels?" questioned Jax.

"Yes, I noticed that, too," replied Augie. "Dogs don't have the best vision, but maybe the energy smells differently; and we all know that Justice has a fantastic nose!"

"True," said Jax, as he recalled the many successful hunting trips with Justice's help. "Maybe it's like smelling ozone or something."

"I smelled ozone when things started happening earlier, but I don't smell it now. Then, you started glowing; and have you seen your arms when the energy ramps up? It looks rivers of intense light under your skin! Sparks fall from your skin wherever you brush yourself afterwards. All in all, it's pretty dang terrifying, but super cool. Honestly, I wouldn't be surprised at all if you had laser vision," concluded Augie.

Jax laughed infectiously in response to Augie's diagnoses and inferences. As Augie joined in on the laughter, Justice barked happily, too, and it seemed like the whole clearing "cheered up" around them.

"Augie, I'm starting to buy into your superhero mantra!" said Jax between outbursts of laughter.

"I don't know if you've noticed, but the weather seems to echo your mood; at least when you're happy. I sure hope it doesn't start to storm when you get angry," said Augie.

"Quit joking around," protested Jax.

"I'm not," he deadpanned. A smile spread slowly across his face. "I wonder what's going to happen when you fall in love!"

"Enough!" shouted Jax, more out of embarrassment than anger, and a cool gust of wind hit the back of Augie's neck. Jax saw his friend's hair blown forward and his own jaw dropped open. He had just imagined knocking him on the back of the head.

"Did you see that?!" Augie demanded. "You just shout, and a gust of wind pushes the back of my neck!" he exclaimed, gesturing for emphasis.

"Wow," hollered Jax. "I didn't mean . . . I mean I don't . . ." stammered Jax. He immediately sat down on the low wall and placed one hand firmly in the dirt to drain energy.

"Maybe," Augie started, then hesitated. "Man, I was thinking; maybe you should 'practice,' you know – experiment – while we're out here. Try to figure out what you can and can't do, Jax." Augie spoke in a tone that told Jax he was dead serious.

Jax quietly weighed Augie's suggestion.

"That's probably the best idea you've had all day," confirmed Jax. "So, what do you recommend I do or try for Lesson 1, Superhero 101?"

Without a moment's hesitation, Augie blurted out his response. "Flying!" You need to see how far you can go, and if you can take things with you. But please," he joked, "start by trying to keep your clothes on."

"You know how I like to make an entrance," Jax said, smiling, "but I'll see what I can do." He thought about tasting the sky and instantly his stomach grumbled, reminding him of how hungry he actually was. Unbidden, his thoughts turned to Franklin's barbeque. And bam! An energy shift hit him, and he was transported to Franklin's back yard, next to the barbeque pit, naked as the day he was born! Then, before the thunderclap could begin to roll over the barbeque pit, he was back in the clearing by the still.

Jax bent over to pick up his clothes, unintentionally mooning Augie and Justice.

"Noooooo," moaned Augie, shielding his face from the sight.

At first, Jax's hands went straight through the clothes; his molecules were racing so fast that he wasn't "whole." He literally could not pick up the clothes. Milliseconds later his molecules slowed just enough that he was finally able to grasp his clothing and dress. Lowering his hand as thunder faded from the clearing, Augie saw Jax standing in front of him again . . . fully clothed!

"Well," he asked. "Did you keep your clothes on?" "Nope," replied Jax, "but I was able to put them back on before you knew I was naked."

"Better! But that's not going to work in the long run. Some super-fast camera will catch you at some point. Probably when you're old and fat and don't want to be caught naked on film anymore," joked Augie.

"Leave it to you to make me feel better," Jax responded. "Can't you be happy that I didn't burn any more holes in my clothes?"

"Good point. Where did you go," he asked?

"Well, it all depended on what I thought. When I thought about tasting the sky, my stomach grumbled. And when I envisioned Franklin's barbeque, I ended up in his back yard next to the pit." Jax replied.

"So, you also have to work on targeting and either focus or impulse control," conjectured Augie.

"Can't we just go home for now?" asked Jax. "This has all been pretty weird, and now I am really hungry."

"No, Jax," Augie shook his head negatively. "You are not normally a guy at the mercy of his belly, but sometimes you act like one. This is important. You should learn something about your powers while we're out here," he insisted.

"Okay," said Jax with a clear tone of resignation. "I've always wanted to see Disney World. Is that the one in Florida or the one in California?" And then, even before Augie could utter a response, Jax vanished.

Augie barely had time to see the veins in Jax's arms turn white and burn fiercely with liquid power before he disappeared. As the now-familiar roll of thunder filled the clearing he looked around, and this time, there was no pile of clothing. Justice, tired of all the lightning and thunder, once again tucked himself under the relative safety of the old still. As Augie and Justice waited patiently for Jax's return, stray raindrops fell and made hollow rat-a-tat-tat sounds on the still's belly, and clouds eddied in the otherwise clear sky. Then, the clouds simply blew away.

Having seen it before, Augie was more accustomed to the sequence of events, and watched closely as clouds pooled overhead again; soon Jax would be back.

"Bam!" Augie exclaimed as a bright flash and a roll of thunder filled the clearing. As expected, Jax appeared; fully clothed, grinning widely, and holding two maps.

"I figured it out," he exclaimed! "If I think of cushioning things, I can carry them with me," declared Jax as if he'd just discovered the most important thing since sliced bread. He continued, "And voila! Maps of Disney World and Disneyland. Heck! Thought I might as well check them both out," he said as he handed both maps to Augie.

"Cool!" Augie exclaimed as he accepted the maps. "Next time, let's see if you can bring something that's alive."

"Ok," Jax gave an exaggerated sigh, "but can superhero 101 be done for today? I'm starving!"

"Jax, you've earned a feast!" Augie said with a smile. "Come on, Justice, let's go home!"

Now on a mission for food, they picked up their rifles and the three companions headed out of the clearing toward the truck. After crossing a few more clearings they were back at the first meadow in no time at all. Somewhat puzzled, Augie scratched his head and almost wondered out loud. *How, in all the years, have we hunted in the scrub and bayou and never before seen the clearing and the old still?* But they'd never seen nor heard of it before. Not really watching where he was going, he thought curiously about who built it and how long ago that was, when he almost tripped over Justice. The big dog had halted midstride, every muscle taut, nose pointed at a clump of brush.

Augie and Justice hunted so many times that reading the dog's body language was as natural to him as breathing. Augie reached out and caught Jax by the arm to silently draw his attention to Justice. It was then that they heard rustling in the scrub and the telltale "gobble, gobble" of turkey on the move. Without speaking, they both pulled out their weapons and took aim at the rustling grasses. Soon, a covey of turkeys began wobbling into sight. Like synchronized swimmers, both boys took aim and fired in total unison. Two of the birds fell as the rest took flight.

Justice maintained his stance until Augie gave him the "all clear," then bounded forward and picked one of the birds up with his teeth to carry it back to his master. Jax retrieved the other bird himself. As Augie reached down to take the bird from Justice, the dog's body language screamed satisfaction.

"Nice shot," Jax said.

"Ditto," said Augie. "Feel better?"

"Yup. I love wild turkey," stated Jax.

"You think Mamere will tell me how to fix this to impress Jessica?" Augie asked. Jessica was a nurse he'd met at the hospital where he did his clinical rotation.

"Of course!" exclaimed Jax. "You're gonna cook for her? She's that special?" he asked.

"Wait until you meet her," nodded Augie with a smile. "I'll probably have both of you over to eat this bird. Think you can find a date?"

"Maybe," replied Jax, as he quickly went through a mental list of possible companions. "I'll think about it," he sighed.

"Never mind," offered Augie. "I'll ask Jessica to bring a friend!" Augie chirped, as if he were playing Cupid.

The trio's trek back to the truck went without further incident or comment. Unknown to the other, Augie and Jax both pondered the wonderful, pristine silence that only friends share.

8

The Beach

Jax, Augie, and Justice all but tumbled out of the truck in their excitement to tell Mamere and Papere about the turkeys, but no one was home when they got there. They quickly set about the business of dressing the birds, getting one wrapped neatly in the refrigerator and one roasting in the oven by the time the older couple got home. Jax decided to roast the bird in large carved pieces instead of whole. Papere walked in rubbing his hands together and said, "Ooohhh yes! Looks like you got a bird! Cher' we are getting treated tonight!" he called out to Mamere, smiling largely.

Mamere walked in, sniffed the delightful aroma of roast turkey and said, "Te Cher'! Something smells divine! How can I help?"

"By not doing a thing," Jax replied. "This is our treat. Augie's on the veg and I'm on the bird. You just relax," he said with a smile.

"It *does* smell good. I might have to get Jax to teach me how to roast a bird," agreed Augie.

Mamere and Papere went into the dining room and saw the table had already been set so they sat down on the front porch to chat as they waited for dinner. The main topics of conversation were the weather and the recent wedding. Memories rolled over Jax, stirred by his grandparents' voices as they floated back through the house. Throughout his childhood, it was routine for Mamere, Papere, and him to sit on the front porch with the aromas of dinner still lingering heavily in the air. They'd talk about everything from who got hurt on the playground that day to politics and religion. It was a great way to grow up. Those evenings usually included Evie and Augie; just one big happy family.

Even though he was preparing dinner, elbow to elbow with his best friend in the kitchen, Jax felt a strong pang of loneliness. Two things had changed radically in such a short time: their family had a huge hole without Evie's daily presence; and Jax clearly was not the same.

Augie looked up with a start, surprised by the rumble of distant thunder. Looking around him, the silence in the house was eerie, made even more so by a corresponding hush in the chatter between Mamere and Papere. More importantly, Augie saw an undeniable sadness in Jax's face. Neither the renewed conversation about how oddly abundant the lightning and thunder was in recent days, nor his grandparents' light-hearted laughter floating through the house, improved Jax's mood.

Ironically, Papere – completely absorbed by the subject of recent odd weather- commented that one of the local weathermen tried to connect the storms with the unusual solar storm activity over the past few days, along with the associated intermittent satellite and cell phone coverage blackouts. The local viewing audience was tickled by how comically the weathermen danced around the forecasts; one moment absorbed in predictions, the next, saving face for "mis-forecasts."

Concerned about Jax, Augie (oblivious to the power building up inside Jax) reached over and patted him on the back.

Ouch! thought Augie, pulling his hand back sharply as Jax's body transmitted another stinging shock to Augie. Surprised by the jolt, Augie wrung his hands, attempting to dispel the annoying tingle.

"What's wrong, buddy?" asked Augie, keeping his voice low.

"Everything has changed so much these past few days," Jax began. "I know it's silly, but I already miss the way things were," shrugged Jax as he tried to wipe the frown from his face with the hand wearing the oven mitt.

"You're going to be ok," Augie said. "We're all going to be ok."

Papere reluctantly decided to head into the kitchen and check on the cooking progress, leaving Mamere sitting on the porch to watch the last rays of the sunset as they gloriously stained the clouds.

Papere asked, "When is that bird going to be ready, boys?"

"Any minute now," smiled Jax as he turned off the oven. "The meat thermometer says the bird is done, just letting the meat sit. We can start laying the sides on the table. Papere, would you pour some sweet tea?"

"My pleasure," he said, crossing the kitchen to retrieve the jug from the refrigerator. He poured large glasses of tea for each of them before going to the front porch to fetch Mamere.

Augie could see them through the front window as he carried large bowls of mashed potatoes and gravy to the table. They cuddled for a moment and exchanged a quick kiss before coming into the dining room. He nudged Jax, jostling the large plate he carried heaped with beautifully browned turkey. "Do you think we'll ever be that happy in love?" he asked as he nodded toward the happy couple.

"Nope," he answered perfunctorily.

"You always like to stomp on my dreams," Augie said with an exaggerated sigh. "Can't blame a guy for hoping."

"Yup," Jax nodded affirmatively. "I imagine you and Jessica will be married next week, probably before you ever ask her out on a date, and the week after that, I'd better find myself a woman or be forever alone," he moaned, striking a dramatic pose – placing the back of his hand on his brow after setting the dish on the table.

"What's this about being alone?" asked Mamere as she entered the dining room with Papere. She always managed to hear snippets of conversation.

"Just Jax being melodramatic," replied Augie.

Papere gave an appreciative sniff and held the chair for her as she sat down. "Smells wonderful," he said, leaning in to kiss Mamere on the neck. "And the food smells good too," he added as he sat down.

The men sat down, and the little family bowed their heads as Papere thanked the Lord for the meal. It was all Jax could do to keep the tears from spilling down his face. His head was spinning as he tried to adjust to the fast-moving changes of the past twenty-four hours. The sadness on his face did not escape the loving attention of Mamere. Instinctively, she reached over and patted him on the hand.

"Ouch!" exclaimed Mamere as she received an unexpected shock for all her consoling trouble.

"Sorry," mumbled Jax as he fought against tears welling up inside.

"What is it, boy?" asked Papere.

"Sorry for what?" asked Mamere. "Just some static electricity, Te Cher'."

"I'm having a hard time," Jax started.

"Now, now," she tutted. "Don't you worry none. We know you've had a hard time finding an apartment in this little town. Why, I was just telling Papere the other day, that if you ever *did* move out of our house to go live with Augie, I would probably cry for weeks! I think it just might break my heart. In fact," she continued with a dramatic pause, "I've just about decided to have Papere build a little apartment in the yard for the two of you. That's about as far away as my nerves can tolerate!" announced Mamere as she shook her finger at Papere. "And don't you tell me no, old man!"

"Listen here, old woman," Papere began, eliciting a smile from her. "I'm not about to build a shed in the yard for my grandson and his best friend when there is a pair of bedrooms upstairs that would do just fine!" He pointed his finger and shook it at the ceiling to emphasize his point.

Jax gave them a weak smile. Leave it to them to try to cheer him up. Thank goodness Mamere assumed it was about the apartment hunt. He almost spilled the whole convoluted story about the still, even though he knew it would be better to keep silent.

Augie playfully nudged Jax. Again, he was shocked, causing him to draw back quickly. Trying to avoid drawing attention to what happened, Jax pretended to drop his fork; when he picked it up, he reached down and touched the floor to drain his excess energy.

"Next time you want to turn on the little boy charm, be sure to warn me, Jax," Augie said.

"Excuse me," Jax said as he pushed back his chair and stepped away from the table. "I need to blow my nose."

Papere said, "That's enough fussin' over the boys, Cher'. Talk about something else so we can finish our meal in peace."

Mamere pursed her lips, "Yes, sir. There's plenty else to talk about. Augie, Papere and I were just talking about this, but have you noticed how odd the weather is lately? It sure makes the evening news amusing! I like to see the weathermen prancing around predictions of lightning storms!" She chuckled.

Jax just caught the end of her sentence as he got back to the table. He didn't consider this topic much better, since it was too close to his secret, but at least he could try to make small talk. Augie chatted easily about the weather, deflecting attention away from Jax and giving him some relief. Jax regained his composure and warmly rejoined the chatter by the time the tide of conversation turned back to how delicious the meal was.

At the end of the meal, the young men cleared the table and brought the dishes to the kitchen. Mamere shooed them out perfunctorily, pre-ferring to do the dishes by herself. The men grabbed cups of coffee and retired to the porch to take in the lazy evening. They talked about every-thing imaginable, staring at the backdrop of stars glittering brightly in the now cloud- free sky. Justice, after waiting patiently in the yard throughout the meal, perked up when Augie tossed him some turkey scraps. Perfectly content, Justice sat at Augie's feet and wagged his tail. It was the kind of night everyone wished would never end. Despite hav-ing consumed a lot of caffeine, Jax was tired and yawned almost non-stop. Augie didn't want the night to end either but was simply too tired to stay longer. Saying "goodnight," Augie whistled for Justice to follow him and headed home. Jax and Papere watched as they sauntered away down the familiar stretch of star-lit sidewalk.

Mamere finished the dishes and busied herself in the house, allowing the men to visit privately. After Augie left, she joined Jax and Papere on the porch. Jax, finally too tired to stay up any longer, kissed Mamere on the cheek, and went inside.

Jax felt energy surge in his body as he ascended the stairs. By the time he reached the landing his veins glowed softly as if he were a human night light. Once in the safety of his room, with the door securely closed, Jax toyed halfheartedly with the rising energy by allowing it to grow steadily. As the energy within him increased, an echoing light emanated from the box hidden above the ceiling fan blades.

Extremely curious about what was happening, Jax – for the first time – telekinetically retrieved the box. Ever so gently it floated down into his open palms and landed with a slight "bump" that flipped open the lid. There lay the flowers and moss, radiantly beautiful and full of life. Jax blew gently on them and they lit up dramatically. His bedroom filled with a pleasantly earthy, green fragrance.

Jax instinctively reacted to the super bright light and tried to shield his eyes with one hand, only to find that he could see through his hand! Surprisingly, the brightness didn't blind him. Jax's energy surged even higher. Concerned that the box's contents might be destroyed, he securely replaced the lid and telekinetically returned the box to its original hiding place. Then, slipping off his shoes, he willed the energy to dissipate harmlessly through his feet.

This was no way to get any rest, thought Jax as he readied himself for bed by the light radiating from his energized body. Once ready, he opened the window, raised his hand, and drained all remaining excess energy into the night sky. Colors flooded the sky and made it seem as if the Aurora Borealis had slid into the Deep South. Jax watched the display, hoping the changes within him were a good thing. Right now, he was so tired that all he did was yawn over and over. *I'm tapped*, thought Jax, as he climbed into bed, slid under the covers, and fell asleep almost instantly.

When morning came, he woke early, only partially refreshed. He had slept fitfully, plagued by one dream after another. His grandparents were still asleep when he crept downstairs, a cup of coffee on his mind. Step by step he hoped to make it to the kitchen without incident.

Whew, thought Jax as he hopped lightly off the last stair step, walked into the kitchen, and set up the coffee pot. He drank his first cup of coffee, thinking about his options for the day; there wasn't a single thing on his mental "to do" list.

Maybe the beach would be a good idea, considered Jax. *It might be the safest place to practice controlling my . . .* Jax paused in thought before completing the sentence. Then, his mind shouted – *Superhero powers!*

With his mind made up, Jax quickly grabbed a piece of paper and scribbled a note to Mamere and Papere; he didn't want them to worry about his whereabouts. He threw together a quick lunch and headed to the truck before giving himself a chance to change his mind.

Getting to the beach didn't take long, but Jax had to find the right place, somewhere fairly remote and off the beaten paths for locals and tourists. About a half hour later, Jax ended up above a quiet, secluded inlet nicknamed Scoop Bay. There weren't any cars in the parking lot; a good sign that the beach might be completely empty. He parked the truck, grabbed his lunch, and headed down to the little beach. The downward journey was somewhat precarious, rugged, and steeply sloped.

When Jax reached the bottom and walked out onto the sand, he was relieved to find the beach was completely empty. Convinced he was totally alone, Jax set up his practice area; towel neatly spread out, lunch basket pushed down into the sand to keep it from tilting over, and his wrapped up, hidden cell phone.

What a beautiful sight, thought Jax as he sat down on the towel, dug his toes into the sand, and stared out at the gently rolling waves. The ocean breeze lifted his spirits and invigorated his body as it blew across his skin.

Time for a swim, thought Jax as he stood up and stripped down to his swimming trunks. He waded out into the ocean, his concerns and distractions pouring out of him like sweat and mixing with the salt water. The peaceful combination of walking in the surf and letting go of everything that raced through his mind did more for him than coffee and sleep ever could.

Renewed and dripping with salt water, Jax walked out of the water and headed back to the towel. He plopped down and allowed the sun to dry his body. As he lay there, his stomach growled steadily above the sound of waves crashing onto the beach. Sitting up, he reached over, grabbed the lunch basket and dove inside. Jax wasted little time in devouring a perfectly ripened peach and a turkey sandwich made from yesterday's leftovers.

Jax suddenly realized he wasn't alone after all; dozens of sand crabs were scurrying everywhere. He watched idly as the crabs scuttled back and forth in the foam and zipped along the shore. He got up for a short walk after he finished eating. He hunted for shells along the way and wondered what would happen if lightning touched the sand.

With only the sand crabs watching, Jax allowed the energy inside him to build. He blocked out everything else to focus his attention on his hand and soon it rivaled the brilliant intensity of the sun! Still walking, Jax stepped onto wet sand. The familiar sound of sizzling electricity filled the air and warm steam was born beneath his feet and rose into the breeze. Jax bent down and swung his hand back and forth, sending energy into the wet sand. Instantly, lightning branched deeply into the sand, like tree roots or human veins, tracing fine rivers of salty water. Next, Jax released a lightning bolt across the surface of the bay. The lightning skipped like a stone, generating ripples that propelled a myriad of branching colored energy streams in every possible direction.

As the energy intensified in Jax's body, he became more and more curious about the "what ifs" floating through his mind. *What if I touch the water with my toes? Will I short out?* thought Jax, as he casually sauntered closer to the water's edge to get his toes wet. Energy sizzled around his feet as it dissipated into the water, but more importantly, Jax wasn't hurt in any way. Emboldened, Jax placed one foot, then the other, into the surf, letting waves crash all around his feet. Again, as the energy escalated, the water bubbled and sizzled, but never touched him.

A shimmering sphere appeared and cocooned him as he walked deeper and deeper into the water. He paused when the waves reached the level of his chin. The bubble protected him. He took a few more steps, deep enough to be completely submerged in water. The water lit up around him as it absorbed the sphere's energy, and he felt his power begin to drain quickly. He poured more energy into the protective border. All around him, Jax saw startled fish entangled in the irregular energy extensions flowing from the sphere; other fish, further away, fled uninjured. Still unfamiliar with everything that happened, Jax marveled at the bubble's powerful protection.

Is this what keeps me safe high above the clouds? wondered Jax. He couldn't figure it all out; everything was happening and changing so quickly.

Jax allowed his energy level to surge even higher. Slender, vine-like tendrils of energy spread outward and morphed into sturdy branches that coursed through the water. After the energy-infused branches extended beyond his sight, Jax allowed the energy to subside. The decrease in power caused the branches to recoil back into the bubble. The border reabsorbed the energy, brightening in response. Sensing his power weakening as the enveloping blanket of seawater sucked energy from the sphere, he saw the sphere's light dim, almost like turning off the sun's rays or drawing a curtain over a sun-soaked window.

Depleted and weak-kneed, Jax traversed the seabed back to the shore. Once his shoulders were above the water line, he allowed the power to drop completely. Jax relaxed, and the cool water washed over him, pushing his body back to the relative safety of the beach with each wave.

Jax was exhausted when he finally stepped out of the surf and walked over to his towel. Steam rose in all directions as his skin dried rapidly in the sun. More out of habit than necessity, Jax rubbed himself with the towel, then laid it out on the sand to flop down on it. Fatigue took over almost instantly, and he fell asleep.

Jax didn't stir from his nap until he heard voices over the sound of the surf. Shaking off his drowsiness, he noticed that the sun's position was so low in the west that the shadow from the hillside surrounding the inlet almost covered his entire body. He turned his full attention to a young couple hobbling down the same precarious path he took earlier that morning. He got up and jogged into the sea for one last dip but stopped short of the surf. There were dozens of dead fish floating in the water slowly being beached by the waves! No longer interested in swimming, Jax turned and walked back to his towel. He noticed a few odd puddles glinting in the sand. Bending down to examine one more closely, he realized it was a glassy footprint . . . his footprint!

Jax straightened up abruptly, crossed the beach, and quickly gathered his things. He jogged across the sand to climb back up the hillside. Oblivious to Jax, the couple giggled and kissed as if they were alone. Jax heard the girl curse as she stubbed her toe on one of his glassy footprints. The boyfriend had just told her he'd found a fragile glass tube branching down into the sand, a fulgurite tube, when she cried out. Jax smiled grimly as he climbed nimbly up the hillside, eager to leave before they saw the dead fish.

—

When Jax got home the house was empty. He threw away the picnic trash and removed his cell phone, then returned the basket to its proper place in the pantry. Before going upstairs to bathe and change clothes, Jax tossed his dirty towel in the laundry room.

Once showered and dressed again in his favorite outfit (jeans and a clean t-shirt) Jax called Augie. When the call connected, Jax only got Augie's answering machine.

"Hey, it's Augie; sorry I missed you. Leave me a message and I'll call back," said the familiar recording.

Quickly, Jax left a brief message and headed downstairs to read the newspaper. When Mamere and Papere arrived home, they found Jax at the dining room table. Jax had the entire classified section spread out in front of him. It didn't take long for Papere to notice all the red circles and x outs.

"What's going on, Jax?" probed Papere, as Mamere peeked over Jax's shoulder for her own look at the goings on.

"Cher', you looking for a new job or an apartment? Some of these jobs are out of town," she asked.

"I was considering it," Jax replied.

"You don't like working at the lumber yard anymore?" She asked.

"I don't like this at all," admitted Papere. "If you're going out of town to work, you might just as well stay home, let us help pay for college, and get a job after that."

"That's tempting," replied Jax, sitting back from the table. "I'm not sure what I'd focus on though."

"That's part of what college is *for*," Papere replied. "You learn how to study, and during that time you begin to learn what fascinates you. *Then* you have focus. That leads you not only to a job, but to a career."

Jax looked intently at Papere. Although he never went to college, Papere was "life smart." He worked his way up from mechanic to shop manager; and eventually, to shop owner. "You didn't have to go to college to find your focus," he said.

"Nope. I never applied myself in school the way you did. And I'm not as smart as you are. I didn't have a desire for more school. I just wanted to put my hands to work getting all greasy and messy," Papere said.

"Greasy and messy!" agreed Mamere with an overpowering sense of love and approval.

"But you're different," Papere continued, as if she hadn't interrupted. "You've got a spark of initiative and you're smart. You should go to college."

"Go to college," Mamere agreed, nodding for emphasis.

"That is something to consider. I'll think on it," pondered Jax.

"Thank God!" exclaimed Mamere. "Papere, we may have a college graduate in our house yet. Time for me to make some dinner."

"Want any help, Mamere?" Jax asked. "No, thank you, Cher'," she replied.

The rest of the evening flew by swiftly. Jax read about a few different universities and waited patiently for Augie to return his call. Jax knew Augie's shift wouldn't be done until 11:30 pm, so he had more time to wait than he wanted. By 10:30 pm, Jax nodded off on the couch; he was completely worn out from the events at the beach.

"Jackson, why don't you head upstairs? You looked pooped," asked Mamere, gently nudging him awake.

Jax yawned, nodded, and said good night to his grandparents. He went up the stairs to his room. When he got to his room and laid down in bed he was thankful that the short trip was without incident. He fell asleep swiftly and deeply. He never even heard Augie's return call.

9

Lesson Three

Jax woke to the sound of falling rain. He laid in bed a moment longer to listen to the rain's mesmerizing rhythms. The gray sky muted the light filtering into his bedroom and soothed him. He glanced at the phone and saw that he missed a call from Augie. *Good,* he thought to himself.

Jax listened to the lengthy message Augie left that confirmed they would meet later today. *Thank God!* Jax thought to himself, eager to get things off of his chest. He had a lot to say. Jax dressed and went downstairs to the kitchen. He was pleasantly surprised to find Mamere already there making breakfast.

"Morning," said Jax, giving her a warm hug and a kiss on the cheek. Mamere immediately recognized a little extra sizzle in Jax's voice; she could tell he slept well and was rearing to go.

"Where's Papere?" inquired Jax.

"Sleeping in this morning to better enjoy his day off. He'll be down in just a little while. Sit down. I have breakfast ready for you and we can chat about this wonderful El Niño rain shower," commented Mamere.

After breakfast, Jax zipped back up the stairs, brushed his teeth, and noticed that he missed yet another call from Augie. He heard Augie's voice float up the stairs before he could pick up the phone and return the call. Augie entered the kitchen through the screen door and said "good morning" to Mamere. Jax quickly finished up in his room and went downstairs to greet Augie. Mamere had already retrieved a plate from the kitchen cupboard for Augie's breakfast when Jax entered the kitchen. They reveled in early morning, light-hearted banter as Augie ate.

When the conversation wound down, the boys excused themselves and headed outside. A quick jog through the light rain brought them to their agreed destination – Jax's tree house. Located at the far edge of the very large backyard, it was partially hidden by expansive tree branches.

The tree house was the brainchild of their third-grade year. They scrounged the necessary materials from the junkyard and enlisted Papere's help. Even with Papere's expert and gentle supervision, the house took several weekends to build. Every chance they got, they slaved themselves to finish the build before the first day of summer vacation.

When all was said and done, onlookers didn't think much of the completed project, but for Jax and Augie, the tree house was their pride and joy. Evie was just as excited about the tree house as they were. She made sure she was on hand to supervise the project at every opportunity and appointed herself to bring the boys a steady stream of sweet tea.

"Remember how Evie 'helped' us build this place?" reminisced Jax with a twinge of humor.

"Uh . . . all I remember is that whenever she 'helped,' I had to pee a lot more," Augie replied.

"Me too!" mused Jax. "All I know is by that second weekend, we were desperate to give her a new job. It's why I handed her a hammer in the first place!"

"Good thing you did," agreed Augie. "And honestly, she turned out to be more help with a hammer than a hindrance."

They climbed the platform and settled in; pleasant memories of meticulous planning and construction of the lofted hideaway flooded their minds.

"Remember how much work it was to get this done?" asked Jax.

"I had *my* ideas and you had *yours*!" confirmed Augie.

"Man! Did we argue! Sooo glad Evie was able to knock some sense into us." Their main argument was over the roof. Augie wanted protection from the elements, but Jax wanted an unobstructed view of the night sky. Evie's logical suggestion to make it half covered and half open made their fight seem immature, even to the small clutch of third graders.

Over the years, the boys made improvements and additions to their nest; chairs, a table, and carefully stored waterproof sleeping bags. A low railing was added at Mamere's insistence – she didn't want her babies rolling over and off the elevated platform in their sleep. If not for the tree's massively dense, years-old leafy canopy, Jax probably would have figured out a way to add solar power too.

As soon as Jax was convinced that he and Augie were completely alone, he gave Augie a review of yesterday's beach episode. One by one, Jax revealed the details about each unique event. Augie's growing excitement was palpable.

"I'm sure you'll be able to bring me," Augie exclaimed with child-like enthusiasm. "I want to taste the sky, too!"

Jax shook his head from side to side as Augie raced ahead full speed. "No, man, not yet. Let me take something small first. I mean, " he paused. "Sure, I can bring my clothes with me now. And I can carry a piece of paper. But those are inanimate objects. And don't forget about the fish! Just being near them I toasted them! I don't know if I can carry anything live," Jax protested.

"Well, figure it out already!" Augie exclaimed; ignoring the possibility that he, too, might get fried.

"And as for the superhero thing," he continued down the road of un-bridled excitement, "don't worry. I won't make you wear a costume or a cape. But it might be good if you wear a mask. You might want to retain some anonymity."

"It's a thought," mused Jax. "I want to protect my family. Carrying out the 'superhero' theme, don't they all have some sad story about losing one or more family members? Don't superheroes have some problem with a horrible disease or crazy accident that gave them powers?"

"I see what you mean, Jax. I certainly don't want to lose anybody; and I don't want to be a casualty," Augie replied soberly.

The seriousness of Augie's comment permeated the atmosphere and put a damper on their conversation. They said nothing for a while, letting the raindrops punctuate the silence; the sibilant shushing of rain sliding down foliage before puddling on the lawn cocooned them in their own thoughts. Drawn hypnotically inward, they let their friendly silence grow. Mamere watched Jax and Augie from the kitchen door as they jogged to the tree house. She reviewed a mental list of changes: high school was behind them, Evie was married, college options loomed, and what about the exciting prospect of apartment hunting? Such a pivotal year! She wanted to race out after them and rein them back in like wandering toddlers but realized they needed to walk this part of the path alone.

From the beginning, Jax and Augie claimed the tree house as a "safe zone," a place where they could "vent" and still leave as friends. On occasion, the boys would ask Mamere and Papere up to their sacred ground to observe, participate, and sometimes even resolve disputes. But she wasn't invited this time, and Mamere realized she didn't need to lecture Jax and Augie about what to do. Mamere assumed they were discussing the paths their lives would take, and she knew they needed privacy to master that decision making process on their own. But what Mamere *could* do was provide pragmatic support, endless love . . . and she could spoil them! With that in mind, she pulled out two special mugs, filled them with steaming hot coffee, and wrapped up two beignets to take to the tree house.

The rain let up and Mamere decided she couldn't hold back any longer. She placed the items on a tray and headed out to serve the boys. Standing at the base of the tree she called out, "Anybody up there ready for a cup of coffee and a beignet?"

Two eager faces peered over the railing and Jax called down to her, "Absolutely! Do you want to come up?"

"No, Te Cher', just here making a delivery," replied Mamere with a smile.

Augie lowered the basket they strung up years ago for just such a delivery; it was inspired by a movie and very handy. Mamere secured the treats in the well- worn basket and sent them on their way to the boys.

"Thank you, thank you!" hollered Jax and Augie in unison as Mamere waved and walked back across the yard to the house.

"Mamere is the best," said Augie as he blew the steam off his mug of coffee and took an appreciative sip.

"Yup," agreed Jax as he sampled his own coffee. "Couldn't, wouldn't, shouldn't do without her," he said before taking a large bite of beignet.

"What next," queried Augie, his own mouth full of pastry.

"No clue," replied Jax.

"Might as well be Superhero 101 – Lesson 3," suggested Augie.

"We need to find a safe place though. Don't want to set the house on fire," finished Jax.

"Agreed," Augie nodded.

They finished the coffee and pastries before climbing down out of the tree house. They jogged back across the yard and Jax popped into the house to put their mugs away while Augie waited outside on the back stoop. When Jax came back outside he realized the rain had stopped and Augie was staring intently at puddles in the yard.

"What's so interesting, Augie?" asked Jax.

Jostled out of his reverie, Augie looked up at his superhero friend, "Just wondering about the 'ripple effect' of your powers. How far do they go? Do they reach beyond the local weather and things immediately around you? And how in the world were you able to make that ball of energy and hurl it?" Augie's persistence impressed Jax.

"Umm. I dunno," Jax answered with a shrug of his shoulders. "You're the sidekick. You're supposed to help keep me in line, not grill me," he protested with a smile. "Why don't you concentrate on finding this reluctant superhero a girlfriend? We could double date. Well, *technically*, you'd have to ask Jessica out on a date first."

"Hold up!" protested Augie. "I would have asked her to Evie's wedding, but that's a lot of pressure for a first date. Next week is the target. I'll see her tomorrow at work," declared Augie as he hopped in the truck with Jax.

"Rats!" exclaimed Jax as he tried to start the truck and heard the easily identifiable sound of a starter clicking, followed by the telltale silence of no connection with the alternator. Frustrated, Jax tried the ignition again, no luck. Not even stomping on the gas pedal elicited a response from the engine. Both boys were speechless. Jax focused his concentration on the engine. He "saw" a gap in the electrical energy flow around the alternator and the battery that weighed on his senses like a dead rock.

Having located the problem, Jax was determined to fix it. He popped the hood and got out of the cab to prop it open. Augie hopped out of the cab and peered under the hood alongside Jax. Immediately, Jax glowed intensely. Augie watched, fascinated, as Jax touched one of his glowing, electrified fingers to the battery and willed a stout energy transfer into it. That complete, Jax crawled behind the wheel, turned the key, and smiled as the engine roared to life.

Without delay, Augie dropped the hood and climbed into the cab. "Pretty handy," he said. "Lesson 3 begins!"

Jax automatically drove to the old still. Rain fell on and off during the short trip. *Good thing I wore my hiking boots instead of running shoes,* Jax thought to himself.

They rode in complete silence; both men wrapped in their own thoughts. Augie, after hearing about the beach events and seeing Jax "fix" the car battery with his powers, was even more curious than ever. Logically, Augie realized he should be worried about safety, but his unbridled excitement drowned out all caution. He was almost giddy just *thinking* about what they might learn today. Studying for his nursing degree made him more and more fascinated about how Jackson might be able to help people who were really sick.

As they neared the scrub, Jax realized that it was immediately adjacent to an expansive lease owned by one of Papere's closest friends. *How could I have missed that?* he thought as he parked the truck on the far side of the drive, away from where he'd parked last time. They would hike the rest of the way.

Standing by the truck, gazing at the trail ahead of them, Augie raised his eyebrows and looked at Jax. Jax met his questioning eyes with a simple response. "I want to keep the still hidden as long as possible."

Augie nodded as, per their routine, they both reached for the always-available rain gear stowed in the truck. Wearing rain ponchos, they walked briskly to the still, careful not to leave an obvious trail. Though he tried not to show it, Augie's mind raced as they navigated through the brush; but Jax, with the keen connection shared by friends, could feel Augie's unrest.

"Ok, enough!" exclaimed Jax.

"What?" asked Augie innocently.

"You're practically *vibrating* over there. Do you think you can calm down?" Jax asked with a sigh.

"Sorry, Jax," he apologized. "I thought I was keeping a pretty tight lid on it. It's just . . . it's so . . ." stuttered Augie. He thought for a moment, then, completely unexpectedly, words spilled out of Augie in a torrent.

"Your power is *so* amazing! Who knows what you can do? Recharge a car battery? Check! Fly? Check! Cure cancer? Maybe! I don't know how you are keeping so chill about the whole thing!" Augie gestured wildly, bumping a tall bush and causing the rain it had collected on its leaves to fall and dribble down his raised arm to his armpit.

"Yuk," he said, as he dropped his arm quickly in a futile attempt to stop the water from rushing to his core.

"Maybe because it's happening TO me," replied Jax. "Maybe I can't wonder and worry because I'm too close to the physical process itself. Whenever I think about something, my body starts to just DO it."

They stopped walking to talk, and though they couldn't see it yet, they could hear the spring. The cheerful, innocent bubbling washed away their anxiety. Jax surveyed the area cautiously, looking for anyone who might be watching. Convinced they were unobserved, he bent down and pulled a weed up from the rain-softened soil.

"Lesson 3," commented Jax as he closed his eyes and held the weed with its soggy ball of dirt in one hand. Within seconds, an intense light emanated from Jax. Lightning – accompanied by pounding thunder – flashed up into the heavens! The phenomenon was so bright Augie had to shield his eyes.

Augie gasped when he lowered his hand and realized he was alone. Jax WAS the lightning that now raced across the sky, generating rapidly changing color patterns. Augie whipped his head around quickly, trying to track Jax overhead, but the motion made him so dizzy he had to stop watching. He backed away from where Jax stood just seconds ago to wait in a relatively dry spot under a large tree.

In short order, Augie felt static electricity raise the small hairs on his arms. By now he knew that signaled Jax's return, so he covered his ears and turned toward the tree to shield his face. In a flash, lightning – followed immediately by a swell of thunder – filled the area. When the lightning subsided, Augie turned around and there stood Jax, frowning, holding a dead weed.

"Nuts," Augie sighed. "I was hoping that would work. "I've only tried this once, remember?" asked Jax.

"Took me a time or two before I could pick up my clothes. I might still be able to do this," he added as he dropped the dead weed and brushed the dry dirt from his hands.

"Come on; let's get to the still!" demanded Jax as he strode off, Augie trailing in his wake.

A little brisk walking brought them to the still. Augie, watching his footing in the slick grass, didn't notice when Jax stopped abruptly and rammed right into Jax's back.

"Woah!" said Jax, jostled by the impact. Augie regained his footing and looked up to see what made Jax stop so quickly. Jax was captivated by the still; it seemed to have deteriorated at an exponential rate.

The now faded belly of the still seemed whisper thin and looked like an old mirror with rust spots. Spring water mixed with the gently falling rain and ran down the sluice to pour into the empty space that was once the mouth of the still. The mix passed unimpeded through the base of the bowl to become a rusty puddle on the ground before sloshing away to join the stream. Augie crossed the clearing and touched the still. The gentle pressure of his fingertip broke what remained of the fragile surface tension holding the metal together. His eyes widened in disbelief as the metal exploded into dust. Like a biblical story, the falling rain clung to the metallic dust, instantly turning blood red and contaminating the puddle. In utter shock, they watched as the perky little spring tried diligently to wash all traces of the macabre puddle away, as if determined to erase the history of the still from the Bayou's tacit memory.

Jax stood near Augie and looked for signs of the moss and flowers; there were none.

"Wow," whispered Jax.

"What do you think of that?" asked Augie.

"Who knows? Maybe the moss and flowers worked to preserve it all these years. Maybe . . . maybe it couldn't stand up to the passage of time without their support," suggested Jax.

"Maybe that's why we never heard of this one," mused Augie. "It might be over a hundred years old. Hey, do you think you can 'fix' it with an energy transfer?"

"Dunno. Guess I could try," Jax said, shrugging his shoulders noncommittally.

Jax stood still and concentrated. It was easier and easier for him to shift into the state where he could see energy patterns. The atmosphere in the clearing prickled with electricity and rain began to glance off the energy field surrounding Jax without touching him. After a few minutes without seeing a visible change, he bent down to harmlessly discharge the energy into the ground.

"Nope. It looks different," Jax stated. "I can see where there used to be a, umm, "living" type of energy but it's changed, and I can't manipulate it now."

"Hmm," replied Augie. "So, what do you want to do next?" he asked.

"Let me try to carry something living again. Something with a heartbeat," Jax replied.

"How 'bout this?" asked Augie, handing Jax a toad he found hunkered down by the stream; taking a large step backwards for safety.

"That'll do," replied Jax, and he was gone.

"Rats!" exclaimed Augie. "Next time give a guy some warning!" he shouted at the empty sky. He stepped back to the relative shelter of the tree at the edge of the clearing. Large raindrops whispered through the foliage, calming his clanging nerves as he waited patiently for Jax to return. It wasn't long before explosive light and sound filled the clearing again. When the light faded, Augie saw Jax standing with the toad in one hand, gently stroking its back with the other. They heard the toad croak and their faces lit up with huge smiles.

"Man," Augie exclaimed. "You *are* learning fast! Why couldn't you bring the plant?" he asked critically.

"Can't you be happy I brought the toad back?" Jax asked peevishly. "I'm still a superhero rookie struggling to get out of kindergarten!" declared Jax as he gently released the toad near the stream.

"Right, sorry," Augie replied abashedly. "You want to practice something else?"

Jax thought for a moment. "Yes," he said and quickly stepped toward Augie, grabbing him in a bear hug. "Before you change your mind," Jax said as he began to shift.

It felt like a million electric goosebumps jumped from place to place on Augie's body as Jax blurred in front of his eyes. Unlike before, both of them now stood within the "bubble," its edges traced in the air by a thin line of shimmering energy. Then, with a suddenness that took Augie's breath away, they lifted off the earth at an astonishing speed. It felt like the weight of the entire world pressed down on him for a moment and then lifted. He was held upright in the shimmering envelope of power that formed around them. Augie looked where he knew Jax's face must be but all he could see was light. He turned his face away to look over Jax's shoulder and tried to hold on but couldn't get a good grip.

Now unbelievably high above the clouds, Jax and Augie zipped randomly through the Earth's thinning atmosphere. Over Jax's shoulder, past the shimmering border, Augie could see the sky change from what he considered the "normal" integrated shades of blue to deep ebony. Stars blinked coldly, with a fierce intensity in the blackness of space that both unsettled and startled him.

The boys' electrified passage through the upper atmosphere created contrails that looked like kaleidoscopic curtains of color swirling and floating away as they flew; momentarily staining the sky before being torn apart by solar winds. For an instant, Augie wondered if he would die from lack of oxygen. He took a big breath to steady himself, and Augie became calmer. He realized suddenly that he could still breathe, and he hoped they were completely shielded from harm by the energy pocket.

"Woohoo!" yelled Augie as exhilaration and fear erased all other words from his mind.

They zipped crazily back and forth across the sky. Augie gradually felt less threatened by all the chaos and got brave enough to loosen his precarious hold on Jax. Jax, fascinated by what he saw below them, redirected their flight and angled toward what Augie thought might be an ocean. Within a heartbeat, Jax allowed the power surge to weaken, and they were standing on a sandbar. Augie, no longer supported by the power within the bubble, collapsed unceremoniously onto the sand and gasped for air with big, shaky breaths.

"Wow," said Augie. "I can't," he paused as he caught his breath. "I don't. I don't know what to say. We're alive! Thank you?" he almost whispered with disbelief.

"No worries," replied Jax. "How about we call that lesson 3?" he asked.

"Done," Augie replied, still shaken. Then, as if all concern were gone, Augie sat and gazed at the waves gently lapping in all directions around the sandbar.

"Let's go swimming," blurted Augie without a second thought.

"Nope," Jax said with a mischievous smile. Augie, sensing a change in Jax, stood up. Jax placed a hand on his friend's shoulder as the air around them began to shimmer; the shimmer coalesced into Jax and suddenly they were darting through the sky again. Before Augie could register any of the sights he was seeing, they lost altitude and landed at the edge of the clearing by the still.

As they landed, Jax – visibly drained of energy and no longer glowing – stumbled forward and leaned on the tree that so recently sheltered Augie from harm. Survival instinct took over and Jax siphoned power from the tree to replenish his personal reserve. The tree, shocked by the unexpected drain, shunted energy from its massive canopy to its core; the leaves all withered on their stems in response. Jax became visibly refreshed and relinquished his hold on the tree.

"Is that what it's like every time?" asked Augie as Jax finally let go of the tree.

"What part?" Jax asked.

"The wild colors and the sky, the weight resting on your shoulders," he said, musing as he struggled to elaborate.

"What you see is not what I see," Jax replied. "I don't know why, but I see that *and* a lot more, like I reach beyond the normal, visible light spectrum. And I'm not just seeing more, I'm *feeling* energy patterns; like the wind shifting, or waves pushing against me." He paused, "what was your other question?"

"Feeling that huge weight press down on you," replied Augie.

"Nope. I feel lighter than air as everything gets faster and faster," commented Jax as he looked at the ground before continuing. "And each time I tap into my 'superhero' powers I feel like I get smarter," he paused. "That probably sounds pretty stupid," he added sheepishly.

"Jax, you're a smart guy to begin with," replied Augie. "It doesn't sound stupid at all. Maybe it's like playing music. You use both sides of your brain because you're using memory and, and what . . . inspiration? Instinct? Intuition? All at the same time," theorized Augie.

"Maybe," replied Jax. "What I do know is that it feels great every time." Jax's words faded and they stopped talking for a few minutes to let their brains process the recent unbelievable events.

Though loathe to dispel the magic of their easy reprieve from every-day pressures and superpower questions, Jax broke the silence first. "Ready to go home?" he asked.

"Yeah, let's call it a day. This superhero sidekick thing is pretty tiring," Augie replied.

Jax kicked distractedly at the ground and didn't respond immediately. He watched as the last of the rust fought against the spring's insistent flow. Finally, reluctantly, Jax looked at Augie as if to say, "Let's go home."

The rain lessened as they slogged their way back to the truck. Now back in "reality," Augie suggested that Jax take him to the duplex apartment he shared with his mom, and by the time he got home it had stopped raining again.

No one was home when Jax arrived, so he decided to cook some rice and start some laundry before he sat down to weigh the pros and cons of college. When Mamere and Papere finally returned, they found Jax crashed out on the couch. As they went about their normal kitchen clean-up routine, Jax woke up, yawned, and stretched in response to their chatter and the sound of clanging dishes.

"The weathermen don't know what to say anymore," declared Mamere.

"Yup," agreed Papere, dutifully shaking his head in resolute agreement. "They don't have a clue! And what about all the dead fish that were reported in the news? Me oh my! Makes no sense at all," observed Papere.

Mamere agreed. "Yes, I heard about that! Dead fish everywhere; and have you ever seen a fulgurite tube? I never even heard of such a thing before this week!"

Jax joined the conversation as he entered the kitchen. "What's this about dead fish? And what in the world is a fulgurite tube?" asked Jax as if he had no clue at all.

"There were a few dozen dead fish floating in Scoop bay. Nowhere else. Just there. And some say they looked as if the life had just been sapped out of them, all dried up and almost mummified," replied Papere. "And for your information, young man, a fulgurite tube is what happens when lightning strikes sand and turns it into glass." Papere always had answers.

"Now Bishop," Mamere shushed him. "You know you can't mummify a fish swimming in the water! Those boys must have been wrong."

"I've never known them to tell a tale, but there's a first time for all sorts of things," replied Papere. Then, shifting subjects on a dime, "Evie called," he said.

"She's still on her honeymoon, isn't she?" asked Jax.

"Yes," replied Papere as Mamere nodded in silent agreement. "Said she had a fright and just wanted to say 'hello.' Seems there are lightning storms in paradise, too. She was almost struck by lightning on the beach."

Jax's heart sank. "Is she ok?" he asked.

"Of course, Cher'," replied Mamere as she crossed the room and hugged her grandson. "Don't you worry about your Evie. She is just fine. You know how she likes to grab some attention! It just gave her a fright."

Jax relaxed into the hug. He was relieved to hear that Evie was all right. He had been so wrapped up in testing the limits of his new-found power that he forgot all about scaring her. He hoped that he would have a chance to talk to her and Franklin and tell them everything soon.

"Need anything before I head to bed?" inquired Jax. "If not, I'm gonna have a piece of fruit and hit the sack. I'm exhausted."

Papere patted his hand and said, "Not a thing, son. Get some rest."

Apple in hand, Jax headed upstairs. Although he loved his grandparents more than anything, right now he needed some time alone. As he bit into the apple, he thought, *Maybe I do need to find a better job, just earn enough to afford a place of my own.*

Entering his room, he answered himself by shaking his head negatively and smiling as he thought. *I sure don't need to rush into anything that would tear me away from Mamere's cooking! It'll all take care of itself; one day at a time.*

10

What?

Jax devoured the apple before he even got to his bedroom. From the open door he tossed the apple core across the room toward the trash can. He half- heartedly kicked at the door to shut it. Staring up at the ceiling fan, it was impossible for him to ignore the sequestered box. Then, even without his bedroom door completely closed, he didn't hesitate but hopped up on his bed to fish the box out of its hiding place.

Peering inside, Jax saw the flowers blinking innocently; their brightly burning essence injecting Jax with a hefty dose of energy that raised the hair on his arms. A pleasant new fragrance flooded the bedroom.

Jax was so lost in the magical moment that he almost didn't hear Papere's heavy footsteps on the landing.

Hurriedly, Jax put the box away and smoothed out his shirt mere seconds before Papere's heavy knock caused the bedroom door to swing fully open. Somewhat startled, Jax turned around; there stood Papere with an inquisitive look on his face.

"What's up?" asked Jax, regaining his focus and demeanor.

"Son, I know the job market is tough," said Papere as he rubbed the back of his neck. "Why don't you come work with me? I can pay you more than you get at the lumber yard," guaranteed Papere in hopes that Jax would just say "yes!"

"You know, that's tempting. But I've never been good at automotive work," Jax smiled as he gently protested Papere's offer. "Not because I haven't been willing. Remember when I tried my hand at it a few years ago? I was like a bull in a china closet," Jax laughingly confessed.

"Yep, sure do. And that's the only reason I hesitated to ask you before now; but you've changed and grown up a bit. You're not the same Jax. And I have every confidence in you," said Papere with a smile on his face.

"Thanks, but no thanks, Papere. I think I should pass for now, keep the lumber yard job, and keep my eyes open to opportunity." Jax almost laughed when he saw the open relief evident on Papere's face.

Papere crossed the room quickly and gave his grandson a reassuring bear hug. Jax, still full of the extra energy dose from the flowers, couldn't stop his grandfather's embrace; and a loud "snap" filled the room as they shared a shock.

"Ouch!" Papere cried as Jax cut the embrace short.

"Dang static electricity! You ever want to try automotive work again; you just say the word. Meantime, consider college. Jax, you are so smart! It would do me and Mamere proud to help get you a college education."

Jax returned his grandfather's smile. "I'll think about it. Don't know what I'd study though. Augie's trying to recruit me for the medical field, but it's just not my thing," Jax concluded.

"Yup," replied Papere. "I couldn't do that either. I love getting grimy and dirty, but I can't take medical stuff. Well," Papere sighed happily, "now you know how we feel." He let go of the conversation and became aware of the pleasant fragrance in Jax's room. "Hmm . . . Smells pretty good in here. You usin' an air freshener now?" asked Papere.

"Nope, maybe I'm just keeping a cleaner room," Jax replied.

"Cleaner?" Papere queried, "you call this 'cleaner?' he joked, catching a glimpse of the discarded apple core near the trash can. "Maybe that's what smells good," he motioned to the apple core on the floor. "God bless you, son. Sleep well."

"Sweet dreams," Jax replied as Papere left Jax's bedroom and headed down the hall to the room he shared with Mamere.

Jax frowned as he quietly closed the door, picked the apple core off the floor and this time successfully disposed of it in the trash can. Frustrated, he sat down on the bed and tried to gather his thoughts about the accidental dose of energy he'd given to Papere. Would he ever have any control over how the flowers and his new-found energy impacted him?

There's got to be some way to have at least a little control over these superpowers, considered Jax. *What about the "cushion" he wrapped around Augie and the toad? Could that insulate people from accidental discharge?* Questions tumbled over each other in his mind as he wondered if controlling these powers was at all possible. As for right now, "mastering" anything – "normal" and "superhero" life included – seemed like a pipe dream.

A yawn surprised him and Jax realized he was really, really, tired. *First and foremost, I need rest,* thought Jax. *Maybe tomorrow I'll figure something out,* was the last thought that crossed Jax's mind as he crawled into bed and drifted off to sleep.

11

Cheryl

Justice was waiting patiently for Augie when he got home. "Home" was a little two-bedroom house Augie and his mother shared for as long as he could remember. A postage-stamp sized fenced-in backyard – barely large enough to hold Justice's doghouse and a small clothesline – boasted a patch of stubborn grass that Augie mowed regularly to earn a slight discount on their rent. Augie loved every inch of it.

Augie let himself in the front door and patted Justice, then made himself a sandwich to eat while studying. He waited patiently while Justice wolfed down his own meal, then the two retired to Augie's room – Augie to study and Justice to nap.

Augie finished reading two chapters in his anatomy book and was trying to stay awake studying pharmacology when his mom got home. As usual, Justice was the first to know she arrived. The big dog left Augie's side and padded softly to his guard post at the front door so he could be the first to greet her as she entered the house.

"I'm home," Cheryl called out as she opened the front door. Augie's mom, arms laden with groceries, only paused long enough in her trek to the kitchen to kick the door shut behind her. She greeted Justice and the happy dog sniffed at her shoes as she cooed to him, then loped after her to the kitchen.

"Down in a minute," Augie responded. "Do you need any help?"

"Nope! Got it," she said, shoving aside the piles of newspaper and junk mail to make room for the grocery bags on the kitchenette's small table. Cheryl wasn't the most stringent housekeeper and tended toward clutter, but she always made time to wash dishes before and after cooking. She simply could not abide a sink full of dirty dishes.

"Hi!" Augie sang out as he bounded down the stairs to plant a kiss on his mother's cheek. "Mama! You shouldn't carry everything in all at once," scolded Augie as he saw the load of groceries. "See this? I've got a matching one on the other side and they both work," teased Augie as he flexed and pointed to one of his well- developed biceps.

"I know, baby," Cheryl smiled as she hugged her son. "But I also know that you study this time of day; far more important than carrying a few bags for an old lady!"

"Old lady?" Augie queried. "Ha! I've seen the way men look at you. They don't share your opinion."

"Nah!" Cheryl said, blushing slightly. Determined to redirect the conversation, Cheryl continued, "I need to change out of clothes that smell like a greasy diner!" and went up the stairs to change clothes, leaving Augie to tidy up the kitchen and put the groceries away.

As Cheryl took off her uniform and started a load of laundry, memories raced through her mind. More often than not, making ends meet on a waitress' income was challenging. Augie mowed lawns as a young boy just to bring in some extra cash. And recently, Cheryl was working longer and picking up extra shifts to help pay for Augie's nursing school. Life was hard, but worth every struggle; especially if it gave Augie a chance at a more promising future.

The enticing aroma of the dinner Augie prepared pulled Cheryl back to the present and down the stairs. "Smells heavenly," she called out with a smile.

"Nothing special," he said. "Just turkey, potatoes, and greens."

"And a big ol' pot of coffee," added Cheryl. She walked over to the happily gurgling pot and poured herself a cup. "Want some?" she asked.

"Yes, ma'am," Augie replied. "I've got more studying to do tonight."

They sat down at the table together, Cheryl eating with gusto and Augie just sipping at his cup of coffee. "Why aren't you eating, Cher'?" she asked.

"I ate with Jax earlier. Last time we went hunting we were successful. That's some fresh wild turkey you're eating there," he said.

"Absolutely delicious, baby boy!" sighed Cheryl happily. As she ate, Augie and his mom enjoyed small talk about Evie's wedding, Augie's job, school, and the weather.

"How's Jax doin?" asked Cheryl.

"Havin a hard time," confided Augie. Augie was glad she didn't press him for any details. Wisely, Augie changed the subject.

"Mama, I was hoping to host a small dinner party next week. I want to invite Jessica, Jax, and one of Jessica's friends."

"Great!" exclaimed Cheryl. "I've been wanting to meet Jessica."

Augie paused before speaking again. "Mama," he hesitated, "I was hoping you would maybe find a way to *not* be home for this party."

Augie anxiously waited for his mom to respond. He loved her, but sometimes she acted oddly rude. It was almost as if she didn't believe he loved her, or didn't believe that people liked her, or something. She wore sarcasm like some sort of armor. Augie learned to look beyond her sarcastic words to find the love, or the humor, behind the sometimes hurtful, bitter words.

Without realizing it, Cheryl taught Augie at a young age how to twist an expression into an acerbic retort that made her smile wryly and made him think he was clever. Clever or not, Augie couldn't remember how many times he apologized to Jax as tears streamed down his friend's young and innocent face because of something hurtfully blurted out. Augie plainly saw that words could wound and haunt, and he was hard-pressed to understand why his mom spoke in such a manner. He only truly began to understand the hurtful nature of sarcasm after meeting and being around Jax's grandparents; they spoke very differently. As a child, Augie (tearfully confused and embarrassed after a "witty" sarcastic retort) retreated to Mamere's different type of love and greater wisdom as he sought to understand what he did wrong. Even now, Augie's memory of one particular childhood conversation with Mamere echoed clearly in his mind.

"Baby, little ears often think sarcasm is just downright meanness," Mamere said as she mussed Augie's hair. "Jax doesn't understand sarcasm 'cause we don't talk like that. It would break my heart if I said something I thought was clever and all it did was hurt you."

Later that night, when Augie went home, he tried to talk to his mom about what Mamere said to him.

"Wow!" Cheryl said with a harsh laugh. "That is *so* naïve! Jax will have to learn it someday. Might as well be now."

From that day on, Augie could sometimes hear the pain and fear in his mother's laugh and see the calloused outlook that protected her tender heart.

Cheryl paused thoughtfully before she continued. "Ok, honey; I guess you can't flirt with a girl while your mama is watching," she said through a disarming chuckle. "What day are you planning on?" probed Cheryl.

"Not sure yet, Mama," Augie said with a sad little sigh. He knew instinctively that being asked to give him some privacy hurt her feelings; sometimes he felt like he just couldn't win with her.

"What day is best for you?" he asked.

"Let me check my schedule tomorrow. I'm pulling a few doubles this coming week, but I don't remember which days," she sighed. As she continued her meal, the conversation waned. When done, Cheryl excused herself while Augie did the dishes.

"Good night, Mama!" he called out, and quietly closed his bedroom door to study for another hour before going to bed. Drifting off to sleep that night, fitful thoughts about the upcoming dinner party dominated his dreams. In the morning, the insistent buzz of his alarm clock became part of the strange, nocturnal charade as an oven timer demanding attention.

Finally waking, Augie rolled over and smacked the alarm, turning it off. He was still exhausted, but school demanded his attention; he had two classes before his shift at the hospital. It would be a long day without time to muse about his superhero best friend.

"But of course," he thought, *"I'll be able to talk to Jessica."*

12

The Lumberyard

Yawning and stretching sleepily, Jax woke up feeling refreshed. Unlike Augie, he didn't have any odd dangling remnants of quirky dreams clouding his morning. As usual, he took his breakfast out on the front porch to enjoy the peace and quiet of his sleepy little Louisiana town. This morning, he devoured a bowl of grits laced with cinnamon and brown sugar, drowned in butter and milk; and of course, a cup of strong coffee.

Up and down the street, the little town woke up and began to stir. Trash can lids clanged raucously as they were emptied into the gaping mouths of growling trash trucks and being set back down. Full of breakfast and with a full belly, Jax stood up, stretched, and stepped away from the familiar weekly "trash symphony." Work called!

Ten minutes later, Jax was out the door and on the way to the lumberyard. Jax loved everything about working there; the challenging, hard, hot labor, the smell of cut lumber, the chance to pick up stuff with his arms and work his legs. But first and foremost, as an employee, Jax wanted to see happy customers; he strove to satisfy every one of them, no matter how difficult. Sometimes it worked; but sometimes his best intentions got waylaid by those who seemed impossible to please. The least little customer complaint would send him running in circles as he tried to make things better.

One time, Jax noticed a short line of people outside the store's bathroom entrance. Curious, he went over to find out what was going on. A woman could be heard crying inside the tiny room. A few uncomfortable looking men had knocked on the door to no avail.

"We knocked on the door, but no answer," offered one of the waiting customers.

Hmm, what now? thought Jax, as he shifted into high gear and headed for the employee restroom to make it presentable. Within minutes, those waiting were redirected to the employee restroom. Jax returned to the public facility and knocked on the door. Eventually, the woman exited the locked room and cried on Jax's shoulder for a good thirty minutes; all over a failed romance.

Though happy to help the woman, Jax quickly started to feel trapped in her personal drama. He finally caught his female manager's eye, who – resisting the urge to laugh out loud at Jax's predicament – intervened and extricated him by redirecting the woman's attention elsewhere. Jax was never happier to get back to work that day.

As Jax neared the yard on the edge of town, he smelled and saw dense smoke floating skyward. Not long after the first whiff of smoke, the local fire engine roared by Jax, siren blaring and lights flashing. A couple of blocks away from work, Jax had to stop and park the car; the road was barricaded by police.

Walking the remaining two blocks, the aroma of burning wood wafted on the breeze. Now more concerned than ever, Jax quickened his stride. Once he made the final turn toward the lumberyard, nothing but brilliant flames and billowing smoke dominated the sky. The street that ran in front of the lumberyard buzzed with people who were either doing their jobs or just curiously straining to get an up-close glimpse of the inferno. Yellow police tape strung hastily across half the parking lot was all that kept people at a safe distance.

The local news "team" (one reporter and cameraman) stood on the sidewalk as close to the yellow tape as they could get, filming with the blaze in the background. Another cameraman and reporter flanked them, and he vaguely recognized them as the news team from the neighboring town. Firemen – determined to keep the blaze from spreading to the outer buildings and exposed stacks of lumber – stood close to the building as they trained a heavy stream of water on the larger part of the structure that still remained. Sadly, a large portion of the building was a smoldering ruin.

The fire was so large, that in addition to the single fire truck owned by the city, two fire engines from neighboring towns had responded. Jax watched as three firemen emerged from the building carrying an unconscious victim and raced to one of the ambulances where paramedics stood by looking eager for work. Jax wondered about the identity of the person being carried out.

Without warning, Jax's vision blurred, shifted from the paramedics, and refocused on the firemen obscured by dense smoke. He now saw a mixed group of energy signatures clearly etched in the curling grey smoke; some were human, while others pinpointed locations of individual fires and their virulence. With alarm, he realized there was another person lying on the floor in the building near a fire cell that writhed with energy, threatening to burst. Assessing the lone human energy signal, he thought it appeared weaker than any of the others.

The stream of water shifted as the firemen, seeing they were losing the battle to save the main building, decided to put their efforts toward containment and damage control.

"Over there! Over there!" shouted Jax's manager at one of the fire crews as she gestured excitedly, pointing to an area of grave concern.

"It's too late!" responded the fireman closest to her, as he shook his head negatively and patted her on the shoulder before returning his complete attention to the flames.

She turned away from the fire and scanned the crowd, hoping to find someone to help her. In anguish, she wrung her hands, her entire body a silent appeal for help. Catching sight of Jax in the crowd, she jogged over to him.

"What's going on, Marcia? What are you trying to do?" Jax asked.

She bit her lip to stifle a sob and shook her head; flecks of soot fell out of her hair onto her shoulders as she moved. "GH is still in there!" she exclaimed, barely loud enough to be heard above the mayhem. "He and Winchell opened early with me this morning. When I walked into the office, I saw the safe open. The cash for the registers was gone! Winchell went to the back to process inventory and I was just about to call out to GH when I heard a weird 'whooshing' noise." Marcia paused for a moment to catch her breath before continuing.

"The door to the office slammed shut and then I heard an explosion! The fire alarms went off a few seconds later but the door was stuck fast. I banged on it and banged on it!" wailed Marcia as tears welled up in her eyes. "But it wouldn't open! I was so scared! No one could hear me. I thought I was trapped!" She choked the next sob back and steeled herself, determined to finish her story.

"Next thing I know, GH is banging on the other side of the door, telling me to stand back. He hacked his way through with an axe. He made sure I got out, then he went back to find Winchell. Winchell was just carried out by the firemen, but no one knows where GH is . . . and they won't go back in to find him!" she cried, tears streaming down her face.

Instantly, Jax realized that the weaker energy signal he saw in the building was probably GH.

Jax started to respond to Marcia but was interrupted by the same fireman approaching Marcia with an update. With Marcia distracted, Jax easily slipped unnoticed through the growing crowd to the edge of the parking lot. Once there, he jogged quickly down the block and into the first empty alley.

Sensing the urgency of a friend in distress, he allowed his internal energy to build as fast as possible. Within milliseconds he was a burning bright, white-hot bolt of lightning boiling with energy! From the alley, he launched skyward and out of sight high above the clouds before changing course to land in the fire, obscured by the billowing smoke, next to the wavering energy source.

The weak energy source was GH. He was unconscious, a bruise just beginning to show on his jaw, his breathing ragged and shallow. Acting quickly, Jax scanned the immediate area to make sure he didn't need to return to extract anyone else. He calculated that the cluster of firemen working at the far side of the blaze was at a distance safe enough for him to work. He reached down and gingerly lifted and cradled his coworker. Next, he gathered an energy ball in his fist, similar to the one he'd made at Evie's wedding, but larger. He hurled the energized ball at the nearest fire source with calculated precision. The ensuing explosion snuffed out the fire like blowing out a candle's flame. The concussive backdraft of air that rushed in to reignite the fire was muddled and defeated as Jax – with GH securely in his grasp – shot up into the sky.

Hovering in the atmosphere high above the blaze, Jax caught the smell of rain in the distance.

"Yes!" shouted Jax. *Drown the fire,* he thought as he concentrated on waking the power lying almost dormant in the clouds. The atmosphere began to swirl counterclockwise as Jax drew the rain clouds closer and closer to the town and the blaze.

The crowd around the lumberyard grew silent and stopped moving as, one by one, they looked to the sky at the enormous drenching clouds assembling directly overhead; they moved and ran for cover only when the clouds began dumping water onto the flames. Jax agitated the tumultuous weather by flitting back and forth across the sky, coaxing rain out of the clouds to drench the fire.

Finally convinced the fire was under control, Jax returned to the alley with GH still securely in his grasp. The damp ground protested Jax's landing, hissing and sputtering around Jax's feet as steam rose around him. Jax reacted instinctively as tiny flames coiled around his feet, stomping on the alley asphalt to put out the little fires and sending sparks in all directions. Without thinking or skipping a beat, Jax propped GH on his own feet so he could hold him with one arm, pointed his free hand toward the sky, and hurled a lightning bolt into the atmosphere.

Now safely "grounded," Jax picked GH up again, slung him over his shoulder, and jogged through the alley to the street and the nearest ambulance. Creatively, Jax approached the ambulance from a position that looked as if they were exiting the burning building. Paramedics rushed to their aid and initiated medical care for GH, who was semi-conscious.

Those in the crowd who previously witnessed the lightning strike appear to extinguish the fire, were protected from the rain by a kaleidoscope of umbrellas. The rain fell gently at first, almost hesitantly; but under Jackson's guidance it soon increased sufficiently to help suppress the fire.

Both the local news camera crew and the crew from the neighboring town captured the heroic efforts of the firemen, the terrifying flames, and the lightning strike. They all appeared unusually excited and Jax wondered what had them so animated.

Crap! thought Jax as he absent-mindedly raked his fingers through his hair, causing sparks to fly everywhere. *What if they caught me on tape?* he asked himself. Concerned that he might indeed be recorded, he pulled his hand down and willed himself to be calm. It wouldn't do if he'd been caught on tape and it would be worse if he called attention to himself now. Convinced that GH was in good hands, Jax focused fully on the news recordings. Somehow, if they existed, they had to be destroyed.

Surveying the situation, Jax noticed the fire chief relocating the news crews further away from the police tape. He watched the crews, and from the many stops, starts, and restarts in their filming he realized they were recording and not broadcasting live. That gave him an idea and, hopefully, a window of opportunity.

Jax knew that a strong magnet could erase the computer hard drive on which the broadcast was recorded. Finding a magnet and getting it next to the camera seemed Jax's only, almost impossible, option for keeping his powers a secret. Fate seemed to lend a hand when the crew happened to place the camera on a large metal pole that was lying in the parking lot. The pole stretched all the way to an almost out of sight stack of lumber. Jax's mind raced as he formulated a plan of attack.

Inconspicuously, Jax worked his way behind the stack of lumber. Crouching down next to the pole, he saw a piece of pipe lying in the debris. He picked up the pipe, then searched until he found a length of discarded copper wire. Working quickly, he wrapped the wire tightly around the pipe. He held the wire and pipe in his hands while he directed more and more energy through the coiled wire; eventually it was strong enough to magnetize the beam. He smiled when he heard a metallic "snap" as the magnet pulled a paperclip out of the reporter's stack of paper. The photographer bent down to retrieve the paperclip.

Wow, that's strange, thought the photographer as he pulled the paperclip away from the pipe. He had to pull harder than he expected to pick up the paperclip, and when he handed it back to the reporter it flew once again to cling to the beam.

Jax shifted his vision and sensed that the magnet was strong enough to affect the camera. He stopped energizing the pipe and stepped away to let the electricity taper, hoping the impromptu magnet had done the trick. Of course, he wouldn't know if he'd been successful until they tried to play back the recording.

Content that there was nothing more he could do, Jax made his way back to the ambulance where he'd left GH. A couple of minutes later, Marcia saw Jax standing by the ambulance.

Gotta talk to Jax, she thought as she slipped back through the crowd to Jax and GH. Marcia gave Jax a hug, then checked on GH. She thought he seemed ok, thanks to the timely actions of the paramedics. The paramedics couldn't say much about GH's injuries but did tell Jax and Marcia he'd been knocked out, had severe smoke inhalation, and was seriously injured.

"Excuse me, but where did you find him?" Marcia asked the paramedics.

"Uh – we didn't find him; he just showed up," replied the medic, who was more consumed by providing care for his patient than figuring out the exact sequence of events.

Jax took advantage of her distraction and slipped away to eavesdrop on the conversation between the nearest newsmen.

"What do we know about how the fire started?" the reported asked.

"Well, somebody thought fertilizer was involved –which the lumber-yard doesn't even carry – or turpentine," the camera man replied.

"And what *exactly* do you mean when you say you 'didn't press record?!'" fumed the reporter. "Are you telling me we didn't get any of this on tape?"

The reporter's angry tone escalated with each word, making the camera man cringe, but the words were sweet news to Jax. *Thank goodness! No tape*! thought Jax, sighing with relief. Digesting what he heard, Jax also realized that no one knew anything about the robbery yet.

The rain didn't last long, but it was effective. Jax watched the firemen achieve and maintain control over the dying blaze. Marcia found him in the crowd and asked a few more questions but she knew he didn't have any answers. She was quieter now, compared to her earlier "non-stop" talking mode. The shock and dismay started to weigh heavily on Marcia, making her less talkative.

During one of the lulls in conversation, Jax mentally reviewed what Winchell said before he was transported to the hospital: he was taking inventory in the big warehouse; heard the blast; rushed back to the main entrance; heard GH yell. That's when he saw two people run out. They were wearing sweat jackets with the hoods pulled up and bandanas over their faces. One of them carried a large duffel bag.

"That's all I remember," Winchell said, gingerly pointing to the back of his head as he showed Jax the protruding, large lump.

Jax lingered with Marcia as the crisis resolved, not wanting to leave until after she gave her statement to the police. They asked her not to divulge any information about the robbery to anyone, not even to Mr. Credeur, who owned the lumber yard.

While he visited with Marcia, he got a phone call from Mamere. She'd heard about the fire and wanted to make sure he was ok. The relief in her voice as she spoke with him was a bright spark that made Jax smile. "I'll be home soon, Mamere," Jax said reassuringly. "I just want to stay with Marcia until her boyfriend shows up."

"You stay with her as long as she needs you," Mamere instructed. "Don't rush off."

The crowd seemed to become more animated when Mr. Credeur arrived. His quickly scanned the entire, devastating scene. The fire had turned the main building into a smoking ruin but the warehouse and most of the smaller buildings were spared. In some ways he was relieved the damage wasn't any worse.

"Marcia," said Mr. Credeur, making a mental shift from damage assessment to situational analysis. "I need you to send me a copy of the schedule, please. Do you think you can do that? Everyone will get paid this week, just like normal, as if they were working and we were open for business. And . . . how are you, my friend? Have you been cleared by the paramedics?" he asked.

"Yes, sir, I can do that" she said.

"Are you ok?" he asked again.

"Yes, sir," she said.

He patted her on the shoulder and said, "You aren't very convincing. Is Arlo here?"

"Not yet," she sighed.

"Well, I'll be in touch. Call me if you need anything," Mr. Credeur said.

"Jax," he said, "when the fire marshal clears it, I'll need help with the cleanup."

"Of course, sir," he said.

"I don't expect that to happen for a few days, though. Will you wait with Marcia until Arlo gets here?" he asked.

"Absolutely," replied Jax.

Mr. Credeur gave Marcia a hug, then left to talk with the police and the fire chiefs.

The morning seemed to fly by, and it was early afternoon before Jax even thought about lunch. As Arlo arrived, Jax suggested the three of them go to the diner or to his house where he could whip up a quick lunch. Marcia thanked him but said she just wanted to go home and take a nap.

The news crews had departed, and the firemen were doing one last sweep of the site. Jax looked over the entire scene and wondered if "normal" would ever be a word he could use to describe his life again. Turning to leave, he noticed police tape mocking him by flapping "normally" in the slight breeze that followed the rain. He said goodbye to Marcia and Arlo and jogged back to his truck.

During the drive home, Jax mulled over everything. He was grateful to Mr. Credeur for the impromptu "paid vacation." More importantly, he was thrilled that his magnet stunt successfully erased the recordings. He almost laughed out loud remembering how a few metal objects flew over and stuck to the beam. Jax, completely absorbed in his thoughts about the robbery and his injured coworkers, was oblivious to the darkening clouds that began to boil in the upper atmosphere.

As soon as Jax parked the truck at home, Mamere wrapped him in a tender hug. Jax relaxed in her arms and the churning clouds subsided enough to let the sun peek through once again.

"Mamere!" he exclaimed, returning her hug. "I'm ok. The fire trucks got there ahead of me and already had things under pretty good control."

"Just not going to miss an opportunity to hug you, Cher'," she replied, rubbing his back. "Come on inside and get you some dinner."

They walked to the house side by side. Mamere paused as Jax held the door for her and said, "Jackson, you are such a gentleman. Just like your Papere."

He kissed her on the cheek. "It's always a pleasure to hold the door for a lady," he said, sketching a quick bow. Mamere chuckled and blushed, saying, "You go on now," and flounced into the house like a queen. Inside, the table was already set, including a plate of sandwiches. After his exhausting morning, Jax still took the time to hold Mamere's chair as she sat down. Once Jax was settled at the table, Mamere prayed over their meal.

"Dear Lord, thank You for taking care of Jax and all the others at the lumberyard this morning and always. Thank You for returning him safely to our side. And, as always, we give You thanks for that which we are about to receive. By Your hands . . . we are fed. Amen."

13

Outer Space – Another Lesson

Jax and Mamere finished lunch right before Jax's cell phone rang, the distinctive tones clearly identified the caller as Augie. Jax excused himself and got up from the table, plugging in his ear buds for some privacy to answer the call.

"Buddy, we need to talk. When can we meet?" Jax inquired tersely and without preamble.

"I've got to finish my shift first," responded Augie. "Heard about the fire-" was all he could say before Jax spoke again.

"Small town. News flies," Jax affirmed.

Augie continued as if he hadn't been interrupted, "and that two people were hurt. Also heard there was a lightning strike. Some think the lightning *started* the fire, but others are saying that lightning put *out* one of the fires."

Jax paused before he spoke, "Yup. I got there after the fire started. Now I've got an unplanned vacation!" marveled Jax. "Heck, Mr. Credeur gave *everybody* one week's paid vacation." Jax was still stunned by the owner's generosity.

"Sweet," replied Augie. "I'll check with Mom about moving that turkey dinner up and we can talk while we cook before the girls arrive."

"Girls?" asked Jax.

"Uh . . . yeah," replied Augie in a slow, drawn out manner. Jax heard the smile on his friend's face change the way he spoke over the phone. "Jessica has a friend she'd like you to meet. She says the lady's really cute."

"Okay. I guess I can trust her instincts in finding me a dinner date," Jax replied. "Call or text me when you know more."

"Gotcha," said Augie as he hung up the phone.

Before heading upstairs, Jax checked in with Mamere in the kitchen. "Need any help?" he asked; always willing to carry his weight.

"It's all done. You go on with your day. I'm good," she replied.

Jax headed up the stairs, fatigue accentuating each step. "'No wonder I'm tired," he mumbled softly. "Things have been crazy."

Jax closed the bedroom door and sprawled out on his bed. Above his head, the ceiling fan blades spun lazily, still creatively hiding the flowers tucked away near the down rod. Light shone briefly above the fixture, fading almost as quickly as it sprang up. As the light vanished, the flowers dispersed a fresh scent throughout the room. The aroma both relaxed and energized Jax. He got up immediately to lock his already closed bedroom door (he did *not* want to be caught unaware again), then held out his hand. Magically, the box floated gently down and straight into his hand. *Did I do that? Or are the flowers in control?* Jax asked himself, still adjusting to his new world of superpowers.

Landing gently in Jax's palm, the top popped off the box. Without warning, the entire room was flooded with a radiant light and potent fragrance. Instantly, Jax's veins glowed with light and his vision evolved as the energy within accelerated exponentially. Before Jax could blink, he was surrounded by the same kind of shimmering energy sphere he saw at the beach. In his hand the flowers burned more brightly with each passing heartbeat; they soon rivaled the sun in their intensity.

Without thinking, Jax reached out and touched a fiery petal, marveling when it didn't hurt him. Jax closed his eyes to shield them from the light, but nothing changed. In fact, he now saw *through* his eyelids. He heard Mamere knock softly on his bedroom door as he hovered in the sphere a few feet off the floor.

"Cher'?" asked Mamere.

"What is it, Mamere?" questioned Jax, a slight tremble in his voice. *Thank God I locked the door!* he thought.

"Do you hear that humming sound?" continued Mamere. "I can't figure it out."

Listening to Mamere's quiet query, he knew there were things of his own to "figure out." The humming was from the cushion of energy that held Jax suspended above the floor. He thought quickly, scrambling for a logical response.

"It's in here, Mamere. The fan's making a buzzing noise. I'll turn it off if it bothers you."

"Not to worry, Cher'. Now that I know what the noise is, it won't bother me," she said. Content with Jax's response, Mamere continued past his bedroom and down the hallway to her own. Jax saw Mamere's bright splash of energy move away, but – distracted by his current situation – he did little more than notice her departure.

Jax watched as tendrils of energy began to grow and play on the edges of the energy bubble like electrified dancers. Uncontrolled, one of the tendrils blazed toward the trash can and set fire to a piece of paper.

Snuff it out! thought Jax as his mind took over and extinguished the tiny, potentially hazardous blaze.

The chaos in the room escalated as vines emerged from the moss. He focused on them as they climbed out of the box, wrapped around his bicep, and sprouted new, glowing buds. He watched, fascinated as they developed into full bloom. Miniature white sparks shot in all directions like newborn stars birthed from a supernova.

The tiny stars pulsed and hummed rapidly as they were flung into orbit above the flowers that birthed them. In response, the flower petals opened further to expose the anther and stamen within. Puff balls of pollen shot out of the stamens with pinpoint accuracy to paint the tiny sparks white or blue – dictated by the color of the stamen's blossom. The pollen bursts knocked the sparks out of their original orbits into higher positions.

Jax saw the energy bubble expand and felt the power increase in him with each passing second. Alarmed, he realized the sphere now took up most of the available space in his room.

I've gotta get out of here! Jax screamed silently to himself. *If not . . . that trash can fire . . . won't be the last pyrotechnic display!*

Searching for a quick fix, Jax tried to siphon off energy by directing it out the window. Unfortunately, the energy he directed outward simply bounced off the inner boundary of the sphere and back into the bubble – like a superconducting feedback loop – his efforts only pumped more energy into the system. Panic flared in Jax as he tried, and again failed, to drain energy from his body and control the escalating situation.

His body rose even higher off the floor as his panic grew. The energy that pulsed through the room propelled the fan blades and they spun crazily in response. Frantically, Jax dropped the box and pushed against the sphere walls with both hands, trying to push through the barrier. The flowers and moss spilled out of the box and floated in the air on riotous currents of energy. Every effort pumped more energy through him with greater intensity and speed. Tears of dismay and frustration coursed down Jax's face as he opened his mouth in a silent cry. Every tear seemed to strangely intensify the light, colors, and energy coursing through his body.

I can't survive this much longer – it feels like I'm gonna explode! Jax screamed in his mind.

Pushed toward the edge of his consciousness, he worried about Mamere down the hallway. Any control over the raw power now seemed impossible. His only hope: being far, far away; far enough away from prying eyes and cameras and the potential threat of harming those nearby.

Jax fought to free himself, but his muscles just bunched and flexed ineffectually in direct response to the surging current. Caught up in the struggle, he barely noticed when the familiar lines of his bedroom walls and furniture blurred. The shimmering, opaque border of the sphere thickened and became even more incandescent, almost impossibly bright, as his room faded completely from sight.

Can't . . . take . . . much . . . more, thought Jax as he closed his eyes and desperately sought escape from the rampant energy in his body.

Through his closed eyelids, Jax became aware of the black border and blurry center of tunnel vision. He sagged as conscious thought began to slip away from him.

Then, out of nowhere, the power eased. *Thank goodness,* thought Jax, grateful for the respite. He gulped in deep, ragged breaths and opened his eyes. Though his eyes were now wide open, he could see nothing beyond the inside of the bubble.

Eventually, the power stabilized at what seemed a less intense level and the border of the bubble thinned, becoming less opaque. Jax strained to see something, *anything* beyond the sphere. Initially, he saw nothing more than an unfathomable black emptiness looming in all directions. With each interminably slowly passing second, he was able to pick out one, then two, then more, distant points of light. Jax's eyes were irresistibly drawn to one particular cluster of distant, twinkling lights. The quietly peaceful sight relaxed him, and his breathing became easier.

He was calmer now within the protective bubble. *I'm okay,* he thought, lowering his arms inside the sphere. As if responding to him, the shimmering border faded to complete transparency. Now able to see easily far beyond the sphere, Jax brought one hand up and touched the inner margin. The sphere immediately responded by glowing where he touched it. The longer he held his hand in place, the wider the light spread around the sphere, increasing in brilliance and opacity. He pulled his hand back down and the border became clear again; nothing else changed within the bubble. He was still safe.

A curious mix of fear and security held him. Though he felt safe inside the bubble, Jax realized things could change at any moment – the sphere seemed to be in control, and he was just along for the ride. At least . . . he hoped *something* was in control!

Jax pondered the situation and turned to his right, immediately needing to raise his hand and shield his eyes from an extremely bright star! He turned away instinctively, and there, off in the immeasurable darkness, floated a mysterious, rotating blue and white marble paired with a smaller, pockmarked grey stone half hidden in its shadow. Innumerable, twinkling specks of light were scattered throughout the inky black darkness. He suddenly realized that the "marble" was the planet Earth and a burst of bright new fear flooded him.

"Damn!" he exclaimed. *Well, I guess this is far enough away for safety,* he thought to himself, half laughing in shock. He briefly wondered if he'd done any damage to the house when he left the bedroom, but there wasn't a thing he could do about it from here.

Fear and panic now in check, he was more interested in the blue and white flowers. Floating effortlessly in the sphere, they glowed brilliantly, and continued to hit their marks with pollen. Jax watched intently, hoping not to miss any aspect of everything unfolding in front of him. He still had a lot to learn.

As he watched, the vines wrapped around his bicep and throbbed in time with his heartbeat. The sphere expanded and the white and blue targets spread out further. Energy pulsed through the filaments exactly as before. The amount of pollen remained consistent, but the actual targets changed.

How did they do that? Jax wondered. *How could they point a stream of pollen at a target and have it puddle into a ball to knock each target precisely? What was changing?* Peering even more intently, Jax saw what was really happening. It was the opening of the filament tube that changed! It was like making adjustments to the nozzle on a garden hose.

Intrigued, Jax stretched out his hand and tried to hit the flowers by "zapping" them with little energy jolts of his own. He fired at the tiny stars; first using one finger, then two fingers, then one hand, then two hands. He experimented with multiple configurations. He changed the space between his fingertips and tried to make an energy ball form at varying distances, just like the pollen. When he hit them, the flowers changed to a deep red color and changed their position, making his target practice interesting and gradually more challenging. When he missed, which was quite often at first, the energy ball skipped around the sphere before being absorbed into the sphere's border.

Fascinated with his target practice, Jax lost all track of time. The flowers generated a gentle power out here that both sustained him and demanded his attention. He didn't know when the thought first crossed his mind, but Jax was now sure that the flowers were teaching him how to manipulate the energy. The longer he practiced targeting the sparks, the more accurate he got.

A loud growl from his stomach and a pang of hunger distracted Jax from his lesson. He looked beyond the sphere and saw that the moon was no longer in the Earth's shadow and was approaching his position. He wondered just how long he'd been up here practicing. Deciding it was time to go home, Jax instinctively stretched his hands out to either side of him. The sphere shrank until he could comfortably place his hands on the inner surface. Energy coursed through him and the sphere once again shimmered and thickened as it became opaque. Knowing what was happening made it easier for Jax to tolerate and control the energy surge. Within moments he was back in his own bedroom, watching the light recede from the room as the power faded. He didn't hear any thunder.

"Thank You, Jesus," he said out loud. A huge thunderclap in his bedroom surely would catch Mamere's attention and she'd try to break down the door to save him. Jax did wonder, however, why there wasn't any thunderous noise.

The flowers retracted on their stems to snug little resting places in the moss. Gently, Jax unraveled and removed the vines from his bicep. Lifting them, he saw a "stain" on his arm like a tattoo. He smoothed the short sleeve of his t-shirt down over the intricate pattern. Tucking moss, vines, and flowers back in the box, he hid it once again above the blades by the down rod.

Satisfied, Jax unlocked his door and headed downstairs. By now, it was evening, and Mamere and Papere were in the kitchen eating a late dinner. As Jax entered the kitchen, Papere glanced up.

"Good evening sleepy head," teased Papere. "You must have been awfully tired," he continued with a hint of fatigue in his own voice.

"Yes, sir. Good evening, Mamere," he said as he entered the kitchen and stood by the table.

"I knocked on your door, but you didn't answer," offered Mamere, "We waited a while but decided you could eat whenever you woke up," she said. "Go fix you a plate," she clucked at him, always the mother hen.

As if on cue, Jax's stomach growled, even more loudly than before.

"Yes ma'am," he said, and obediently set about fixing a plate for himself. He realized suddenly just how hungry he was. "How was your day, Papere?" Jax asked.

"Exhausting," Papere replied. "'Bout half the town decided they needed to stop by after the fire." Papere's shop was in the middle of town. For a decade, the shop was nothing more than an automobile maintenance facility; only later did Papere add gasoline pumps and a small convenience store. Locals were drawn by both the opportunity to chat and what was arguably the best coffee in town.

"Sold more gas today than we've sold in the past two weeks. Coffee pot was on overdrive," chirped Papere with glee.

"Hmm," said Jax as he sat down at the table. "What were people saying about the fire?" asked Jax, knowing full well Papere had a reputation for an accurate retelling of events. He was known as the one who passed on tales without embellishment or interpretation of the facts. That was a valuable habit, especially in a small town where rumors could spread faster than a summer cold.

"Better question is, what *weren't* they saying about the fire," rebutted Papere. "Jax, that was an awful fire," he offered as he reached over and patted his grandson's hand affectionately. "I'm so very grateful you weren't at work when it happened. And Marcia was sure glad you were there to help her through it."

"You saw her?" Jax asked.

"Yup. She said that GH and that other boy are doing fine. She acted kind of skittish, though. Like she wanted to say more but just couldn't find the words. I 'spect anybody that's been through what she went through today would be just as jittery," Papere replied.

Jax just nodded and started eating. He suspected that Marcia wanted to talk about the robbery, but he couldn't divulge that just yet. He was sure it would come out in the open soon enough. After eating another forkful of food, he asked, "You hear about my vacation?"

Papere and Mamere both nodded. "Pretty nice," said Mamere.

"Parish Credeur has just about ensured that he'll never want for employees. From what I'm hearing, he's ingratiated himself with the whole town," said Papere. "Always thought he was a shrewd businessman."

"Yup. And an all-around nice guy," Jax agreed. "That leaves me with some free time. Thought maybe I'd help Mamere around the house."

"Why, thank you, Cher'," Mamere said. "I don't have a big list of chores right now, but I will work on building one."

"Now you hold on just one-minute, old woman," said Papere, as he pointed his fork at her for emphasis. "I've got a lot of extra work at the shop that didn't get done today because of all the visitin' people wanted to do. I'd like to capitalize on this opportunity and have Jax with me tomorrow."

Jax held up his hands in protest. "There's a whole week of volunteering at your fingertips! I think I can help you tomorrow, Papere, since Mamere doesn't even have a list drawn up yet."

The older man smiled and said, "That'll do. Mamere, ok with you?"

"Yes, Bishop. That'll do," she matched her husband's smile. They finished the rest of the meal in easy silence.

After supper, Jax helped Mamere with the dishes exactly as he'd done dozens of times before. Meanwhile, Papere sat out on the porch and rocked. As Jax put the dishes away, he reached up to store a small stack of plates and his t-shirt sleeve shifted, revealing the stain on his bicep.

"Jackson Timothy Arceneaux!" exclaimed Mamere when she saw the tattoo.

Jax whipped his head around, wondering what had startled his grandmother. Normally, she only used his full name when he was in big trouble.

"What?" Jax asked sheepishly.

"Is that a tattoo on your arm?!" she asked. Though the words were phrased as a question, her tone made it a statement. She shook her head back and forth. "What next? A brand?"

Curious, Jax looked at the stain. The kitchen's bright lighting revealed that the stain had evolved into an intricate, alien-looking tattoo.

Man, I like it, thought Jax, really looking at the stain for the first time. *I couldn't have designed it better myself.*

"Uh, no, ma'am! No branding. Just a harmless tattoo," Jax stammered.

"When did you get that?" she asked incredulously.

"A while ago." Jax said, searching for a believable explanation. "There's been so much going on lately that it slipped my mind and I just plain forgot to show you. I wasn't trying to hide it from you," he said, almost apologizing.

"It's beautiful," she whispered, surprising him. "I never thought I would like a tattoo, but I like that one. Have you shown it to Papere?"

"Not yet," he replied.

"You are changing so much, Te Cher'!" Mamere was quiet for a moment. "So much," she continued and shook her head from side to side, "and still the same. It's a wonder."

Dishes done, Jax and Mamere joined Papere on the front porch. It was a beautiful evening. The three of them talked effortlessly about everything and nothing in particular. A refreshing breeze ebbed and swelled. It cooled them and tickled the leaves of the large pecan tree dominating the front yard. During one of the lulls in conversation they were surprised by the appearance of Justice. The happy dog bounded down the sidewalk, nudged open the front gate, loped across the yard, and plopped down on the porch at Jax's feet as if the spot had been reserved for him. He sat there panting and nudged Jackson's hand, mutely asking for a scratch behind his ears. Before he could even be seen, Augie's familiar whistling was heard down the block.

"Beautiful night," Augie called out when he reached the gate.

"Oh, yes," agreed Mamere.

"Quite right," said Papere.

"Hi, Augie," said Jax.

Augie entered the garden and closed the gate behind him. He stood in the little oasis and took a deep breath. Though the sidewalk stretched from the road toward the house at a 90-degree angle, the rest of the front yard was a refuge of soft angles and hidden treasures created by Mamere. Here, at ground level, the hustle and bustle of the street was hidden by an old stone wall and muffled by breezes whispering in the pecan leaves. The only glimpse of the mundane was through the gate. From the porch, one could look through the iron bars and see the middle of the street and a sliver of the opposite sidewalk sandwiched between the top of the stone wall and the heavy curtain of tree branches.

In the far corner of the yard, a small cluster of banana trees flourished. The breeze ebbed and flowed, shushing the outside world by rustling the pecan leaves. Joining everyone on the porch, Augie clearly heard the murmurings of the small water fountain.

Though the street could be seen from the porch, the pecan's height and breadth shielded the quartet from casual observation by passersby. Augie looked out at the quiet street and bent to scratch Justice. "That's a good boy," he whispered to the dog.

"How was work?" asked Jax.

"Pretty slow," replied Augie. "You know, if one of the nurses had asked me that, I would have had to tiptoe around the truth."

"What do you mean?" asked Mamere.

"Well, you know," Augie began in a conspiratorial tone, "medical people are superstitious. They pretend they are not, but they truly are."

"I'm not," Jax volunteered.

"Whatever," Augie replied dismissively, continuing where he left off. "We can be having an easy shift with everything running smoothly, but if someone asks a nurse how his or her day is going, they will say they're busy, even though they're not. If they mistakenly say, 'it's so quiet!' – then all the other nurses will immediately scold the tattle tale and say things like, 'now it's going to be awful! You said the 'q' word!' And they believe it."

"All that science and medicine, and still superstitious?!" Mamere asked.

"Yup," replied Augie. "They will also open a window a smidge in the room of someone who is going to pass on so that the spirit has a 'way out.' Trust me, I could go on and on."

The quartet sat in silence to consider Augie's revelations. When Papere spoke up, he said, "You know, it's just the opposite in the Bible. We're taught that you reap what you sow. You speak and it is. For instance, God didn't say, 'Let there be light,' and quickly follow it with, 'Oops! I shouldn't have said that! Even karma teaches 'what goes around comes around.'"

Augie and Jax laughed while Mamere just shook her head in agreement. She said, "Amen, old man! Tell it like it is!"

"Yes, sir!" Jax agreed. Then he turned to Augie, "you picked a nice night to take Justice for a walk."

"More like Justice took me for a walk tonight," replied Augie. "I checked with Mom, and we can roast that wild turkey for Jessica on Wednesday. That a good day for you?"

"Wednesday?" asked Jax.

"Jessica?" asked Mamere.

"Yes," replied Augie. "Jessica is a girl that I want to get to know better, Mamere. I think you'll like her. She's a nurse."

"A nurse," said Mamere. She smiled coyly and pointed her elbow at Jax. "You bringing Jackson here as a chaperone?"

"Chaperone? Heck no," laughed Augie. "Jessica is bringing one of her friends as a blind date for Jax."

"Blind date?" asked Papere. "Sometimes those work out quite well." He reached over and patted Mamere gently on the hand. They shared a smile and Mamere blushed.

"What?" asked Jax. "I thought you met at a dance."

"Well," Mamere began and paused but Papere interrupted before she could continue.

"Best thing that ever happened to me. My life wouldn't have been any good without that date. My brother Jed, the one that was killed in the war, he wanted to go dancing one night before shippin' out. I didn't want to go, but he begged me. He said he knew there would be a woman waiting just for me."

Papere shook his head, remembering.

"I never could refuse him anything. He had a knack for getting me into trouble! But I digress. He wanted to go dancing and dragged me along. Best decision I ever made! Prettiest woman I ever laid eyes on walked into that dance hall. Boys flocked around her like flies on a sweet, so I just bided my time. I waited for them to get turned down because I knew she outclassed them by a mile! It was quite entertaining to watch her shoot them all down; one by one. Every single one of them walked away so very disappointed."

Papere smiled as he remembered it all.

"So, I limped past her to the punch bowl and made a big show of leaning on the table, almost spilled my punch!"

"Limped!" Mamere said, laughing. "You drug your foot along the floor and stubbed my toe!"

"Jeb caught on fast," Papere continued, ignoring her interruption. "He made his way lickety split across the hall, had me lean on him and helped me over to a chair, apologizing loudly about abandoning me. Even apologized to Mamere, like I might have edged too close to her."

Jax and Augie looked at each other and grinned. They'd heard this story many times before but never tired of it.

"Bishop, you sorry old man," Mamere interjected.

"You can't deny that it piqued your interest," Papere said.

"I wondered what kind of disability you had!" Mamere protested. She sat up straighter in her chair and put on an air of indifference. "I was interested from a purely *medical* standpoint," she said slowly and distinctly, emphasizing the word "medical."

Papere waved her protestation aside with one large hand. "Boys, I knew that beautiful creature had to have a pure heart. She just *had* to come to my aid. After that, well it was just my animal magnetism that kept her interested." Papere gave Mamere a sly grin.

"Pshaw! You were so adorable! Trying so hard to get my attention. I figured anyone that desperate to meet me deserved a chance. But Jackson's right. That wasn't exactly a blind date." She stood up. "Good night boys." Mamere kissed Jax's forehead, then leaned over and kissed Augie on the forehead as well. She turned and kissed Papere full on the mouth before sashaying past him, her hips swinging as she went inside.

Papere let a slow, satisfied smile spread on his face and looked at the boys. "Wonderful woman. Best blind date of my life. Have fun boys." With that he followed Mamere inside.

14

The Garden

Jax and Augie leapt down the front porch steps into the garden two at a time. A light breeze wound its way through the pecan trees; every leaf shivering involuntarily, creating a tremulous sighing tenor counterpoint to the crisp splashing of water in the fountain. Jax always liked the garden. It wasn't fussily ornate, and it wasn't particularly old, but it had character. They sat down on the stone seat that ringed the base of the fountain. Justice followed them, drank some of the water, then laid down at Augie's feet. Jax relaxed with his best friend, his mind wandering back over years of memories.

Augie, unaware of Jax's reminiscent daydreaming, was completely lost in his own ramblings about the dinner party. Augie's verbal onslaught started when Mamere and Papere excused themselves and showed no signs of slowing. Finally, after having ignored much of Augie's commentary, Jax looked around furtively, held a finger to his lips and said, "Shhhh!"

Augie stopped talking abruptly and looked over his shoulder. Leaning in toward Jax he asked in a conspiratorial whisper, "What is it?"

"Nothing," Jax whispered back. "You just aren't letting me talk. You are so wound up about this dinner party that you're talking a mile a minute but not making much sense! Augie . . . take a breath."

"It's not that bad, Jax!" Augie protested.

"Yes, it is," Jax asserted. You've already suggested three different ways to roast the bird. By the way, I'm not going to fry it. I do like your idea of the dry brine." He paused, considering recipes. "I think I'll add bacon strips while roasting, but we'll have to rinse them first so it's not too salty. But now I'm getting off track. Who is Jessica bringing as my date? Anybody I know?"

Augie just sat and stared at Jax for a minute. "Dude," he said, "you are such a nerd!"

"What?" Jax asked innocently.

"Who knew you were such a geek about cooking?" Augie replied. "And, no, I've got no idea who Jessica is bringing. But she told me the girl is beautiful and smart," he said, rubbing his hands together in anticipation.

"Hmm . . ." said Jax, nodding. "I like that combination."

"I just told her you'd be there and that she should bring someone so you wouldn't be a third wheel," Augie replied.

"Ok. Two days, right?" asked Jax.

"Yup." Augie paused. "Can we talk about 'you know what' or do we have to go to the tree house?" he asked.

"As long as we're not loud, no one can hear us over the water fountain." As if on cue, Justice got up and crept away to the banana trees, sniffing the ground as he went. "You will not believe what happened today!" Jax whispered excitedly.

"Well, go on, spill it," Augie whispered back. In hushed tones, Jax told Augie about his day. When he got to the part about realizing he was in outer space, Augie held up his hand, stopping Jax in mid-sentence. "Hold on, I need a minute." He stood up and paced slowly around the fountain. He put his hand under the spout and let the water play on it as it fell into the basin. His flitting fingers changed the paths of the water drops.

Jax watched in silence and waited for his friend to digest the information. He knew that what he had to say next would be equally hard to believe, if not harder. Absentmindedly, Jax rubbed his right hand on his left bicep and briefly exposed the tattoo. Augie had been watching the water play at his fingertips but looked up at just the right time to see the tattoo.

"What . . . is that?" he asked incredulously.

"That . . . is what happened next." responded Jax as he pulled the sleeve up and exposed the alien-looking tattoo. "The moss sprouted vines and they wrapped themselves around my bicep. Left this mark," he said. "I didn't notice it at the time because I was so engrossed in the target practice."

"Does it hurt?" Augie asked.

Jax rubbed at his bicep as if smoothing a wrinkled sleeve. "Nope," he replied.

"Wait, wait, wait," Augie began and held both his hands up as if stopping traffic. "Target practice?" he asked.

"Target practice," Jax affirmed. "The flowers zapped little specks of light with balls of pollen."

"What?" Augie asked, leaning forward slightly and almost shouting in his disbelief.

"Shh," Jax whispered urgently. "They'll hear you," he said, as he pointed up at Mamere and Papere's bedroom window.

Augie sat down on the edge of the water fountain but stood up again almost immediately to start pacing back and forth. "Can you demonstrate?" he asked.

Jax shrugged his shoulders noncommittally and stood up. He moved away from the fountain out of sight of both the street and his grandparents' window. Augie followed close behind.

Jax stopped and said, "Stand back, Augie. I don't know how much control I've got over this."

Augie stopped, moved back about twenty feet and asked, "How about here?"

Jax nodded and stood with his feet about shoulder width apart. He closed his eyes and relaxed. He stopped fighting to keep control of the energy around and in him and just let it build. This time, he felt as if he were drawing energy from the ground itself. The spherical field quickly formed around him, and he felt heavier and heavier, as if he were becoming rooted in the core of the Earth. Then, without warning, Jax was rapidly and deeply pulled into a disorienting experience that he would struggle to explain later.

His entire body was flooded with a simultaneous series of external stimuli. He felt the massive speed and momentum of the planet itself as it rotated on its axis; sensed the dizzyingly powerful hunger of the sun's all- consuming gravitational pull on the planet. He felt an intense sense of relief as he realized the Earth would miss that target and instead continue to fall headlong into orbit. He was so rapidly and consumingly pulled into the experience that he forgot where he was. The energy on which he drew seemed limitless and he felt supremely powerful. Opening his eyes, he fully expected to see stars and the deep black expanse of space before him. Instead, he was jerked back to his senses when he saw Augie standing in front of him, mouth open wide in absolute shock.

Earlier, when Jax first closed his eyes, Augie had absently picked up a small rock and tossed it in the air over and over. He noticed that the energy build-up was different this time. It smelled like fresh dirt instead of ozone. Idly, Augie tilted his head to one side as he observed Jax and wondered about the change in aroma.

Augie tossed the rock into the air again. It flew immediately away, toward Jax, and stuck to the outside of the energy sphere. Eerily, the ground shook, at first gently, then more insistently. Small rocks, twigs, leaves, and debris in the yard began to fly off the ground and stick to the sphere's exterior. Augie, face now awash with shock and confusion, was fearful as he felt his own body being pulled gently forward.

"Jax!" Augie cried out as the tug on his body grew stronger and stronger and drew him perilously close to the tornadic winds that began to encircle Jax and his sphere.

Augie's outcry made Jax open his eyes. Swirling debris encompassed the entire sphere, partially obscuring Jax's view of Augie. Instinctively, Jax tried to drain off some of the escalating energy, but his connection with the Earth remained strong and was increasing exponentially by the second. Unable to control the surge, Jax paradoxically felt more powerful and more out of control than ever. In desperation he expanded the sphere to envelope Augie.

Now completely surrounded by the bubble, Augie dropped to his knees and gasped for breath. "Dude! You are making a mess," spat out Augie between his ragged breaths.

Jax didn't reply as he stretched out his arms and touched the bubble's inner lining. Unexpectedly, the bubble shrank around him and Augie. As the space narrowed, Augie was forced to stand up within the chamber.

Once Jax's hands touched the bubble's interior, the energy changed tenor and the sphere thickened and became opaque. The dirt and debris that coated the sphere fell away and puddled around them. Jax's only thought then was to get far enough away to prevent any more damage. Augie, unable to make sense of the external chaos, seemed completely unaware of the structural transitions of the bubble itself.

Then, for no apparent reason, the tiny interior space expanded and became fully transparent. Gently, Jax and Augie floated effortlessly in the bubble's middle space. Relieved that it seemed they were no longer endangering the house, Jax lowered his arms to his sides and asked Augie if he was okay.

Augie nodded dumbly as his body spun uncontrollably and awkwardly in the zero-gravity environment. Augie's eyes opened wider as he analyzed what was happening and where they were.

"Are we . . . did you . . . are we in space?" asked Augie as his body shook involuntarily.

"Yup," replied Jax, as he nodded in affirmation. "Had to get far enough away to keep everyone safe." He smiled wanly and patted Augie on the back. "Congratulations! You've just earned your astronaut wings," Jax joked as Augie's body spun in a more logical, organized pattern.

Augie opened his mouth to speak, stopped and closed his mouth, then opened it again.

"You look like a catfish," commented Jax.

Augie took a deep breath and spoke haltingly. "How long can we stay here?"

"Long as we need to," Jax answered. "Don't want to stay long, though. I want to get back and make sure everything is ok. But, since we're here, might as well explain what I meant by target practice."

Seconds later, Augie noticed something shockingly unexpected. Right before his eyes, Jax's tattoo morphed into a glowing, vibrantly green, three- dimensional . . . "thing." It sprouted tendrils that extended outwardly from Jax's arm. White and blue blossoms budded and opened at seemingly random intervals, each surrounded by twinkling, hovering specks of light. Then, like something out of a sci-fi movie, the blossoms puffed bursts of pollen toward every floating light speck. Magically, the pollen transformed each light particle into the color that perfectly matched the flower that dusted it.

"How in the world is this happening?" asked Augie as he and Jax both watched the pollen puffs head unerringly to their intended targets. After each hit, the floating sparks reeled away from the flowers, propelled by the pollen balls, then held position as if waiting for the next barrage. When the sparks had all been dusted at least once Jax took aim.

Augie watched intently as Jax floated in the sphere's center. Though nearly impossible, Augie tried to absorb all the physical changes taking place in his best friend's body: the veins inside Jax's exposed arms glowed brightly; his skin glistened with escalating energy; and his arteries pulsed uncontrollably with embedded light.

An astoundingly loud "Shwwash!" filled the air as Jax released a fiery ball of energy that traveled down his arm and coalesced in his palm. Augie winced as the sound reverberated on his eardrums. Jax propelled the energy ball toward one of the floating lights. Again and again, he conjured up energy balls and unleashed them at one light after the other.

Occasionally, when Jax missed his intended target, the discharged energy pulse dissolved into an opaque splash on the far side of the sphere. When on target, the hurled ball destroyed each floating light and caused it to burst into showering, multi-colored sparks that resembled mini fireworks. In turn, each cascade of light dispersed and intensified as if it were preparing for the next onslaught.

In no time at all the entire bubble was lit from within by the little lights, making it more difficult to see beyond the sphere. Jax stopped his target practice and each little light winked out. Without explanation, the flowers and vines retracted into the tattoo on his arm and the light within the sphere dimmed.

"There!" said Jax to his stunned friend. "It's a lot easier to show you than to explain it with words," said Jax, somewhat unaware of Augie's stunned condition. Augie nodded. He simply couldn't speak at the moment. The entire display fascinated him beyond words. As Augie gazed all around him and at his super friend, he was taken aback by the vast expanse of space. Everything he saw simply took his breath away. In the far distance, bathed in utter silence, satellites orbited around the Earth, and the moon's edge peaked above the planet's rim.

"It's all so beautiful," mumbled Augie. "And so very crazy-quiet."

"Peaceful," agreed Jax. For the first time in a while, Jax quizzically looked over at Augie, who was shaking uncontrollably. "You ok, buddy?" he asked.

"Supremely frightening," continued Augie. "Depends on what you mean by 'ok,'" he replied. "The terrarium in which we live is way, way over there," said Augie, as he pointed at the Earth. "And I'm wayyyy over here in some sort of see-through bubble with my best friend." He put one hand on his chest and stretched the other hand out, fingers touching the inner side of the sphere. "Man, that looked like some sort of crazy Fourth of July target practice!" Augie's voice, accompanied by the gestures with his hands and probing fingers, got louder and more frantic with each passing word. "But hey, don't get me wrong; I think what you're doing is awesome, even if I can't wrap my head around any of it," confessed Augie.

Jax nodded. "It's hard for me, too, Augie. And honestly, it's easier if I just don't think about it. You ready to go home?"

"If there isn't a bathroom up here, then we'd better go home soon," replied Augie as he smiled and shifted back and forth. "And dude, got any astronaut food? Starving!" Augie added.

"No, but next time remind me, and we'll bring a picnic basket," joked Jax.

"Next time?" Augie queried. "If you bring me up here again, I want to bring a camera!" Then, Augie paused as a curious, puzzled look blanketed his face. "You think any of those satellites or NASA telescopes . . . heck, even someone with an awesome backyard telescope, are getting pictures of us?"

A worried look crossed Jax's face. "Wow; I never thought about that!" he exclaimed. "I was up here for a few hours last time, who knows?"

"We'd better head home to decrease our risk of discovery," cautioned Augie.

"You got it, buddy," agreed Jax. He stretched his hands out to touch the sphere and the sphere responded by shrinking and becoming opaque again. Cocooned in the smaller space, Augie let the inner boundary of the sphere gently nudge him into position next to Jax.

Once Jax's hands touched the sphere the energy circuit was completed, and his veins glowed with savage intensity. Then, astoundingly, before their hearts even finished a beat, the boys were back in Jax's front yard. This time, Jax was able to release the energy before getting caught up in the same type of feedback loop that caused him to lose control earlier.

Augie took a step away from Jax and looked over the yard. There was debris everywhere! It looked like a storm had swept through and knocked the trees for a loop. Fortunately, the house seemed to be intact. Jax was also appraising the damage.

"Thank God I didn't do any more damage," said Jax.

"Do you think they heard anything?" Augie asked, nodding in agreement and pointing toward Mamere and Papere's window.

"Better question, Te Cher', is 'do you think they saw anything?'" came a deep voice from the shadows. Slowly, the boys turned toward the familiar voice.

"Woops!" Augie said sheepishly.

"Papere," Jax began, "I didn't see you standing there."

"Heard the commotion and came down to check on things. Found Justice cowering here in the corner." He reached down to pat the big dog's head. "Thought it was a storm blowin' through. Got a look at the yard and thought it might have been some sort of freak dust devil, what with all the strange weather we've been having. But now, I'm changing my mind. Son . . . what's going on?" asked the older man.

Jax hesitated and glanced over at Augie, who simply shrugged his shoulders and gave him a questioning look. "Jax," interjected Augie. "Why not tell him everything?" he suggested.

"Papere, I don't know how to begin," Jax said.

"Jus' better start at the beginning," said Papere as he stepped completely out of the shadows and stomped the dust from his shoes.

"Let's go inside and brew a pot of coffee," suggested Jax. "It's a long story."

The three men climbed the stairs to the front porch and quietly entered the house; they didn't want to wake Mamere. Soon the rich scent of freshly brewed coffee filled the kitchen. Jax toasted some bread while Augie rummaged around in the refrigerator for lunch meat, mustard, and butter. Papere, though eager to hear their story, just sat quietly at the kitchen table. He never could have imagined what was coming.

Jax poured each man a cup of coffee and busied himself finding cream, sugar, and teaspoons. Augie simply sat down with Papere.

Finally, Papere broke the ice. "Te Cher', sit down," he commanded. "Talk to me."

Jax sighed as he sat down at the table and immediately started tapping his fingers nervously on the lip of his coffee cup. Augie pushed the plate of hastily made sandwiches in the center of the table, then held his own steaming cup of coffee up and took an appreciative whiff of the delicious aroma. "Ahh," he said. "Nothing sets the tone quite like a fresh cup of coffee."

"Boys, somebody'd better start talking," said Papere as he gave stern looks to both young men.

"Papere," Jax started, then hesitated again. "I don't completely understand what's going on. It's all happening so fast!" He ran his hand over his hair, grazing the design. "You ever heard of an old still?" asked Jax, beginning his explanation. Hours passed. Dawn streaked the sky with gold and pink before Jax finished telling his grandfather the fantastic story. Augie was content to occasionally interject his own, rather limited, observations. When Jax finished, Papere reached over and touched the green tattoo on Jax's bicep.

Augie spoke first. "Every time he tells me something new, it's harder to believe. Even though I'm seeing most of it with my own eyes, I still ask myself if I actually saw what I saw! Or if it's really happening. And it's not even happening to me!" Absolute astonishment filled Augie's voice as he sat back in his chair and fiddled with his empty coffee cup.

"That dust ball you stepped out of in the garden," began Papere, "that was some sort of . . . spaceship?" Papere could hardly get out the word "spaceship."

Jax shrugged his shoulders. "I guess that's as good a description as any other."

"But you can also travel like lightning?" Papere asked.

"Yes," Jax answered.

"The lightning is pretty cool," interrupted Augie. "And I like calling him 'White Lightning' in honor of the still. But I guess "Moonshine" would be ok. It just doesn't have the same zing to it," babbled Augie.

"Augie," protested Jax, "I think giving me a superhero name is a bit much."

Papere smiled and chuckled softly. It was the first time the frown had left his face since they started talking. "I like it. It *might* be a bit much, but there's something about it that I like. I *do* think you should be more careful. Probably shouldn't let on that you've got special powers."

"Heck, he could handle the press!" joked Augie before he was interrupted by Papere raising his hand in protest.

"Not the press I'm worried about," said Papere. "I don't know that the government wouldn't reach down and sweep our Jax off to some hidden place for their own reasons. Don't know that I'd trust their intentions to include having Jax's best interests in mind." Papere rubbed at his chin before he continued. "There's a lot to think about. Right now, best get breakfast started for Mamere or *she'll* start asking questions. Her first question would be: why are three grown men staying up all night and chatting into the wee hours of the morning?"

"Yes, sir," replied Jax.

Augie stood and stretched. "I can't stay. I've got to get ready for work. It's been an adventure." He shook Papere's hand and without thinking, clapped Jax on the back. "Zzzt!" filled the room as Augie received a shock. "Ouch, dude!" Augie yelped.

"Sorry, Augie," Jax apologized. "I didn't realize how much 'juice' was running through me." Jax stood and walked over to the kitchen window, raised it, and held out his hand. Immediately, energy drained into the atmosphere. Papere's jaw dropped as he watched the energy stream exit Jax's hand and briefly color the sky.

"Whatever," Augie said playfully unfazed. "It's not like you tried to hurt me. Good night. Umm, good morning. Gotta go," mumbled Augie as he walked through the house, down the front steps, and called softly to Justice, who slept patiently outside during the whole sensational conversation. Jax and Papere heard the dog's bark in response to his master's call, then heard the creak of the gate as it was opened and shut behind the departing companions.

Papere looked over at Jax, who had gotten up to make Mamere a breakfast. He cleared his throat and asked, "When you get that under control, how 'bout you show me that lightning thing?" he asked.

Jax looked over his shoulder at his grandfather. "Ok. Anything in particular you want me to bring back? Augie wanted a map of Disney World."

"Nope," Papere replied. "Just watching you fly off and return will be sufficient."

Jax was stunned by the sense of normalcy that filled Papere's tone and comments. "Ok," Jax said, then turned to his task. In no time at all he whipped up some grits, poached an egg, and brewed a fresh pot of coffee.

"Good morning!" said Mamere as she peeked into the kitchen. "I wondered at the gorgeous smells wafting through the house. What a wonderful way to wake up!" Mamere smiled warmly as she gave Jax a kiss on the cheek before sitting down at the table next to Papere. As was his habit, Papere reached over to caress Mamere's cheek and tenderly squeeze her hand.

"Good morning, Te Cher'," Papere said to Mamere.

"When I woke up this morning, your side of the bed was cold. Didn't you sleep well?" Mamere asked.

Papere smiled and met her questioning gaze. "A big wind blew through the garden in the early morning hours; it woke me up, so I got up to check on things."

Mamere looked quizzically at him, "Any damage?" she asked.

"No, ma'am. Just some debris to clean up," he replied. "I've got Jax to help me whip it back into shape today, thanks to Parish." Parish Credeur and Papere had been good friends for a very long time.

"Just don't get used to monopolizing his time. I'm still working on a list of my own." She stopped speaking as Jax laid her breakfast on the table before her. She smiled up at her grandson, picked up her coffee cup and took a tentative, careful sip and smiled before she sat back in her chair; she was happy with the world. "Yes sir, what a wonderful way to wake up," she repeated.

Jax bowed to his grandmother. "Don't worry, Mamere. I've got you prioritized!" clarified Jax.

"You playing favorites?" asked Papere with a smile.

"Absolutely!" affirmed Jax. "I know where the power lies in this household." He winked at Papere. As if to prove it, he turned to his grandmother and asked, "May I be excused?"

"Yes, Te Cher', you may be excused," she said with a grand wave of her free hand. "And thank you for breakfast." Jax bowed deeply.

"Papere, I'll meet you in the garden; gotta bathe first. Got a whiff of myself earlier. Whew! No matter how much manual labor awaits in the garden, I need to get a fresh start on the day." And with that, Jax left the kitchen and trotted up the stairs to his room.

Papere sat with Mamere while she finished eating. Once she was done, he excused himself and headed into the garden; work awaited. There wasn't much to do, just enough to keep him occupied until Jax joined him, which wasn't long.

Jax breathed a deep sigh of relief as he showered. Being able to confide in his grandfather lifted a huge weight from his shoulders. Besides, Jax was never very good at keeping secrets. The fog of trepidation that secret shrouded him with was finally gone. Of course, he realized that he needed to tell Mamere, too. *All in good time,* Jax thought to himself. *All in good time.*

Jax bounded into the garden with a brighter countenance than he'd worn in several days when he finally joined Papere in the garden. Papere noticed that his grandson's demeanor seemed lighter.

"You're looking pretty fresh for a man without any sleep," Papere observed as Jax jogged lightly over to join him.

"You can NOT imagine how good it feels to have finally told you everything," Jax said in a low voice, not wanting Mamere to overhear. "Augie and I talked about telling you and decided to wait. We didn't want to worry you unnecessarily. He shrugged and smiled, "now you know."

Papere smiled back. "Jax, I knew something was going on. You have a 'tell.' That's why you don't win when we play cards against each other," he said.

"What?" Jax asked. "You never told me that before."

"Of course not," admitted the older gentleman. "What good would that do me? An old man needs some tricks of his own to keep ahead of the next generation." He paused, glancing around to make sure no one was watching. "How 'bout showing me one of your – tricks?" broached Papere.

"Ok," said Jax. "Sure you don't want me to bring something back for you?"

"Nope. Just show me how you can move," Papere said.

Jax backed away from his grandfather and thought about where he wanted to go. Just the thought of "traveling" caused the veins in his arms to glow and his arteries pulse with light. Suddenly, lightning filled the small space. Reflexively, the older man drew his hand up in front of his face. Thunder rolled with a majestic crescendo as the bright flash faded. The sound swelled before it bounced back from the garden's stone wall and completely washed away, reverberating like so many ripples running riot in a small pool after a large stone disturbs the water. Without hesitation, Papere covered his ears with his hands for protection.

Then, the front porch screen door slammed open; there stood Mamere staring into the horizon, looking for the storm. Papere didn't notice her arrival; his eyes were shut, and his ears covered.

Thunder and lightning completely overwhelmed the space. "Oh my goodness," mouthed Mamere as she retreated into the relative safety of the house and, as Papere did, closed her eyes and covered her ears.

In the garden, Jax stood before Papere. Unlike before, Papere's eyes were wide open and he was smiling at his grandson's heroic presence. Again, Jax's veins flowed with radiant, fading light.

After recovering from her initial surprise, Mamere courageously took a few steps forward and peered into the garden. *Is that fire?!* she wondered, fully expecting to see burns and devastation from a direct lightning strike. But what she saw truly took her breath away. "Jackson!" she screamed as she ran down the stairs into the garden, only to be intercepted by Papere's strong arms. There she stood, motionless, locked in the safety of Papere's embrace.

Together, they stared at their grandson. The sight was almost beyond belief! Yet, there stood Jax; feet shoulder width apart, arms akimbo. His veins glowed like rivers of light. His arteries vividly echoed his heartbeat. The whole display faded to normalcy as the energy surge ebbed.

Never in a million years could Mamere and Papere have ever imagined these moments.

15

Telling Mamere

Jax caught a glimpse of Mamere on the porch as he returned to the garden. She ran down the stairs and into Papere's waiting arms. The entire scene seemed to move in an exaggerated slow motion. Jax sighed with a mixture of relief and trepidation as he gladly embraced the elimination of one more screen of protective anonymity. He hated keeping secrets from her.

Jax was deeply moved by the immensity of what was happening to him and those whom he loved. He watched intently, gauging their reactions, as Mamere and Papere clung to the safe familiarity of each other. Staring at their heroically transformed grandson, their eyes were open beyond wide, and their lips trembled in response to that which they could not explain.

What now? Jax thought sadly, as an electrically charged, glowing tear trickled down his cheek. Sparks flew from Jax's fingertips as he wiped the tear away.

Protectively, Papere squeezed Mamere tightly and gently stroked her hair. "Jax," he began haltingly. "I think Augie is right," he said, clearing the lump in his throat before continuing. "White Lightning is a good name!" He crooked a finger under Mamere's chin and gently drew her gaze away from Jax, physically coaxing her to look him in the eye. "'Te Cher'," he said, "our boy has a secret, one it's time you knew. Let's go inside."

The trio slowly climbed the stairs from the garden and entered the house. Pausing on the porch by the old rocker, Jax gave it a push. The familiar whisper of wood on wood intensified the vague feeling of sorrow that presaged a change in the seasons of his life.

They entered the kitchen in complete silence. Mamere and Papere sat down at the breakfast table in their usual chairs. Jax methodically poured each person a glass of tea but still no one spoke. Jax was clearly stalling before taking his seat. They sat together, each toying with their own glasses of tea without drinking. Jax finally cleared his throat and said, "Mamere, the weathermen haven't been able to accurately predict the lightning storms because . . ."

Papere interrupted him saying, "Jax, start at the beginning, she needs to hear it all."

Jax nodded and sighed. He started again. "Remember the day I came back with Evie's boar?" he asked.

Mamere nodded mutely. She hadn't said a word since calling out his name in the garden. Having told the story twice already, Jax spoke more easily and concisely to his grandmother. Little by little, Jax revealed the most unbelievable events, starting with his first traveling attempt that ended with his "au natural" return, and ending with his experience on the beach.

Most of the time, Mamere simply nodded or shook her head in disbelief. No detail was too small; he left nothing out. Then, Jax told her about taking Augie with him on a trip to outer space. Immediately, Mamere shot up from her seat and motioned for Jax to be silent. Shaken by his words, she paced briskly around the kitchen twice before stopping to stand behind her chair. She clenched and unclenched her hands nervously on the familiar backrest. When she finally sat back down, she scooted her chair closer to the table and reached for Jax's hand. "Go on, Cher'," she gently prompted.

Calmed by Mamere's words and tone, Jax leaned forward and continued his narrative. Mamere's stunned silence punctuated the improbable end of Jax's superhero tale. Reaching over, Mamere gently traced the exposed green tattoo on his bicep. "Um, um, um," was the only response she could muster at first. Then, after a brief pause, and in typical Mamere fashion, she asked, "Jackson, how are you doing?"

Mamere's concerned, grandmotherly inquiry, though comforting, took Jax by surprise. He sat back in the chair, silent for a moment. "I guess I'm ok, Mamere," responded Jax as he moved his hands aimlessly on the table. "Honestly, it's all a bit much. And . . . I'm sorry I didn't tell you sooner."

"No, Cher'," she sighed. "It was good that you waited. Besides, what could you have said that wouldn't have sounded too unbelievable?"

Jax watched Mamere as her voice fell silent, but he was unable to decipher the puzzled looks that raced across her face. "Mamere," began Jax. But Mamere immediately held up her hand to stop Jax in mid- sentence.

"My treasured grandson, if anyone can handle supernatural power thrust upon them it's you!" declared Mamere. Both men smiled in response, though Jax's smile was more of a grimace.

"True enough!" said Papere as he nodded his complete agreement. "Jax, you know full well we'll do what we can to help you with this. But I think . . . for now . . . you should stop worrying about college or moving out. No other changes need to happen for a while."

"Yes!" interjected Mamere. "You've got enough to deal with."

As Jax listened, energy surged within his body. In response, his skin glistened involuntarily. Without hesitation, Jax stood and walked to the kitchen door, propped it open with his foot and raised one hand to release energy into the sky. Clouds flared brilliantly into color briefly as the energy bolt excited the atoms within them.

"Yes, ma'am," sighed Jax. When he turned back toward Mamere she was staring at him with her mouth and eyes wide open. *STUPID!* Jax scolded himself, realizing how strange and unexpected his action was. Just the thought of disappointing and surprising her again bothered him. "I'm not interested in any more changes right now either," he added quietly, dragging his boots back and forth across the floor. *Dang it,* thought Jax.

"I just scuffed the floor with my big ol' boots," he said aloud as his shoulders sagged and his eyes aimlessly searched the floor.

In reassurance and out of concern for his shocked wife, Papere reached over and patted Mamere's hand. She realized suddenly that her mouth was wide open and hurriedly closed it, rubbing her hand across her chin.

"'Te Cher'," she said to Jax with a hint of regret. "I didn't mean to embarrass you. I just need some time to get used to . . . this," she finished awkwardly, as one of her hands fluttered in the air.

Slowly, Jax lifted his eyes and glanced briefly at Papere before looking back at her. "I know. I'm not used to it either," he admitted. "Augie actually joked that he wished there was something like 'superhero.com' so we could get advice."

The older man smiled again, this time relieving some of the tension on his face. "I've always liked that boy," he said. "Well," he continued, pushing back his chair and getting up from the table, "I think that's enough for now. Jax, you'd better get some rest."

Mamere also rose and approached Jax. She was about to give him a hug but stopped and asked, "Is it alright if I hug you?"

He nodded in affirmation and pulled her into a tight embrace. "Sometimes there's a shock, but if I drain off some energy first, it's ok." Returning his embrace, Mamere's familiar arms and scent comforted him. Tension ebbed away from him and he realized how tired he truly was. "Papere's right, I need to get some rest."

She patted his back before releasing him, stood back a pace, and traced the tattoo again. "How do you know you're not going to hit a bird or a plane when you shoot at the sky like that?" Mamere asked playfully.

"I don't," answered Jax as he shrugged his shoulders. "For now, what I'm aiming at is what I hit."

Mamere shook her head in wonderment. "There are more things in the universe that I do not know. And I don't understand the few things in the universe that I do know," she said. "Go on and get some rest."

Jax smiled at his grandmother and kissed her gently on the forehead. "Yes, ma'am," he replied. He hugged his grandfather and headed to his room. Flopping down on his bed, he sighed contentedly. Sinking into the familiar mattress made him smile – at least his bed hadn't changed! Determined to get some rest, Jax closed his eyes and listened to the hum of the ceiling fan. Exhaustion and relief came like furtive thieves and carried him to a deep, restorative sleep.

16

Papere's Shop

Mamere and Papere tried to act like everything was "normal" for the rest of the morning. Though Papere needed to go to work, he took the time to putter around the kitchen with his stunned wife. Trying not to disturb Jax's nap, they tried to work quietly. Mamere washed the breakfast dishes, rambling nonstop about the wild and previously unimaginable facts that were presented that morning. Most of her thoughts emerged as truncated questions and partial statements that were in synch with the familiar routine and didn't require Papere to respond. Nevertheless, he listened intently.

Then, without warning and in mid-sentence, Mamere headed out to the front porch.

Normally, Mamere confronted issues while rocking on the porch. Today, she didn't even bother to sit down in her therapeutic rocker. She found it impossible to sit still. Standing erect, her mind reeled with what seemed like almost too many uncontrolled thoughts. And she kept talking – completely unconcerned about who might overhear. Barely pausing to breathe, Mamere verbalized one daunting, chaotic superhero detail after another. She tamed them, reigned them in, and tried to set some solid, logical boundaries.

Though Mamere didn't see him, she knew Papere followed her outside, but she would have kept on talking with or without him there. As it was, he simply stood near her side. He meticulously filed away every salient point of her verbal, disjointed litany. Though he was a few steps ahead of her in processing Jax's astounding evolution, it helped him to listen. For the moment, it was one of the ways that they, as a couple, could focus fully on Jax's mental and physical condition.

When Mamere finally ran out of nervous energy and sat down in the rocker, Bishop took it as his cue to get ready for work. It was his habit to walk to the shop on a daily basis; one of the reasons they'd chosen this house was because it gave him that option. He liked the exercise. He got enough heavy lifting at work but would quickly admit that he couldn't lift the heavy things now as easily as when he was younger. The light cardiovascular exercise to and from work every day was something he really enjoyed.

Not too many people on the street today, he thought to himself as he let his mind wander over the night's activities, his feet automatically trekking the path to work. Though he was still a few blocks away from his shop, he heard the familiar, pleasing sound of metal on metal; a sure announcement that his employees were hard at work.

Turning the last corner, his senses were assaulted by the mingled smells of oil, grease, and gasoline. Short bursts of laughter and light-hearted chatter wafted to Papere's ears on the gentle, cooling, late morning breeze. The entire scene was a welcome distraction from everything on his mind.

Like flipping a switch, Papere's thoughts instantly shifted. The two cars up on lifts and four other cars lined up in front of one of the stalls matched his mental checklist of scheduled repairs. All four gas pumps were busy and there was a pickup truck parked off to the side. A few customers lounged near the pickup's passenger door, lost in conversation and the steamy clouds that rose from their coffee cups.

A steady stream of cars cycled through the gasoline pumps all day long. Papere greeted every customer. His shop's reputation for prompt, quality service earned him such a regular patronage that customers brought their own mugs from home instead of messing with disposable cups. Papere provided coffee, milk, cream, and sugar at the shop. No frilly creamers or newfangled chemically derived sugars. If a customer wanted something that wasn't offered, they never complained. There was a waiting room, but it was only pressed into use during inclement weather. Today, the customers were clustered on and around a spray of folding chairs under the trees at the side of the building, and at the picnic table he'd set up years ago for lunch breaks.

"Mornin' ma'am," said Papere as he shook the hand of a young mother parked at a gas pump. "Fill 'er up?" he asked.

Before the lady could even answer, one of the two children in the backseat piped in. Waving her hand in front of her face, she exclaimed, "Ewww! Did you just fart at me?" she asked her older sister.

"No," replied the sibling. "I just made an elephant noise . . . with my butt!" This made them both dissolve into peals of laughter.

The mother hid her slightly embarrassed smile from her girls by turning her head to look at the numbers slowly spinning on the pump. Papere just smiled at the children playing in the back seat. After what he'd seen and heard this morning it was good to hear normal kids saying normal things. As the young mother drove off, he greeted everyone outside before retreating to his office to attack the stack of paperwork waiting on his desk.

"Mornin', sir!" Leroy's cheery voice greeted him. Leroy had worked for Papere for the past five years. He started out as a pump jockey and cashier but soon showed an avid interest in mechanics. Papere resisted training Leroy at first, but the boy always managed to find a way to watch everything the mechanics were doing. In return, the mechanics were glad to have someone to chat with and act as a gopher. They eventually taught him, and soon Leroy was doing some of the smaller jobs by himself.

Leroy's interest in every aspect of the repair shop was clear, and after earning his business degree at the community college, he presented an expanded business plan to Papere, one that included his newly degreed self as shop manager. Bishop was so impressed with Leroy's proposal that he promoted him on the spot. Three years later, the shop was running smoothly, and with a noticeable increase in revenue that could only be attributed to Leroy's supportive and efficient management style.

"'Morning, son," replied Papere, looking up from the stack of papers in his hands. "Things are looking good today, as usual."

"Got it under control," Leroy agreed. "Lots of chatter again today. How's Jax doing?" he asked.

"Just about as you'd expect," he said. "I wanted him to come in and help us out, but Mamere has him pigeonholed at home. I'll probably be able to sneak him out tomorrow. Would that help?" he asked.

Leroy smiled wryly. "I remember the last time Jax came in to help. Are you sure you want to pry him away from Mamere?" he asked.

The inference was not lost on Papere. "He could probably run the register without causing any damage." What he really thought was that it would be good for Jax to get out of the house and hear what the townsfolk were saying.

"You're the boss," Leroy said, whistling happily off key as he returned to the garage.

There wasn't much to review. Once finished, he was free to go out and check on his mechanics and mingle with the customers. In reality, he hoped to catch more of the gossip about the lumberyard and the freak lightning strikes. Papere mingled, and soon heard an interesting piece of gossip.

Parish Credeur had been by the day before for gasoline, but here he was again, refilling his gas tank. Papere went over and shook his hand. "Morning! Do I need to check your air filter?" he asked, curious about Parish's fuel consumption. "Seems like I remember you fillin' up your tank yesterday, Parish," he commented.

Almost everyone in town called Jax's grandfather "Papere." Parish was one of the few exceptions. As one of the first people who met and befriended him when he moved into town as a teenager, Parish called Bishop by his given name.

"No, thank you, Bishop," Parish replied. "Had to drive to Baton Rouge yesterday on business. That'll drain a tank."

"Baton Rouge," Papere repeated wistfully. "Beautiful city. Worth a trip."

"Yes, sir," Parish agreed. "But I don't like the big city prices. I had to squeak back here on fumes," he said. "Can't get a decent cup of coffee there either. How do you do it, Bishop?" he asked.

"Trade secret," Papere answered, winking. "I need something to get people to want to come by! Get 'em to enjoy comin' in, share their time, and spend a little money with me. Coffee's a good draw. If I told you, I'd lose half my convenience store business to your lumberyard."

Parish smiled back wanly. "Not losin' any business to me this week."

"How are the repairs comin'?" asked Papere.

"Slowly," he replied. "Any chance I can get a cup of that coffee and bend your ear for a while?" he asked.

Papere nodded his assent. "'Course. I'll wait for you in my office. Just come on in when you're ready." They shook hands and Papere went back to his office. He wiped some dust off a shelf behind his desk and moved the books piled in the spare chair so Parish would have a place to sit.

Papere's parents were born and raised in the south, but moved to Milwaukee, Wisconsin shortly after they were married. Papere himself was born a "Yankee." It took about a dozen years before the harsh winters wore his parents down and they moved back home. That first week of school in Louisiana would have been awkward if Parish hadn't gone out of his way to make the "new kid" his friend. They'd been friends ever since. Now, they sat on the city council together; the other members often joked it was like going to church if both Parish and Bishop were at a meeting.

Parish entered the office and sat in the newly cleaned chair. Sipping his coffee, he thumbed through the magazines on the small table next to the chair without reading them. Papere asked, "What's on your mind, Parish?"

"The police haven't released this information yet, but they're not just looking into what started the fire, they're looking for who robbed the safe," Parish stated bluntly.

"They don't think Jax . . ." Papere began but was interrupted by Parish.

"Of course not, Bishop," Parish said, raising his free **hand** to placate Papere. "I'm telling you this as a friend. Whoever did it might be looking for more than one score. You need to double check your safeguards on this place," he said, circling one finger in the air for emphasis.

Papere nodded in understanding. "Of course, thank you, Parish. How is the investigation going? Do they have any leads?" he asked.

"Nothing concrete enough to tell *me* about," Parish responded. "Funny thing, though," he paused, thinking. "There was some sort of an incident with lightning. Right now, the fire marshal is lettin' on that the fire was accidental; but he told me he thinks it might have started with a lightning strike. I don't know. Maybe so. I was there when the lightning struck, and it looked for all the world like the lightning helped put the fire out. One of the news crews interviewed me, but I don't think the cameraman was quite right in the head. Claimed he had video of the lightning strike."

"That what makes you think he's a bit 'off?'" Papere asked quizzically.

"No, that's not crazy. The crazy part is that he claims he saw a person in the lightning bolt," answered Parish.

"What?!" exclaimed Papere.

"Yup," replied Parish. "But he can't prove it. He knows what it sounds like, but he insists it's the truth. And he thinks some weird magnetic surge erased his hard drive. Now he's determined to photograph lightning in this town." Parish shook his head. "Some people need real jobs."

Papere smiled half-heartedly. "Hmm," said Papere. He suddenly realized he was nervously tapping the table. Attempting to appear calm, he picked up a pencil and doodled on a piece of scrap paper. "What do *you* think?" The knowledge that the cameraman was actually correct put an odd edge on Papere's voice.

Parish looked at him quizzically. "What do I think?" he asked. "At first, I thought he was just plumb crazy. But his partner claims to have seen the same thing. Now they'll be getting into everybody's way! Setting up motion sensitive cameras and whatnot! That's just too much of an invasion of my privacy! I told them that they couldn't set up any cameras around the lumberyard, but they maintain they can set cameras up anywhere they want, as long as it's not on private property." He shook his head from side to side in frustration. "Bad enough I got to deal with a robbery, a fire, injured employees, and loss of business. Now I'm looking at an invasion of privacy."

Papere didn't respond immediately. He just nodded in agreement. "How much did you lose?" he asked.

"Don't know yet. Won't know for about a month. We'll be able to partially reopen next week. That's where you come in," said Parish as he scooted his chair toward Papere.

"How can I help?" Papere asked.

"I need Jax to come back to work early and help me whip things back into shape," he answered. "Marcia is a wreck, and both GH and Winchell are recuperating in the hospital. I know you probably planned on using him here at the shop, but could I impose on you to send him back to work for me?"

"'Course, Parish," he replied. "I was just going to try to keep him busy and out of trouble. Do you want him as early as tomorrow?" he asked.

"No," Parish replied. "Let's give him one more day of rest. Day after next," clarified Parish as he stood up and offered Papere his hand.

Papere stood with him. He grasped Parish's hand in both of his and shook it warmly. "Let me know if there's anything else I can do, Parish."

"Sure thing, Bishop," he said. "And thank you."

They walked out to Parish's car together in amicable silence. Once there, Papere said, "Thank you, Parish. This is troubling news but thank you all the same." He watched Parish drive off, the information about the reporter and the cameraman seeing Jax disturbed Papere far more than the idea of being targeted by persons unknown.

Papere mingled with the new customers now at the pumps before going back in and checking on how the repairs were progressing. He knew everything was under Leroy's meticulous eye, but it made him feel good to touch base with the customers and the mechanics. That done, he retreated to his office to sit down and think.

He mulled over the idea of tampering with the cameras and discarded it. He was not a spy, nor was he versed in criminal activities. He would surely get caught and that would expose Jax. He considered sending Jax away, maybe send him on a trip to Wisconsin. But then, his sudden disappearance and the immediate cessation of lightning activity might be noticed and considered too coincidental, yet another red flag.

No, he thought . . . continue daily life as normal. Discourage Jax from exploring his powers for now, let the interest abate. Maybe the reporter's cameras would work to the town's advantage. Maybe it would help them find those persons responsible for robbing and setting fire to the lumberyard. He puttered around his office, straightening the items on his desk again even though he'd placed them right before Parish sat down. Finally, after exhausting every reason to stay at work, he said "goodnight" to Leroy and boys and walked home. He had to talk to Jax.

17

New Orleans

Papere's mind raced through every troubling aspect of his conversation with Parish as he walked home. Absorbed in thought, he lost track of time, so the walk home seemed infinitely faster than the walk to work. It was as if time itself had somehow contracted. *Not possible! Superhero time,* he thought to himself, chuckling at his flippant reference.

The worn gate latch and hinges barked no resistance to Papere's familiar touch, allowing him to enter the garden unnoticed. Mamere and Jax were laughing, talking, and working nearby, and didn't hear him enter the hallowed area. The garden was Mamere's personal oasis. Without doubt, this trio, and others close to them, understood the garden's importance. It also served as Jax's private playground for many years. Papere watched affectionately as Mamere and Jax shared a laugh. He wanted to hear more, but only caught snippets of their conversation as he crossed the yard toward them.

"I'm home," chirped Papere as he planted a kiss on his wife's cheek and patted Jax on the back. Jax and Mamere both jumped, startled by his sudden appearance.

"Oh my!" exclaimed Mamere. "I didn't even hear you come in," she said as she kissed him in return.

"You're home early," commented Jax.

"Yup, Leroy has everything under control, and I caught up on enough gossip for one day," Papere said. "Did you get some rest?" he asked.

"Yes, sir," Jax replied, without any trace of the fatigue evident earlier that morning. "Hear anything worth repeating?" he asked.

"Umm hmm," Papere replied affirmatively. "Somethin' you should hear. Parish said some reporter's putting up cameras to monitor lightning strikes. Says he thinks the man is slightly touched (he tilted his head and tapped his forehead gently with a finger) as he's talking about seeing a man in a lightning bolt."

Jax's easy smile evaporated instantly. Mamere put a hand over her mouth and said, "Oh Lord!"

"Son," Papere began hesitantly, "Now that I've had some time to think, I suggest you stop using your powers until things settle down."

Jax shrugged his shoulders. "Maybe so," he replied. "Right now, the hardest part seems to be draining off excess energy."

"No more shooting at the clouds," insisted Papere, with a tone in his voice that reached beyond suggestion. "Is there any other way for you to, um . . . cool off?" he asked.

"Yes, sir," Jax replied.

"Don't tell me," said Papere, as he held up a hand in gentle protest. "For the time being, it's best Mamere and I don't know all there is to know about your powers." Mamere nodded in agreement.

"Yes, sir," Jax said again.

"Also, Parish wants you to help whip the lumberyard back into shape instead of languishing here on vacation – though it looks like you haven't been idle." Papere said, looking around the garden in appreciation of the day's work. "Looks even better now than it did yesterday before everything happened."

"When does Mr. Credeur want me back to work?" Jax asked.

"Day after tomorrow," Papere replied.

"Good," said Jax. "I've got a dinner date with Augie and Jessica tomorrow night."

Mamere's smile grew playfully curious. "Know who Augie's got picked out for your date yet?" she asked, raising her eyebrows and cocking her head sideways.

"Nope," Jax sighed. "But – same rules apply as the ones for Evie's wedding: I'll be friendly and polite. You know you're the only woman in my life, Mamere."

"For now, Te Cher', for now," she replied.

"I'm sure everything will be just fine," Papere said. The three stood and surveyed the garden in silence. "Guess our work is done here. Anyone hungry?"

"Supper's on the stove," Mamere responded. "You boys get washed up."

"Yes, ma'am," said Jax as he headed toward the garage, collecting the yard tools on the way.

Filled with a sense of pride, Mamere and Papere watched Jax walk away with his usual easy sense of self confidence; his newly acquired power didn't seem to be weighing him down. Without doubt, he was a man on the brink of a startling adventure.

"That's a good boy we've got there," confided Papere.

"Yes, sir," agreed Mamere. "Only had to beat him until he was eight years old," she teased.

"Old woman, you know you never laid a hand on him," scolded Papere. "He was just born good." As Papere glanced at his wife, he saw signs of Jax in her face: proud, chiseled chin, straight nose, and high cheekbones. "He takes after you."

"Fibber!" exclaimed Mamere as she lightly slapped him on the shoulder. "He is *your* shadow!" Anyone could see that Jax had Papere's coloring, temperament, and stature.

"I know," Papere admitted with a tiny smile. "I just wanted to make you feel good."

"I feel plenty good enough without you telling stories!" she retorted. She turned away and headed toward the house. "Thank God that boy is more intelligent than the both of us combined!"

Papere smiled and nodded. There was no denying that. Following Mamere up the front steps and into the house, the smell of dinner tugged at his stomach and made him step more enthusiastically.

Even after taking the rake and other tools to the garage, Jax reached the kitchen and washed up before his grandparents entered the room.

"I think I'll call Augie and see if he wants to go to New Orleans tonight," said Jax.

"Tonight?" asked Papere.

He nodded. "Do something fun before my vacation runs out. Mamere, do you want me to bring anything back for you?" asked Jax.

She thought for a moment as she washed her hands. "No, don't think so. Does that mean you're not eating here tonight?"

Jax fished a piece of meat out of the stew pot with a fork, blew on it and popped it into his mouth. He closed his eyes and said, "Yumm . . . Yes ma'am. I'll grab a bite in town with Augie, but I'm hoping there'll be leftovers tomorrow."

"Go on, Jax! Get on out of here," urged Papere. "If you let Mamere talk, she'll guilt you into staying home. Maybe we can have some quiet time here ourselves, Te Cher'," he said with a wink that made Mamere giggle and blush.

Jax smiled coyly at his grandfather as he ducked out of the kitchen and flew up the stairs, two steps at a time. He pulled his cell phone out of his pocket as he went, punching in Augie's familiar number. Augie answered before the phone finished ringing the first tone.

"Augie," Jax began, "let's go to New Orleans tonight. My vacation is over day after tomorrow. Let's have some fun."

"Hmm," replied Augie. "Let me see about getting my shift covered tomorrow. Call you back," he said as he hung up the phone.

Jax showered quickly and changed clothes; all the while hoping Augie would be able to come. The phone rang as he was tying his shoes. "What's the word, buddy?" asked Jax.

"Go!" Augie replied enthusiastically. "When can you pick me up?"

"I'm ready now. I'll be right over," said Jax. He jogged lightly down the stairs, grabbed his car keys, called out "good night" to Mamere and Papere and strode out the kitchen door.

Outside, the sun still hung low in the western sky. A slight breeze pushed the humidity aside, hinting at a cool evening ahead. Jax hopped into his truck and revved the engine with a light and happy heart. He was eager to get out of town and have some fun. When he arrived across town, Augie was pacing the sidewalk and talking on his cell phone. He waved to Jax with his free hand and got into the truck, still talking. Jax just sat and listened to Augie's half of the conversation.

"Tomorrow's still ok then?" asked Augie. "What? Of course! That'll be fine. Yup. Leaving now. 'Bye." Augie abruptly ended the call and turned his attention to Jax. "Let's go!"

"What's up?" he asked.

"Just getting everything set for tomorrow night with Jessica," Augie replied.

"We still cooking?" queried Jax.

"Yesss," Augie sighed. "I've got Mom out of the house. I don't have to study or work. My best friend is going to help. And the girls are coming over," he said, tapping the fingers of his left hand with his right index finger in succession as he identified each task. All that's left is for us to have some fun tonight!" He smiled at Jax as he inquired further. "Do we have an agenda?" he asked.

"Nope!" Jax replied. "Totally unscripted fun" said Jax, smiling from ear to ear and driving down the road. "We need it. Papere met with Mr. Credeur today and picked up some gossip."

"Anything interesting?" asked Augie.

"Umm. Yes." Paranoia made Jax turn on the radio and crank up the volume to cover their conversation. As music filled the space between them, he said, "seems that reporter I was worried about and his cameraman are determined to find a 'guy' they saw in a lightning bolt," explained Jax.

Augie's mouth dropped open. "What?! I thought you destroyed that film!" he exclaimed.

"I did. They don't have the film. But they saw me. Guess I'm hard to forget!"

"*Whatever!*" exclaimed Augie, rolling his eyes. "Your ego sure hasn't been damaged! But seriously, this is a problem. Are they going to try to do something about it? Like – are they planning on catching you, uhh, *him*?" he asked, editing himself midstream. "And if so, how?"

"Papere said something about cameras being set up around town to monitor the increased lightning activity. He suggested I stop experimenting with my powers for now, probably a good idea. And we should think about using some sort of secret code. Who knows? What if those cameras catch us talking on tape?" Jax thought quietly for a moment and paid closer attention to the road ahead as the sun dipped below the horizon.

Augie also fell silent, searching for answers to the problems they were now facing. He cleared his throat before he spoke again. "So . . . superhero lessons are on hold for a while?"

Jax nodded affirmatively, saying, "no 'planned' lessons, anyway. Can't promise total cessation of activity. I mean, what if somebody really needs help?"

"Rationalization!" Augie coughed the word into his hand.

"Call it what you like!" retorted Jax. "You have to admit that it's fun."

"Scary fun" agreed Augie as he fiddled with the radio controls. The further they travelled out of town, the worse the reception got. Three words made him stop channel surfing – ". . . unusual lightning activity." They listened attentively as a reporter bandied a few theories around about the increase in lightning strikes, fulgurite tubes, dead fish, flashes of Aurora Borealis in the Deep South, and finally the "man" seen within a lightning bolt itself.

Trying to hold onto the broadcast, Jax pulled the truck to an abrupt stop on the highway's shoulder. The reporter's galling interview of an unidentified government official continued. The disembodied voices spit out snippets of distressing information one after another. He pressed the official to explain the sunspot activity, algae blooms, and mass hallucinations. Fortunately, no real conclusions were drawn. It all boiled down to getting the lightning strikes on film; hence, the proposal to set up cameras. When the reporter asked if satellite reconnaissance would be used as well, the official just laughed and said, "I don't really have the budget for that . . . yet."

Interview concluded, a last query about satellites seemed to hang in the air. Augie said, "What a buzz kill," reaching over to turn off the radio.

"No, no, maybe this is good," said Jax as he turned the radio back on.

Augie looked over at his friend in disbelief. "What?" he asked. "How could you say that? The only thing they haven't talked about is that old still and the handsome childhood sidekick." He whispered forcefully and pointed at his chest to indicate himself. "Next thing you know, they'll be at the shop sipping coffee with Papere and scratching Justice behind the ears!"

"But right now, we're going to New Orleans. Maybe the 'unusual lightning activity' could spread. That would make it harder to pinpoint a source or even a suitable place for investigation," Jax suggested.

"No, no, no," started Augie, "there shouldn't be any activity in New Orleans tonight. Too many people know where we're going. There should be an increase in activity somewhere else."

Jax nodded in agreement and said, "Exactly! Flip a coin!" he commanded.

Catching on, Augie dug in his pocket and pulled out a quarter. "Call it," he said, expertly tossing the coin and catching it. He slapped it onto his forearm, keeping it covered with his hand as he waited for Jax.

"Heads," Jax said.

Augie picked up his hand, looked at the coin, and said, "Tails. Where are we going?"

"Not we," corrected Jax. "Me. You drive. I'll go spread some 'unusual lightning activity' around Baton Rouge, then catch up with you before you get to New Orleans. Ok?"

Augie nodded, "Sure you don't want to think this through, first?" he asked.

Jax shook his head negatively. "Just a quick flash or two out and back; no frills."

"Not my first choice, but it sounds like a plan," said Augie as he hopped out of the passenger side and walked around the truck. "Be careful, Jax." But before he could say anything else, the flash of light and thunderous swell that he now associated with his best friend filled the roadside . . . and Jax was gone!

"Don't know if I'll ever get used to that," muttered Augie to himself, shaking his head and instinctively ducking for cover.

As agreed, Augie jumped in the truck and resumed the drive to New Orleans, humming along with familiar songs on the radio. Less than half an hour later, a huge lightning bolt streaked across the sky and struck the side of the highway about one hundred yards in front of the truck.

"Damn it!" yelled Augie, bringing the truck to a screeching halt. Nerves raw, he plopped his head onto the steering wheel and concentrated on breathing, ignoring Jax as he jogged over to the truck.

"That's done," said Jax as he hopped into the passenger side of the truck.

"Jax," started Augie, "you've got to give me some time to get used to this 'popping' in and out business. You have no idea how overwhelming the light and noise is when you, um, fly," he finished.

"Sorry, dude," apologized Jax. "You're right. I don't know how to fix that."

"Whatever, Jax," he said. "Just realize that it's a lot to get used to, and it's all still really new."

"Yes, sir," Jax said.

"So, what did you do?" Augie asked.

"Well," he began, "there are some pretty impressive burns on sidewalks. Some folks in rocking chairs got an extra 'push,'" he laughed, "and there was a brief yet brilliant display of multi-colored lightning. I don't think anyone had time to pull out a camera."

"Fingers crossed, Jax," said Augie. "Thank goodness you figured out how to travel with clothing."

"Will you never let me forget that?" asked Jax.

"Umm," said Augie as he considered the question, nope. Just serves to help keep the superhero humble."

"Thanks, Augie," Jax said with a hard edge to his voice.

"No need to thank me, Jax," he said, "all just part of my job. As 'sidekick,' I don't get paid. So, I get satisfaction where I can find it," offered Augie playfully.

Jax just stared at Augie. "Fine then, do what you can to keep me humble. In the meantime, I think I'm going to nap. Drive on," Jax instructed. Yawning, he closed his eyes and settled deeply into his seat.

"That means you get to drive home." Augie smiled as he drove and listened to the radio.

"Deal," Jax mumbled without even opening his eyes.

The cab of the pickup was lit by the soft glow of the radio and the lights on the dashboard. Suddenly, a pulse of light permeated the cab's interior. "What in the world?" asked Augie out loud, stunned and now night blind by the light. He slammed on the brakes and pulled off the highway onto what he hoped was the shoulder. He glanced over at Jax just as the pulse faded. Although the light ebbed, Augie still saw the increasingly familiar road map of Jax's veins and arteries dim. Jax was sound asleep. A little unnerved, Augie just stared at him, unsure if he could or even should nudge Jax awake. Augie finally decided to just let Jax sleep, but his thoughts were now edged with a touch of fear. New Orleans wasn't much further.

Reaching the outskirts of New Orleans Augie leaned over and shook Jax gently by the arm to wake him, receiving a shock for his trouble.

"Ouch!" Augie yelped.

Jax woke with a start, yawned groggily and asked, "What? Who? Are we there already?"

"Just outside of town," replied Augie, rubbing his hand on his thigh in a vain attempt to stop the stinging sensation. "I got shocked reaching over to wake you."

"Sorry, dude," Jax apologized. "I had the weirdest dream," he confessed.

"Almost as weird as you glowing in your sleep?" Augie asked.

"What?!" Jax asked incredulously. "Hmm . . . that goes along with my dream; this could be a problem."

"Yup," agreed Augie. "You'll need to fit your room with blackout curtains so no one can see you "light up" at night while you're sleeping. And maybe even no catnaps outside of a draped room."

"Good idea," Jax agreed, rubbing his hands together gleefully. "But that's enough of that! This is Nawlins,' The Big Easy, Creole City! Let's have some fun!"

"You probably need to drain off some power before we get any closer to town," suggested Augie.

"Good idea," agreed Jax. He rolled down his window and pointed at a small boulder on the side of the road, aimed, and released a burst of energy. The rock heated quickly and exploded, the glowing debris narrowly missing the truck.

"Dude!" exclaimed Augie. "Thank God no one else was on the road!"

Jax looked over at him sheepishly. "Oops!" he said. "I'll be more careful next time."

They drove to the French Quarter and parked in the first parking garage they found, already caught up in the sights, sounds, and smells. The friendly chatter of the city helped erase Augie's earlier trepidation. As they left the garage, Augie quickly found himself deep in conversation with a friendly couple walking on the street next to them. As they strolled along the river, breathing in the exotic, intoxicating atmosphere, Jax relaxed as well.

Venturing deeper into the city, different strains of music lured them on like musical breadcrumbs. The strains made by ethereal pied pipers wafted to the street from the open doors of various establishments, and from musicians performing on the sidewalks. The melodies mingled and wove together; not seeking individual dominance but partnership. The unscripted symphonies overlapped each other like couples exchanging partners in midair, creating an intricate, disembodied dance.

A few more streets, just *that* much deeper into The Quarter, a thick, sugary horn moaned a sad tune. It was pursued furtively by a trembling guitar that seduced Jax and Augie. The tune pulled them with it past a jazz- laced funeral procession to a second line parade. Swept up in the celebration of people waving handkerchiefs, raising exotic parasols, and holding fragrant candles, Jax and Augie chatted about nothing in particular to everyone around them.

The press of happy revelers squeezed Jax and Augie out near a small restaurant where they decided to eat dinner. Though the restaurant was stuffed full of people they were seated immediately. Jax ordered a large meal, while Augie just ordered an appetizer. Waiting for their food to arrive, Jax spoke up, "This was a great idea! I really needed some space . . ." Jax stopped in mid-sentence as his hand was rubbed by the backside of a restaurant patron passing close to their table.

"Space, huh?" asked Augie with a laugh.

"You know what I mean!" Jax exclaimed. "I needed to have space to *think*! There are so many things happening. I needed to do something normal to make me feel like a real human being again."

"I know what you mean," agreed Augie. They stopped talking as the waiter magically appeared and set glasses of ice water and sweet tea on the table. Taking an appreciative sip, Augie sank against the back of his chair and sighed with satisfaction. He was knocked forward almost immediately by a patron passing behind him. "Dude!" he said, turning to glare at the diner but still speaking to Jax, "I don't think we picked the largest restaurant, but it seems like it just might be the most popular!"

"Right!" exclaimed Jax. "We don't have to shout to hear each other, but it couldn't hurt."

Jax and Augie had little to do while waiting except watch the flow of people in and around their table. There was plenty to see. The host had seated them near the entrance in a tight little space right next to the path where patrons walked in off the street to order at the bar instead of waiting for seating. Their table location was great if Jax and Augie wanted to "people watch," but didn't afford them much privacy.

Despite the crush of people, their order arrived quickly. Their waiter appeared, gracefully lifting a steaming plate from his serving tray, just as a clumsy patron squeezed by. The patron stumbled and leaned on the waiter, knocking him completely off balance. One hand clutching the serving tray and the other balancing a heavy plate of food, the waiter fell precariously across the table. To the casual observer, it looked like he leaned over to delicately balance the dish on an imaginary shelf on the other side of the table. He froze, trying not to drop the dish, when yet another distracted customer passed. Concentrating on balancing three drinks and walking toward his friends, the man didn't see that his path would intersect the steaming plate the waiter held at waist level in front of him.

Augie instinctively reached forward to grab the serving tray while Jax stretched out in an attempt to catch the hot dish. The chaotic combination was just enough to tip the hot plate directly onto the passing customer.

"What the . . . ?!" the customer exclaimed in surprise, tossing his drinks forward, dousing Jax.

Their server, now free of everything he was carrying, tried to stand and get himself under control. Beyond angry and off balance, the customer slipped as the hot food slid down the front of his pants, crying out in instant agony! Falling on Jax's outstretched arm, Jax and the rattled customer ended up in a tangled pile on the floor. Jax, heart pounding from an immediate rush of adrenaline, felt energy surge precariously within his body.

Gotta get away, thought Jax, trying to extricate himself from the customer before inadvertently shocking him.

Jax's skin started to glow and Augie knew they were in imminent danger of being found out. He sprang into action. Standing quickly, he dropped the serving tray on the floor and lifted the fallen customer from Jax's grasp.

Unencumbered, Jax now turned his attention to dealing with the rising energy within him. Instinctively seeking a place to "ground" the surge, he grabbed hold of one of the wooden table legs. The energy immediately found the path of least resistance and funneled into the wood. Unfortunately, the poorly made furniture wasn't up to the task and the table-top exploded from the energy-induced stress. The waiter was dumped unceremoniously on the ground and hundreds of dagger-like wooden splinters were propelled into the crowd.

"Geez! I'm so sorry . . . are you ok?" Augie apologized to the soggy, disheveled customer. "Here . . . have my napkin . . ." he offered as he gently turned the man toward the men's room and pushed him away from the danger and confusion. Urged along by his friends, the customer stomped off to assess the damage in private, cursing fluidly.

The waiter, now completely nonplussed, tried to gather his wits and stand, but only succeeded in wrapping himself in the tablecloth. Jax watched as a red stain spread distressingly on the white cloth. The shock and surprise of his fall receding, the waiter groaned, finally realizing he was hurt.

Most of the energy surge was gone, funneled into the destroyed furniture, but the latent energy in Jax enabled him to easily assess the energy patterns in the waiter. *There's the problem!* Jax thought to himself. A dinner knife was piercing the man below the rib cage, lodged precariously close to what Jax thought must be his spleen.

The spreading stain also caught Augie's eye. He carefully removed the man's shirt to get a better view of the damage.

"Call 911!" Augie shouted to a second waiter standing nearby, making eye contact with the man. Using the fallen waiter's shirt, Augie held pressure on the wound while being careful not to manipulate the knife. "I'm gonna wait here with you," Augie said, speaking calmly and softly to the injured man as they waited for the paramedics to arrive.

Jax knew he could "fix" what was wrong with the waiter, but the previously fluid restaurant crowd was now a stagnant puddle of people stopping to see the excitement. Using his power here would mean certain exposure; there would be no going back. Jax's quick assessment of energy patterns assured him that if things stayed the way they were, the man would be ok. Paramedics would arrive soon and handle the situation. Preparing for their arrival, Jax politely pushed back the crowd to give Augie as much room as possible and tasked the hostess with creating a clear path for the paramedics.

Two policemen passing by stepped in off the street and took control of the stunned crowd. Their intervention freed Jax up even more to help Augie and the staff. "Here!" one of the waitstaff said to Jax, pressing a dustpan into Jax's hand so he could use both of his own to wield he broom as he swept.

Wow . . . my superhero job is less than glamorous, Jax thought, grinning sheepishly at Augie.

Augie smiled back grimly. At the moment, he wasn't really completely aware of Jax. Rather, he was fully focused on the injured man's fear, fatigue, and first aid needs.

The crowd's relief was palpable when the familiar "Waa. . . Waahh. . . Waaaahhhhh" heralded the imminent arrival of the paramedics.

"Ladies and gentlemen," a policeman shouted to be heard above the crowd, "Step back! Please make way!" The crowd shifted sluggishly, reluctantly giving up their "front row seats" to the paramedics.

Appearing magically at his side, the paramedics gingerly yet expertly freed Augie from his first-aid responsibilities, holding pressure on the waiter's wound and keeping the knife still. With the practiced ease of long experience, they lifted the waiter onto their stretcher for transport, started an IV, checked the waiter's vital signs and quizzed Augie about what actually happened.

Surreptitiously, one of the policemen lingered closely and listened to the exchange between Augie and the paramedics.

"So how did the injury happen?" interrupted the policeman. "Stabbing?" he asked.

"Absolutely not," responded Augie. "It was all a completely innocent accident." The policeman quickly appraised Augie and obtained his contact information, then followed the paramedics to interview the injured waiter.

Augie sighed with relief after relinquishing responsibility for the injured man to the paramedics. He looked around the crowd, trying to find Jax. After the police arrived, Jax stepped back and wedged himself into the fringe of the crowd, a timely, safe, and inconspicuous haven. Jax wanted to protect his anonymity and tried to stay close enough to monitor the waiter's injury but not so close that he'd be noticed. Jax caught Augie's eye and motioned nonchalantly that he'd wait for him near the restroom. Augie nodded and noticed his hands were covered in blood. *Gotta clean up,* Augie thought, as he started to push through the throng to the bathroom.

Jax snaked his way anonymously through the crowd to the restroom, but Augie couldn't walk more than five feet at a time without someone trying to thank him for being there. The grin on his face broadcast how much he enjoyed the attention. By the time they met at the men's room, someone had given him a wet towel to remove most of the visible blood from his hands.

"Gross!" grimaced Jax once he was close enough to see Augie's hands and the bloody towel.

"Just blood. Hey, it happens. Let me wash up. I'm *famished!* Are you still hungry?" he asked.

"I could eat," replied Jax. "I'll see if they can find us another table wayyyy in the back. If not, we'll go someplace else."

"Sounds good. The food smells wonderful, but I'm not committed to staying here if it's on the main thoroughfare again!" he replied.

"Agreed," Jax said as he moved off to speak with the hostess. She surprised him by already having a table waiting for them in an empty room usually reserved for private parties. Before sitting down, Jax texted Augie to let him know the location of their table.

The attentive hostess pulled out Augie's chair to seat him when he arrived. "Here you are, sir," she said. "Don't bother ordering, gentle-men. The wait staff would like to thank you for your help." Before they could respond, the hostess waved her hand and a waiter appeared with a tray of salads, ice water, and tea. "Do either of you have any food allergies?" Both men shook their heads in a silent indication of "no." "Good," she said, backing away to make way for the server. "I hope you enjoy your meal," she inclined her head gracefully and left them alone to eat.

"This is amazing!" declared Augie as he looked at the artfully arranged salad and started eating. Wasting no time attacking the plate in front of him, Jax's mouth was already full so he only nodded in agree-ment. Some sort of garlic encrusted fish on a bed of dirty rice with wild mushrooms magically appeared as soon as their empty salad plates were whisked away. The mouthwatering aroma exploded when they cut through the crisp skin into the tender flakiness of the fish, only to be trumped by the chorus of tastes that serenaded their senses in true New Orleans fashion. They ate with the speed and gusto of men who'd been deprived of real food for days.

They ate in silence until Jax finished off his ice water and picked up the pitcher to replenish both his glass and Augie's. He said, "Man . . . this is *so* good!"

"There's real art in this cooking, but it's not so fussy you can't eat it and enjoy it," Augie replied. His words hung lightly in the air as the chef personally brought out two cups of coffee and some of his very own green tea and sweet mint gelato. Chatting briefly, the chef thanked them for taking care of his waiter, while Jax and Augie thanked him in turn for the amazing meal. During the exchange, they learned that the waiter was the chef's favorite nephew and that he was doing well at the hospital.

Standing to leave, Jax reached for his wallet, but the hostess refused to allow him to pay. She did accept the hefty tip he pressed into her hands, saying it would go towards the waiter's hospital expenses.

Jax and Augie walked leisurely back down the street, both waddling a little as they felt the reassuring heaviness of the meal and enjoyed the carefree city atmosphere.

After all that transpired in the restaurant, Jax and Augie didn't linger much longer in the city. A little more people watching as they walked back to the truck was all they could handle.

"Your turn to drive," said Augie, making himself comfortable in the passenger seat. Augie was fast asleep before they reached the outskirts of the city.

Fortunately, the drive home was uneventful. There were no wild animals lurking near the highway. They encountered no stranded motorists. And the truck gave them no trouble on the road home. Driving, Jax relaxed to the sound of soft music from the radio, the soft glow from star-lit skies above his head, and the monotonous hum of the truck engine.

Parking the truck in front of Augie's house, he reached over and gently shook Augie's shoulder. "Wake up, Sleeping Beauty," he said.

Augie stretched and yawned. "Wow!" he said, rubbing his eyes and face. That was one of the best naps I've had in a long time!"

"Thanks for coming along tonight, buddy," said Jax.

"Any time, Jax. See you tomorrow?" he asked.

"Yup," Jax confirmed. "I'll try not to 'nerd out' on the cooking stuff."

"Whatever," replied Augie. "If you do, it'll just make me look cooler! 'Night!" he sang happily, lightly hopping out of the cab of the truck.

"'Night," replied Jax. As he drove home, Jax thought back over all that happened in the past twelve hours or so. *Wow . . . this has been a crazy day!*

18

The Grocery Store

Jax was completely exhausted, but happy, when he got home and tumbled into bed. Mamere and Papere were already in bed and fast asleep. The upcoming day was the last of his impromptu vacation days, and he was looking forward to sleeping in late. He was also pleasantly surprised when he realized he was really looking forward to the dinner date with Augie, Jessica, and whomever Jessica was bringing.

He fell asleep easily and slept soundly until he was teased awake the next morning by the heady aroma of coffee and the familiar clatter of Mamere making breakfast in the kitchen.

He dressed and went downstairs to greet his grandparents. They were already seated for breakfast when he entered the kitchen. Mamere started to push back her chair as she greeted Jax, "Good morning, Te Cher'."

Before she could rise, Jax picked up her hand, brushed it with his lips and said, "Good morning, ma'am." Laying his cheek on her soft hand he added, "You stay seated. I can fend for myself. Morning, Papere," Jax smiled over at his grandfather.

"Morning, Jax," Papere returned. "You have a good time in New Orleans?" he asked.

"Yes, sir!" said Jax. "We had a little excitement," he said.

He looked quizzically at Jax and finished the bite of food in his mouth before speaking. "Saw a blip on the news this morning about some unusual lightning strikes over Baton Rouge last night. Don't suppose you know about that, since you were in New Orleans . . ."

Jax sighed and told them about "spreading" the sightings around, and about the incident at the restaurant. He mentioned the emotional turmoil of knowing he could help the waiter while being determined not to reveal himself. He also talked about the meal they were served, knowing Mamere would enjoy hearing about it. Rubbing his belly, he concluded with, "All I need this morning is a cup of coffee.

Probably won't see Augie until later this afternoon. He was pretty tired when I dropped him off last night."

"Speak for yourself," Augie called from the kitchen door."

"The energies of youth," Papere whispered loudly to Mamere, "continue to amaze me!" "Morning, Augie," Papere said warmly.

"Good morning everyone," Augie singsonged happily, stopping the screen door from banging behind him on the way in. "Is there a cup of coffee for me, too?" he asked, knowing full well he was always welcome at the table.

"'Course!" replied Mamere. She started to push her chair back again to get up but Augie put his hand gently on her shoulder.

"I can pour for myself," he said. "Anyone else want a fresh splash of coffee?"

"I could use a cup, sunshine" replied Jax. I didn't expect you up so early."

"My nap in the pickup on the drive home was really refreshing," Augie stated. "Even stayed up to chat with Mom when I got home," he elaborated, bringing two steaming cups of coffee to the table.

"She still 'ok' with not being around tonight?" asked Jax.

Augie shrugged his shoulders noncommittally and said, "She says so. I just need to believe she's telling the truth."

Mamere and Papere exchanged a quick glance. They knew this was a sensitive issue for Augie and Cheryl. Mamere chewed on her bottom lip to keep quiet, steeling herself not to say anything that could be interpreted as interfering. Papere stuffed a forkful of eggs in his mouth and kept quiet, too. Jax, oblivious to his grandparents' discomfort, said "Of course she is, Augie. She's working anyway, right?"

Augie nodded affirmatively. "I just want everything to be perfect tonight."

"Don't stress so much about it. It's just a dinner date," Jax grinned. "Jessica likes you enough to come and eat your food and bring a witness."

Augie responded by hiding his expression behind a sip of coffee.

"Mamere, Papere," said Jax, "if you'll excuse us, Augie and I have some shopping to do."

Augie groaned. "Can't we just sit here a minute longer?" he asked.

Jax laughed and said, "Sure can, sunshine!" They sat at the table and chatted lightheartedly while Augie and Jax finished their cups of coffee. Sighing happily, Augie pushed back from the table and thanked everyone for the coffee and conversation.

Jax stood and excused himself, following Augie's cue. Outside, the morning sun warmed their shoulders. A cool breeze wound its way around the boys under the clear blue skies of another truly beautiful Louisiana morning.

Jax automatically drove straight to the only grocery store in their little town. When they arrived, there was an unusual knot of customers in the parking lot. Jax parked at the far end of the little lot, but neither one made a move to get out. Something looked odd about the crowd, so they just sat and stared. No one was entering or exiting the building. Most of the people were standing close together, shifting their weight from foot to foot. Others paced back and forth like anxious cats.

Intrigued, Jax and Augie got out of the truck and headed toward the group. One of the women turned and saw their approach; it was Marcia. Deftly, she moved through the crowd to join them.

"This is too weird for our little town!" exclaimed Marcia as she hugged Jax.

"What is?" asked Jax.

"There's a guy in a hoodie holding the clerk at gunpoint telling everyone to stay out. Says that if anyone calls the police, he'll shoot," Marcia said fearfully.

"No one has to call," said Augie. "If we just wait out here all huddled together, Chief Flournoy will figure it out all by himself."

Marcia responded with a tense, little humorless laugh and said, "You're probably right. But who knows how long that'll take? And will that nasty 'so and so' think *we* called him anyway?" Marcia's naturally good- natured sassy tone creeping back into her voice; the edge of her fear blunted now that Jax was there.

"If he's a local, he knows the Chief is always around and that he's got a very limited time frame to do whatever it is he thinks he's going to do," Augie interjected. "I'll bet the clerk is scared stiff! Can you imagine? Showing up for work and getting assaulted?"

Marcia just stared at him.

"Oh," Augie said, abashed, "I'm so sorry!" He lowered his eyes, embarrassed at what he'd just said to a woman who was so recently assaulted at her own job.

Marcia sniffed. "I'm probably more emotional about this than I should be." Augie gave her a quick hug.

Just then, the automatic grocery door swung open; the sensor triggered by a shopping cart full of large, 5-gallon water bottles that rolled slowly to a stop in the doorway. An urgent, muffled voice offered a chilling warning to those in the parking lot.

"Get outta here! If y'all stay in the parking lot I'm a goin' ta shoot you just like these here bottles!"

The horrifying sound of a shotgun blast filled the air as the first bottle exploded. Obliterated, the bottle spewed water in all directions. Although everyone was at least thirty feet away the crowd instinctively ducked down.

"Oh my God! He's shooting at us!" screamed a woman, her words hanging in the odd silence that followed.

Without needing to be told, everyone outside scattered and hid behind the vehicles dotting the parking lot. Augie, Jax, and Marcia took refuge behind Jax's truck.

"That does it," said Augie. "I'm calling the Chief."

"You can't!" protested Marcia.

"We've got to call, Marcia," Jax agreed with Augie. "If we don't, someone will surely get hurt. This guy hasn't done anything to make me think the clerk, or anyone else here, is safe."

Augie didn't hesitate; he dialed the Chief's personal cell phone.

"Flournoy here," answered the chief, slightly annoyed to be getting a call while finishing a bite of breakfast.

Augie started telling the Chief about the situation. The Chief interrupted him several times, firing more questions than Augie could answer. Frustrated, Augie handed the phone to Marcia.

"I can't!" Marcia protested. "I'll be putting a friend in grave danger!" The mute appeal in Augie's eyes won her over, and Marcia reluctantly accepted the phone. Surprisingly, the conversation – though informative – was quite brief. After she hung up, Marcia handed the phone back to Augie and sat down on the ground with her back against one of the truck's wheels.

Crouched behind the pickup, Jax peered over the bed of his truck at the front of the store. He concentrated and focused on trying to interpret the puddles of energy inside the store. Something familiar about the man in the store wearing a hoodie caught his attention. He tried to put his finger on it, but the more he concentrated the more it eluded him.

Scanning the rest of the store, Jax easily pinpointed the clerk's location. It was obvious to Jax that the clerk, though scared, was uninjured. Jax wished he could just use his powers and BE a superhero. He wanted to "flash" into the building, "take out" the robber, and rescue the clerk. His main hesitation was the promise to Papere about "laying low." Right now, that promise was rubbing his conscience raw.

Jax ached to form a plan . . . and then take action! He looked over and caught Augie's attention, raised his eyebrows, and tipped his head toward the store, silently hoping Augie would understand his question. Augie shook his head negatively, clearly indicating superhero intervention wasn't a good idea at this time. Jax sighed, quietly frustrated.

Glancing down, he noticed Marcia's shoulders shaking as she sobbed silently. Jax crouched down to give her a hug. "Everything's going to be fine," he whispered, trying to reassure her.

Marcia wilted as she laid her head on his broad shoulder, releasing the tension threatening to overwhelm her. "This is just too much for me," she admitted. "I've got to go home . . . now," she said, choking back a fresh sob.

"Maybe Jax can take you home," said Augie. "It's not too far, right? You can walk?"

Marcia nodded her head and said, "I can walk. You don't have to come with me, Jax."

"I'd be happy to walk you home, Marcia," he said. "Augie can wait here for Chief Flournoy." He stood up and offered Marcia his hand to help her get up. "I'll come right back, Augie."

"No worries," assured Augie, his attention already returning to the people cowering behind all the vehicles in the parking lot. *How many are out here?* he thought, silently counting them.

Staying low, Jax and Marcia slipped away to the opposite end of the parking lot, using the parked cars for cover. Jax was surprised at Marcia's speed; her nervous energy fueled her feet to a trot that was almost a jog. Fortunately, her apartment was only three blocks from the grocery store. Jax saw her safely inside before calling Augie for an update.

"Hey, Augie, Chief showed up yet?" he asked.

"Nope," answered Augie. "Everything looks the same over here."

"Hmm. What do you think, sidekick?" he asked.

"I think it's time for an intervention," said Augie. "But it would have to be sneaky."

"I think I can throw a curveball with some stink on it," Jax said with a mischievous smile.

"Now that's something I'd like to see," said Augie.

"I'm on it," said Jax, hanging up abruptly.

Relieved to finally have some sort of a plan *and* "permission" to act, Jax jogged one more block away from the grocery store, toward the apartment complex's playground. He picked up his speed as he passed the empty swings and monkey bars and sprinted toward the clump of trees at the far end of the park.

Approximately 20 feet into the stand of trees, Jax stopped and glanced around for possible onlookers. Satisfied no one was watching, Jax acknowledged the energy he now always felt brewing in his core. Relinquishing what little control he enjoyed over it, the power surged. His skin started to shimmer as liquid light pulsed in his arteries and his veins glowed with light as the circuit was completed. With each subsequent heartbeat, the light intensified, and soon, Jax was gone! Lightning flashed and thunder filled the empty space he left behind in the little stand of trees.

Hovering far above the grocery store, Jax's tattoo glowed bright green, blue, and white. Attracted to the immense energy, dense, boiling clouds formed around him. Jax's excellent vantage point provided an encompassing view of the grocery store and surrounding area. He quickly picked five prime target areas around the grocery store.

"Zzoom, zzoom . . . zzapp . . . zaoom, pow!" In rapid succession, Jax launched five lightning bolts. Rolling thunder accompanied each bolt, effectively drowning out all conversations among the people in the parking lot.

The first bolt hit the dumpster at the far end of the parking lot, sending it into an impressive, but harmless spin. The second and third bolts hit the shopping cart corral near the front of the store, sending an eye-opening fountain of sparks skyward. The fourth bolt zeroed in on the flagpole. *"Ddjjjzzapp!"* filled the air as the ammo sizzled its way down the metal beam from the gold-colored ball perched at the top. Searching for ground, the bolt snapped at the sidewalk and small pieces of concrete flew everywhere. The final bolt unerringly connected with the store's power line. As Jax hoped, the last energy mass split and rolled along the power line in two directions. One ball of rolling electricity exploded spectacularly on the store's surge protector.

Down the street, away from the store, the power flashed over another surge protector and split again. The tempered energy that continued along the line was once again dampened by the next surge protector. Residual electricity flashed directly into the ground.

Done with the sideshow, Jax was now ready to address the dangerous situation inside the store. He held his arms out to the side and imagined himself standing in the grocery storeroom. Instantly, a sizzling, energized sphere formed around Jax; the next moment he was no longer hovering in the atmosphere.

"Kkkaaboom!" swelled inside the grocery store as Jax materialized in the storeroom. Wasting no time, Jax – moving faster than any human could actually see with the naked eye – entered the main body of the grocery store. There, in plain view, stood the store clerk, hands flat on the conveyor belt. Nearby stood the man in the hooded jacket. A shotgun was propped against the culprit's leg so he could hold a duffel bag stuffed with cash.

Jax immediately took aim and fired a deadly energy pulse at the shotgun. *"Ddjjjzzapp!!"* it took the hooded man by surprise.

"What the . . ." shouted the man as his weapon inexplicably melted. The shotgun's metal barrel bowed and fluxed as it fell toward the man, badly burning his leg.

Thinking the thunderous boom was yet another shotgun blast, the clerk fainted. Falling to his knees behind the register, he rolled on his side and knocked over a big stack of grocery bags, his head narrowly missing the open till.

Outside the store, though relatively safe behind the truck, Augie ducked reflexively in the wake of the thunderous explosion. Across the parking lot, everyone followed suit. Only Augie had any kind of calm, almost humorous inkling of what was really going on.

Inside, Jax was slipping between the aisles, still busy with his superhero rescue efforts. He scanned the parking lot, closely analyzing all the energy signatures. Unexpectedly, he saw Chief Flournoy approaching the storefront, weapon drawn.

Concerned he could be seen by the Chief, Jax immediately ducked behind rows of shelves and scooted back into the storeroom. Thankfully, the last discharge into the shotgun drained enough power to quiet the storm of energy illuminating his blood. Jax was able to hide as he patiently waited for the Chief to take the robber into custody. Flournoy's nonchalance as he took control of the situation was all Jax needed to reassure him it was a good time for him to leave. He slipped quietly out the back of the store and jogged down the block before he could be discovered.

Jax got back to the front of the store by way of the little park near Marcia's apartment. Jogging the route didn't take long, but in comparison to his new-found method of travel it felt like it took forever. By the time he saw Augie in the parking lot, one of the deputies was hauling the would-be robber off to jail, and Chief Flournoy was taking statements from the witnesses. Finishing an interview, the Chief shook hands with Augie, waved across the lot to Jax, and turned to the next witness.

"Guess I missed all the action," Jax called to Augie, loud enough to be overheard.

"Yup. Marcia feel better by the time you got her home?" asked Augie as he met up with Jax at the pickup truck.

"Not really. She was starting to cry a little, but she needed some space," Jax replied. "I wouldn't be surprised if she takes a few more days off."

Augie nodded as he watched one of the deputies move a shopping basket out of the doorway and stretch police scene tape across the entrance. "Guess shopping isn't happening right now," he mused.

"Ah, nope," agreed Jax. "Is there a plan B?" he asked.

Augie smiled mischievously. "Plan B?" he echoed. "There has to be one now," he said, opening the door of the cab and jumping in. "Let's go!"

Jax hopped into the driver's seat and started the engine. "Where to?" he asked.

"My place," answered Augie.

Jax revved the engine and carefully steered the truck through the people still milling around in the parking lot. Near the edge of the lot, the deputy that taped off the store entrance waved them down. Jax rolled down his window and greeted the deputy. "Bunch of craziness going on," he said.

"I'll say," responded the deputy. "Chief get your statements?" he asked.

Augie nodded affirmatively and Jax said, "Not from me, but we got here after it all started. From what I hear, I was walking Marcia home when it got really exciting."

"Chief'll call you if he needs you, Jax," the deputy replied. "We could do without that kind of excitement. "Y'all be safe," he instructed as he touched a finger to his cap and waved them on.

Jax rolled his window up and drove off the lot, not speaking again until they were at least one block away. He sighed, only then realizing he was holding his breath. "Wow," he said, "wonder how long I'll be able to remain anonymous."

"Not long," Augie replied, "not if you keep insisting on helping people. I still think you need to work on the aspect of healing people."

"There's *no* anonymity in that!" Jax protested. "And seriously, Augie, I'm not some saint! Maybe if I became a doctor and just healed my patients . . . but I'm not that guy!" Jax shook his head. "*You* are that guy. I wish this was a power that you could use."

Augie sat quietly for a moment. "I know," he said quietly. "Sorry, man. I don't mean to make things worse for you." Augie looked out the window at the passing scenery; a convenient way for him to avoid Jax's questioning gaze.

"You ok, Augie?" he asked.

Augie didn't answer for a long moment. "I guess I'm jealous," he finally said.

Jax started to laugh.

"Don't laugh at me, Jax! I'm serious," Augie protested.

"Dude," Jax chortled. "I have been jealous of you my whole life!"

"We're not a couple of girls, Jax," said Augie. He continued in a high-pitched, whiny voice, "I'm jealous of you . . . no I'm jealous of you! Tee-hee!"

"Geez, Augie! Get a grip," Jax replied, all trace of merriment gone. "I'm totally serious. You're the guy who can talk to anyone, make friends with everyone, and can date the prettiest girls. I've been trying to learn those skills from you since we met."

Augie stared out the window. Above them, the previously clear sky darkened. Clouds boiled up out of nowhere and the weather threatened to turn foul. Augie looked back in Jax's direction and saw confusion and frustration knit in deep furrows across his brow. Concerned, Augie started to empathetically tap his friend's shoulder but stopped midway. *Again?* Mused Augie as Jax's skin took on the now familiar glow; a sure sign that Augie would be shocked if he touched Jax.

"Man . . . you're amping up!" Augie said in amazement.

Quickly, Jax pulled the truck onto the side of the road and hopped out. "Dang it!" hollered Jax as he dropped to the ground and shoved his hand into the dirt to drain off energy. "I can't just nonchalantly stick my hand in the dirt every time I start to glow!" The confusion and frustration evident on his face ebbed as he scanned the sky and realized the formerly angry clouds were now calm and the sun once again burned brightly through scattered white clouds.

"Nope," Augie agreed as he also got out of the pickup. "Not the most convenient problem to have." He snapped his fingers. "Hey! What if you can get a rechargeable battery and . . ."

"Drain the energy into the battery?" interrupted Jax. "Dude! That could work!"

"Providing you don't cause the battery to explode," added Augie."

"Ok, so, maybe not the little ones. But maybe the little ones would be good for hiding in my pocket and taking the 'edge' off until I can get to say, an automobile battery . . ." mused Jackson. Then, they smiled at each other, their earlier jealousies forgotten; best friends once again.

"Let's get going," said Augie. "Mom's got to have at least one rechargeable battery at home." Jax nodded in agreement as he and Augie hopped back into the pickup and headed to Augie's house.

19

The Date

By the time Augie and Jax got to the duplex Cheryl was already at work. The events of the morning had made time fly and it was already midafternoon. They frantically cleaned and made the house as presentable as they possibly could. After a little digging around, Augie found a couple of long forgotten rechargeable batteries in the kitchen's disorganized "everything" drawer. They were tucked away where Augie's mom put all the little things she occasionally needed. He handed the batteries to Jax, who slipped them into his jeans pocket. A little brainstorming and searching through both the refrigerator and the small pantry yielded the makings of a dinner that evoked comfort, if not affluence.

Jax and Augie sat down and watched the news on the kitchen television set while they waited for their dinner dates to arrive. Listening intently, they were surprised that weather coverage trumped airtime over their small-town crime wave.

"The unexpected, dramatic spike in lightning strikes in our region is all but beyond explanation," reported the weatherman. "And honestly, I confess I am at a complete loss regarding the spectacular solar flares. As reported by many of our viewers, and NASA correspondents, the number of meteorite sightings has skyrocketed! Unfortunately, NASA has not yet released footage of these odd events." Jax frowned deeply when he heard about NASA's unreleased footage of the "unusual meteorite" sightings. It was impossible to miss the hint of confusion that infused the meteorologist's voice. The coverage of the incident at the supermarket was almost an afterthought by the anchorman, who speculated vaguely about ties to the lumberyard incident.

Augie was about to ask Jax what he thought about the unreleased footage in the news report when he heard a car drive up. He looked out the window and saw Jessica parking her car. Two beautiful women got out and approached his front door.

Although Augie reached the door before the girls did, he forced himself to wait until Jessica rang the bell before he opened it. For the moment, he didn't want his eagerness to be so blatantly apparent. After the bell rang, Augie took a deep breath, smiled, and opened the door to invite the women into his home. Jax was silencing the news cast and turning on the stereo. The soft strains of New Orleans-style jazz magically transformed the living room into a very cozy space.

Turning from the stereo, Jax could clearly see the front door. His heartbeat kept pace with the pulse of mesmerizing music. The girls' radiance coupled with the intensely romantic music filled the room with a more than human electricity. Augie greeted the girls with an enviably comfortable grace.

"Hello, Jessica, glad you could make it," he said, taking her hand.

Without hesitation, Jessica leaned in and kissed the air by Augie's cheek. "Hello, Augie. May I introduce Patrice?"

"Patrice," echoed Augie. "Welcome!" He turned and nodded toward Jax. "Ladies, may I introduce Jax?"

Still standing by the stereo, Jax – though locked into the conversation – felt as if his feet were glued to the floor. No matter how hard he tried, Jax simply couldn't move his overwhelmingly heavy feet. Clearing his suddenly dry throat, Jax mustered up the courage to respond.

"Hello," Jax croaked, willing his feet to cross the room. He shook hands gently with each woman and repeated their names, "Jessica, Patrice."

"Please, call me Jess," said Jessica.

"Jess," Augie and Jax echoed in unison.

"Jax?" asked Patrice. "Are you a card player?" "No," replied Jax, smiling. "It's short for Jackson." "Great name," said Patrice.

"Make yourselves at home," Augie invited. "Would you like something to drink?"

"I would love a glass of sweet tea, if you have some," replied Patrice. "I just got back from visiting relatives up north, and they do *not* know what sweet tea is! Now I don't think I can get enough of it! You should've seen their faces when I ordered tea instead of 'soda pop.' And the tea I got was hot, weak, and bitter!"

"Ouch," said Jessica with a pained expression. "Sweet tea would be wonderful," she added.

"On it," said Jax, popping into the kitchen to grab the pitcher of sweet tea he'd prepared earlier.

Augie followed him and picked out the glasses his mother usually reserved for guests. Concern put a hard edge on his voice when he whispered, "Jax, you might drain off some energy now, you're starting to glow."

Jax looked down and saw that his skin was indeed glowing slightly. He hadn't even noticed the "buzz" of energy until Augie mentioned it. He placed his hand flat on the wooden table in the kitchen and concentrated on draining energy. He was careful not to drain too much into the table, just enough to take off the edge. Nevertheless, the table shook finely before he was finished. "Better?" asked Jax.

Augie nodded and smiled. "I don't need you looking all 'shimmery' and taking Jess' attention away from me," he joked.

"No need to worry there," replied Jax. "Her attention is squarely on you. I'm just happy to chat with Patrice. She's pretty."

"Yup," agreed Augie. "Jess said she would be. I've never known her to bend the truth." Augie put ice in the glasses and waited as Jax poured the tea. Placing the glasses on a tray, he carried them into the sitting room while Jax brought the pitcher of iced tea and placed it on the small decorative table next to the couch. Augie handed a glass to each woman and sat down.

Patrice took a timid sip, then smiled and took a larger drink of the sweet tea. "Yum," she said appreciatively. "I really missed sweet tea."

I've never been north of Louisiana," said Augie, "and I've always wanted to see the Rocky Mountains. Now that I hear there's no sweet tea, I'm not sure I want to go."

Jessica smiled and said, "Forewarned is forearmed! You could bring tea with you. There must be some good reasons to travel north. Plenty of people go more than once."

"Your family's up north but you live in Louisiana?" probed Jax.

"Cousins in Wisconsin," she replied. "I also did my first year of nursing school in Chicago."

"Brrr," said Jax, "sounds cold."

"That's *precisely* why I only did one year there," she said, nodding in agreement. "After that, I moved back home to finish my degree."

"You work with Jess and Augie at the hospital?" asked Jax.

Patrice nodded again. "But I don't think I've ever met Augie before."

"Nope," agreed Augie, "I don't think we've met before."

"With a hospital this size," Jessica interjected, "it's not all that unusual." The hospital at which the three of them worked was a regional trauma center located approximately 10 miles from town on the way to New Orleans. Jessica and Augie worked on the neuropsych unit and Patrice worked in the emergency department, so, all three didn't cross paths very often.

"What do you do, Jax?" Patrice asked.

"I work at the lumberyard," replied Jax.

"Oh, really?" Patrice asked questioningly. "Were you there the day of the fire?"

"Yup. But I got there after it started," Jax replied.

"Will you be able to go back to work?" asked Jessica.

"Yes," replied Jax. "Tomorrow."

"Wow!" Patrice said, "it's one thing doing fire drills in a hospital, being prepared to evacuate patients, but completely different when it's at a lumber yard. At least the hospital isn't tied to a stack of wood that can easily catch fire."

"True," replied Jax. "But doesn't the hospital have all kinds of explosive chemicals and gasses? That sounds more dangerous to me."

Jessica laughed. "Yes! But I never thought of it quite that way before."

Augie shook his head before commenting, "Leave it to Jax to find a way to make healthcare scary!"

"Hey man," Jax said, "it is *not* my thing. And please don't start a discussion about how 'cool' some wound or procedure is while we are eating." He raised a hand as if surrendering. "It'll make me gag."

Augie said, "I'll try to restrain myself," as he, Jessica, and Patrice started laughing.

"I know what you mean," replied Jessica. "My parents can't stand that either. Thing is, it's such a fascinating thing for us to see how bad a wound can get and how things either heal or fail . . ."

"On that delicious note," Augie interrupted, "shall we eat?"

"Yes!" Patrice exclaimed. "I'm famished!"

"Me, too," echoed Jessica.

"This way, ladies," said Augie, bowing as he and Jax led the girls to the small, but intimate, dining area.

Earlier, Jax meticulously draped the table with a simple cloth. The vase in the middle of the table was stuffed with an eclectic arrangement of discarded flowers Jax rescued from Evie's wedding.

As the others took their seats, Augie excused himself, went to the kitchen, and quickly returned with a platter of grilled crawfish, cheese sandwiches, and four bowls of tomato soup. "I hope no one is allergic to shellfish," joked Augie as he placed the platter in the center of the table.

"I love shellfish," stated Patrice, taking an appreciative sniff.

"Me too!" said Jessica, nodding in agreement. "Smells wonderful."

"We'd planned on serving wild turkey, but with the robbery at the grocery store today, we couldn't get the right sides. Hope you don't mind homemade," apologized Jax.

"I would have fainted if Augie walked in here with a homemade turkey dinner!" joked Jessica. "This is *far* less intimidating."

"Less intimidating?" asked Augie.

"Yes," Patrice said.

"And here I am, hoping to blow your minds with my culinary expertise," he admitted, tongue in cheek. "Jax. We blew it," he sighed.

"What do you mean, *we*?" asked Jax, chuckling.

"I reserve the right to decide on whether or not you've 'blown it,'" Jessica interjected, "until *after* we get a chance to sample the meal."

"Well then," said Augie, offering her a sandwich, "don't stand on ceremony! Take a bite."

Sitting down, Jessica accepted the sandwich he offered and chose a bowl of soup. Patrice, Jax, and Augie all watched as she picked up her spoon and dipped it into the soup. Steam curled delicately off the rich concoction above the bowl of the spoon. Timidly, she tasted the soup, then smiled. "Yum!" she exclaimed. "It's perfect."

Patrice sat next to her, chose a bowl of soup, and waited for Augie to hand her a sandwich. She tore off a bit of the sandwich, held it up over her bowl of soup and hesitated. She looked up at him questioningly, mutely asking permission. Augie nodded affirmatively, and she dipped the tip of her sandwich in the soup before sampling it. A smile spread over her face as she chewed and swallowed. Nodding at Augie she asked, "Homemade tomato soup, too?"

Augie nodded as he pulled out his chair and sat down. "But don't give me too much credit. We just warmed up Mom's tomato soup. She's a whiz in the kitchen!"

Jax sat down and both men started eating after choosing sandwiches and bowls of soup of their own. Before long, the four of them polished off their meals. Patrice finished first, which seemed to embarrass her.

"Anyone want seconds?" asked Jax, trying to put Patrice at ease. "Plenty more where that came from." Both women declined politely, but the boys each dove in for a second sandwich.

Comfortably full, the cozy quartet got up from the table and returned to the living room to listen to music. Patrice, Jessica, and Augie sat on the old, comfy sofa, leaving Jax to sit in the rocking chair. Chatting happily, the soulful notes filled the natural lulls in their conversation, Jax caught himself staring at Patrice more than once. Pulling his eyes away from her, he glanced at Augie, who grinned foolishly at him. Jax searched fruitlessly for something witty to say when he saw Augie's expression darken with concern. Augie tilted his head toward the kitchen but didn't want the girls to look in Jax's direction, so he didn't speak.

That was when Jax glanced down and noticed he was starting to glow. He nonchalantly slipped one slightly glowing hand into his jeans pocket and touched the little cache of batteries. Holding one between his thumb and index finger, he siphoned off the energy buildup. The small battery heated faster than Jax thought it would, quickly, sizzling and popping unexpectedly! Yanking it out quickly, Jax tossed it into a decorative vase on the end table before it could burn a hole in his pocket. The clink caused Patrice to look up, but the overheated battery was already safely hidden deep in the bottom of the vase. More importantly, Jax no longer glowed.

"Patrice, would you care to dance?" asked Jax, politely standing up to twirl her into the middle of the small room. Not to be out done, Augie held his hand out to Jessica in a silent invitation to join him on the impromptu living room dance floor. Fortunately, the dancing provided a way for Jax and Augie to steer the girls away from the acidic smoke inexplicably curling above the lip of the vase.

Patrice was so light and confident on her feet that Jax felt he needed to pull her closer, just to keep her from floating away. Breathing in the amber and lavender scents that clung to Patrice's body, Jax's heart quickened. Jax closed his eyes as they danced, absolutely content to be close to her. When Jax drew her nearer, Patrice laid her head on the center of his chest and effortlessly let her footsteps mirror his.

Jax's strong heartbeat tugged at Patrice's emotions; so much so that she shivered inside. In response, Patrice laced the fingers of her right hand between Jax's fingers and traced the strong line of his shoulder blade through his shirt with her left. Her featherlight touch generated a line of cool goosebumps that warmed as they raced towards his spine.

Jax knew instinctively that the energy building in him couldn't be drained into a small battery, so he pulled brusquely away from Patrice. A loud "snap" of static electricity arced and bridged the new distance between them, and she yelped painfully at the unexpected jolt. Jax mumbled an excuse and almost jogged out of the room. Startled and confused, Patrice didn't even have time to respond before he was out of sight in the kitchen. Augie, completely entranced with Jessica, barely noticed Jax's exit, but Jessica disentangled herself from his embrace and asked, "What happened?"

"I just got zapped with static electricity!" Patrice said, shrugging her shoulders and looking slightly perplexed. "I guess we were shuffling our feet on the carpet. Be careful, Jess." Looking quizzically at Augie she asked, "What happened to Jax?"

"What happened to Jax?" Augie echoed, feigning ignorance. He guessed what made Jax leave the room hastily. *Thank goodness he was able to get out of here quickly,* thought Augie. "Uh . . . beats me! Excuse me a minute," offered Augie as he left the room to check on Jax.

Patrice looked at Jessica and said, "I guess my personality is electric!" Jessica giggled.

Jax was through the living room and halfway across the kitchen before he heard Jessica ask what happened. Opening the door quietly, he went out into the tiny backyard. Crouching down, Jax placed one hand in the dirt and siphoned off the power buildup, easing the pressure he felt along his spine. Breathing a huge sigh of relief, he stood and looked at the peaceful backyard.

He'd always liked it here. It was familiar, unpretentious, and comforting, perfect for odd little moments like this evening.

Jax didn't notice Augie standing in the doorway behind him until he spoke. "You ok, buddy?" Augie asked quietly, his voice filled with an unmistakable sense of concern. Augie was looking out through the screen but couldn't see Jax, who was just off to the side and out of his line of sight.

Jax nodded and said, "Yup. Kind of freaky. It's like playing with fire, Augie."

"Literally," he replied.

Reluctantly, Jax turned toward the house, opened the screen door, and stepped back inside.

"Dude, you don't have to act so disappointed about coming back inside," joked Augie.

"I'm not disappointed!" Jax protested. "Patrice is nice."

"Whatever! I'm just playing. Just keep it together a little longer, man," Augie said as he led the way back into the living room.

While Jax and Augie were out of the room, Jessica and Patrice talked about the pictures displayed on the sitting room walls. Jessica stopped mid-sentence when Augie walked up behind her and interjected, "Mom has a flare for picking the most embarrassing pictures."

Jessica slipped her hand into his and said, "It's a learned behavior. I thought I was *so smart* when I 'redecorated' the parlor before my high school graduation party. But Mama noticed before my guests arrived and put all the embarrassing photos back up where she wanted them. It was a shocker."

Patrice smiled. "Wish I'd have thought of that!"

"If I even *think* of moving a picture to a less conspicuous place, Mamere is already at my side, letting me know how much she likes this one or that one, where it is and *why* it's there," Jax said with a half-smile. "I'll bet there isn't one bad picture of you anywhere, Patrice" he said, taking her hand to twirl her around the living room once again. "Sorry I shocked you."

"That was odd, wasn't it?" Patrice asked. "I'll try not to rub my feet on the carpet again."

Jax pulled her in close as they danced. Letting Jax guide her around the room, Patrice closed her eyes and focused on the music. Their bodies moved to the sultry jazz. Jax's close proximity teased and excited her senses. Patrice caught herself fantasizing about kissing him. As they danced, she unwittingly tilted her face towards his.

Observing Patrice's subtle movement, Jax smiled playfully. Confidently, Jax slowly dropped his hand from behind Patrice's shoulder blade to the more intimate small of her back. Without hesitation, Jax narrowed the space between them even more, pulling Patrice slightly nearer to him; how he enjoyed her closeness. Jax's smile deepened when Patrice's body responded with a delicious, involuntary shudder. The enjoyable tension between them rose even higher when Jax dropped his head and let his cheek brush lightly against Patrice's.

Ill-timed, Jax heard and felt a familiar, slight electrical buzz. Trying to protect Patrice, Jax reluctantly removed his hand from the small of her back to slip it into his pocket. His primary goal was to drain energy into the small battery. It overheated much quicker than the last one. Fortunately, just as the battery started to smoke and buckle from the power surge, Jax instinctively tossed it into the vase.

Augie looked over at Jax and Patrice as soon as he heard the "clink" of the battery landing in the bottom of the vase. The lack of daylight between their bodies clearly communicated their intense attraction to each other. *What if they keep dancing?* Thought Augie. *If Jax surges again, I can't help him . . . all out of batteries!* Augie's brain raced as he searched for a way to protect everyone.

"Cards!" exclaimed Augie out loud as the song ended. "Anyone want to play cards?"

"No, thank you, Augie. I still have to unpack," Patrice said reluctantly as the song ended and they stopped dancing.

"I'll have to decline, too," chimed in Jessica. "In fact, we've got to call it a night. We both work a day-shift tomorrow."

"Aww," groaned Augie with exaggerated disappointment. "Well, he continued while rubbing the back of his neck. "I can't say I'm happy to hear that, but I do understand." Pulling Jessica close, he gave her a kiss on the cheek. "I'm really glad you came tonight," he confessed.

Jessica put her free hand on his chest and said, "Thank you for the invitation," and kissed him lightly on the lips.

Surprised, Augie grinned and whispered, "You are most welcome."

Across the room, purse in hand, Patrice added to Jessica's comments. "Yes, thank you. It was nice to finally meet you, Augie. Jess has told me so much about you." Embarrassed, Augie started to protest, but she held up one hand and clarified. "All good! Jax, it was a pleasure to meet you, too."

"Pleasure was all mine," replied Jax.

Augie and Jax accompanied the girls outside to Jessica's car. They lingered on the sidewalk as the intimate quartet wished the evening didn't need to end. Jax looked up at the stars and commented on the expansive beauty. "Wow! Now that's a beautiful sky!" In unison, everybody agreed. Eventually, the girls got into the car and headed home.

"That was a good night," observed Augie as he and Jax watched the girls drive away.

"Nope . . . it was a great night," Jax corrected.

"I thought it was touch and go for a while, though. I don't think those batteries are going to be enough," said Augie.

"Nope," agreed Jax. "I need a better idea. But at least no one got hurt."

"Yup," said Augie.

"I'll help you clean up," said Jax.

"No worries, man. I got it. See you tomorrow," replied Augie.

"Ok. See you later," said Jax. He started the pickup as Augie walked back to the house, whistling happily.

Jax wasn't in a hurry, but it didn't take him long to get home. Again, he was glad that Mamere and Papere were asleep. He wasn't in the mood to answer questions about tonight's dinner date. Glowing softly, Jax moved confidently through the dark house, finding it unnecessary to turn on any lights.

Tumbling gratefully into bed, Jax relaxed and focused on letting the power go. The gently glowing light faded. By now, he was pretty comfortable managing the little, less volatile energy spurts. The larger surges were another matter entirely.

Lying in bed only half-awake, his mind was flooded with thoughts about Patrice and the evening. *What's wrong with me . . .* he thought. *Flirting? Really?!* That was totally out of character. *And almost kissing her in Augie's living room?* Jax wondered if Patrice would have slapped his face if he'd have tried. *Do I have any self-control at all?* The whole situation left him feeling out of his depth and floundering, especially where his emotions were concerned. Sadly, he realized that avoiding romantic entanglements was probably the best plan of action for now, even if it wasn't much fun.

Rechargeable batteries aren't the answer, Jax conceded as he debated the best ways to release energy . . . and manage romantic urges. *Priorities! Gotta put Patrice on hold for now,* were his final thoughts as sleep finally captured him.

20

Salvage

Jax woke up before his alarm went off in the morning. Lying in bed, he wondered why he was wide awake so early. Down in the kitchen, he heard the low murmuring of Mamere and Papere quietly going about their normal morning routine – soft conversation accompanied by the muffled clatter of dishes. Nothing unusual.

What time is it? wondered Jax. A quick glance at the alarm clock revealed he was awake a full hour earlier than necessary. *Hmm . . .* thought Jax, rolling over in a vain attempt to squeeze in one last hour of sleep before actually getting out of bed.

Five minutes later, Jax rolled onto his back again. Eyes wide open, he stared in frustration at the ceiling. *Why in the world can't I go back to sleep?* Jax thought, baffled as to why sleep was viciously eluding him.

Finally, Jax gave up on getting more sleep. He threw back the covers with a deep sigh, swung his legs over the side of the bed and got up.

The second he stood, he realized what had woken him so early. He was energized! The tattoo on his arm was tingling and a cushion of static electricity popped and sizzled between his feet and the floor.

Hovering above the floor, Jax struggled to maintain his balance, wobbling on the unpredictable electric cushion under his feet. Taking great pains, he kept himself upright, then effortlessly skated across the room. Experimenting with the electric charge, Jax discovered that the faster he moved, the thicker the cushion became. As tall as he was, Jax quickly had to duck down to keep from knocking his head on the blades of the ceiling fan.

Jax was starting to find the whole situation entertaining. Smiling, he slowed down a bit to allow the charge to wane. As it dissipated, he skated over to his bedroom window, raised it, and pointed at some clouds in the sky, then changed his mind. *Better choose a more inconspicuous target,* he thought to himself. He saw the cluster of stones in the backyard and chose a large one.

"*Dzzbboom!*" resonated impressively as Jax fired unerringly with practiced precision of an expert marksman. The stone glowed red-hot for a fraction of a second before evolving into a color so bright it defied description. Then, "*Blaaammm!*" The awesome sound filled the air as the entire stone exploded into a dense shower of fine pebbles and dust.

Dang it! Jax thought, scowling in disappointment. *That explosion was way bigger than I thought it would be*, he admitted to himself.

More than ever before, Jax was beginning to realize he'd have to keep a tight leash on where he aimed in the future. *I can't just aim at the sky*, he thought to himself. *What if I accidentally hit an airplane?* The very thought of that terrified Jax; besides, additional, unwanted attention was the last thing he needed.

Safely discharged, the cushion of static electricity under Jax dissipated, dumping him unceremoniously on the floor. He sighed again, got dressed for work, and went downstairs for breakfast. Mamere and Papere were staring out the kitchen window at the spot where the rock had been. They turned in unison to look at Jax as he entered the kitchen.

"Interesting morning already?" Papere asked, nodding toward the backyard.

"Yes, sir," Jax agreed. "Couldn't be helped. Woke up floating on some sort of a cloud of static electricity. Augie gave me some rechargeable batteries yesterday to drain energy into as needed. They helped a little, but it's not perfect."

"Hmm," Papere said, rubbing his chin, lost in deep thought. "Rechargeable batteries. Not a bad idea. But maybe you need bigger reservoirs, like a car battery."

"Maybe, but that's a bit awkward to carry around," joked Jax.

"Yup. Any other ideas?" Papere asked.

"Not yet," answered Jax. "But I can't just go around blowing up little boulders or lighting up the skies. I wish Superman was real. I'd love to ask him some questions."

Papere snapped his fingers. "That's actually a good idea!"

"What?" Jax and Mamere both asked, surprised.

"Why couldn't you 'transport' yourself to Antarctica or someplace equally remote, discharge, and return?" asked Papere.

"I like where you're going with that," Jax began. "It's worth exploring. But first, I need some breakfast." He got a bowl out of the cabinet.

"Do you want an egg?" asked Mamere.

"No, ma'am, just some cereal this morning," replied Jax.

"How did your date go last night?" Mamere asked Jackson.

"Good," replied Jax. "Nerve wracking, but good."

"First dates are a bit unnerving. And this one was a blind date. That's understandable, son," replied Papere.

"Not exactly what I meant. My energy built up faster and more frequently than I expected. I drained energy into two of those little rechargeable batteries Augie gave me and just about blew them up. Tossed 'em into one of Miss Cheryl's vases and they smoked a bit. Still had to go outside and drain the rest," explained Jax.

"Hmm," said Papere.

"My word!" exclaimed Mamere. "Are you getting stronger?"

"I'm not sure," began Jax, "the energy seems to build up faster every day, but I don't know if that also means I'm actually more powerful. Papere, so you think I should travel to a remote area, discharge, and come home?"

"Maybe," he replied. "But just flying is a discharge of energy, right?" he asked.

"Yes, sir," said Jax. "Of course, flying draws attention, something I do not need right now because of those reporters. It's really simpler to just bounce up into the atmosphere and come back."

"It won't be for much longer," said Mamere. "Those reporters are bound to get tired of looking for a needle in this tiny haystack of a town. Then, they'll go home. Someone's got to think it's just an oddity of the El Niño or whatever storm system we've got going through."

"I hope so, Mamere," replied Jax. "There was a blurb on the news last night about NASA observing some 'unusual meteorite' activity. That's got me a little concerned too."

"I heard that too," said Papere. "They're also yappin' 'bout a solar flare that'll probably mess up satellite communication in the next day or so. You'll need to figure out where those satellites and telescopes are to avoid detection, or you'll have to keep below the clouds."

The entire conversation distracted Jax so much that he forgot about pouring cereal into his bowl. "Honestly, the more I try to avoid exposure, the more impossible it seems," he said, tensely rubbing the back of his increasingly stiff neck.

"Too bad your powers don't involve some sort of short-term memory loss on the part of the observer," said Mamere.

"Could you imagine?" asked Jax, chuckling. "I'd have to tell you the whole story again, every time you found me out. That would be *so* frustrating! Everyday this superhero thing seems more of a hindrance than a blessing," Jax added softly, suddenly subdued. "I sure hope that changes soon."

Jax's frustration and emotional heaviness caught Mamere's attention. She looked at him more intently, her eyes narrowing with deeper inspection. What she saw made her move without hesitation. She rushed over to him to throw her arms around him and hold him. Jax held back at first, afraid he would shock Mamere. But when nothing happened, he pulled her closer and returned the embrace.

"Jax, you'll never be too old or 'hero-like' to get some sugar from your Mamere." In spite of being "grown up," Jax reveled in Mamere's love and tenderness. "Now pour you some cereal!" she ordered, tenderly kissing him on the cheek.

"Yes, ma'am," agreed Jax, holding her just one second longer before grabbing a box of cereal out of the cabinet.

Sitting down to eat, Jax shook his head. For as long as he could remember, everything was always better after a hug from Mamere. Papere sat near him, quietly sipping his coffee and reading the paper. Mamere kept busy tidying up the kitchen. After finishing his cereal, Jax excused himself, grabbed an apple out of the fruit bowl, and headed out the door for work. What a great way to start the day, he thought as he bounced down the porch steps.

Jax tossed the apple in the air and caught it, then buffed it on his shirt as he walked to his truck. The slight friction caused the apple to smolder. He stared at it as it warmed and puckered in his hand. Tossing the apple into the air again, it blossomed into flame.

"Sheesh," mumbled Jax, stepping aside to let the tiny fireball land in the driveway. As soon as the flames died, he stomped out the smoldering pulp, then scraped the burned, mashed apple off the sole of his shoe.

Turning the key in the ignition, the truck's engine roared faithfully into life, music blaring triumphantly from the radio. Jax whistled happily and drove to work; Mamere's tender attention had done the trick.

Jax parked on the street next to the lumberyard. The flimsy wire fence that stretched around the fire site to discourage trespassers was broken only by the small opening that served as a gate. Jax saw Winchell and Marcia already chatting in the parking lot when he arrived. The entire area was still wet, the sad scene even dampening their polite "Good morning" greetings. Inside, Parish wandered around the store taking stock of the damages.

"Wow," remarked Jax, joining Parish and surveying the situation inside.

"Yes, 'wow,'" Parish echoed, nodding. "There's a lot of work to be done. But right now, let's get that small area straightened out," he said, motioning toward one of the only still-standing parts of the building. "We'll open for business there. The engineers have checked it out and it's safe. The rest will have to be razed and rebuilt. Taped off areas aren't safe; so, don't go exploring!" stressed Parish. "For now, we can use that area over there as a breakroom," he continued, pointing to a table and chairs set up in a tiny puddle of "clean."

Jax nodded as he took in all of Parish's observations and instructions.

"Thank God, most of the lumber was spared!" Parish sighed. "Even still, I don't expect we'll be ready to open for a few days. Probably more like weeks. Anybody wanting a cup of coffee first, just help yourself," he concluded, pointing to a large thermos and coffee fixings set up on a stack of wet lumber near the table.

Marcia and Winchell followed Jax inside and heard everything. They helped themselves to coffee while Jax hunted up some brooms and dustpans. It took them most of the morning just to clear out and clean up the area near the counter they'd use for the cash register. Eventually, Parish left to meet with the electricians he'd hired to get the power back on and run wires where needed. GH, fresh out of the hospital and still sporting his hospital ID band, stopped by to say "hello" and surprised everyone by bringing a picnic lunch and a jug of ice cold sweet tea. He told them he wasn't cleared to work yet, that would take a while longer. Nevertheless, GH looked pretty good for a guy who'd been knocked out and left for dead in a burning building.

Jax chewed on his sandwich as he listened to Marcia, GH, and Winchell hash over the events of the day of the fire, trying to figure out who started it and why. He debated the same issues. For sure, the robbery wasn't the only thing on his mind lately.

GH listened as Marcia and Winchell continued to visit, but Jax's attention wandered. He was only marginally interested in their conversation. The energy waves emanating from the piles of debris tugged at him constantly. They were much more interesting to him, and though he couldn't mention it to anyone, their potential danger was physically and emotionally taxing. Now tired from the morning's exertion, it was harder and harder for him to avoid absorbing the energy generated by the decay. He was frequently forced to kneel down and discharge the excess energy into the cement floor or "push" a pile of lumber – with a hopefully discreet energy pulse – just to stay in control of his body.

All these energy forms . . . amazing, Jax pondered silently. His hero transformation opened his formerly oblivious eyes to the different forms of energy all around him.

After lunch, Jax wanted to experiment with using a faint energy bubble as a type of shield to deflect energy away from him. Of course, he'd have to find someplace to practice unobserved. Jax finished his sandwich and was reaching for his tea just as the sheriff arrived. "Afternoon, sir," Jax said after finishing one big swallow of tea.

"Afternoon, folks," replied the sheriff, politely tipping his hat toward Marcia. "Is Mr. Credeur around?" he asked.

"No, sir," replied Marcia. "But may I help you?"

"Just stopped by to update y'all about the investigation," he said. "We can all rest a little easier and get back into our old routines. The same bunch of hoodlums that robbed and burned the lumberyard were caught in New Orleans last night."

"Thank God!" said Marcia, visibly relieved.

"How do they know they're the same ones?" asked GH.

"Well," replied the sheriff, rubbing his hands together. "They were picked up trying to rob a convenience store. During processing they couldn't seem to stop talking. Bragged to anybody that would listen about how they'd pulled the wool over the eyes of a small-town sheriff!" he grinned, pointing to his chest. "They were even taking credit for attracting lighting with the 'brilliance' of their arson." By now the sheriff was clearly enjoying how the little audience was hanging on his every word.

"Stupid!" exclaimed Winchell.

The sheriff shook his head in disbelief. "They'll be prosecuted for robbery, arson, and attempted murder."

"What about the grocery store robbery?" asked Jax.

Sheriff Flournoy nodded and said, "That was one of them, too. Seems he was the 'smarter' one. The other two babbled on and on, holding nothing back once the detectives started asking questions." He smiled wryly as he continued. "Evidently, these two assumed their partner'd already given them up. Guess they thought they would be treated more leniently if they came clean."

"Wow," said Jax.

"What about those reporters setting up surveillance cameras?" asked Winchell.

"Never did like that idea," said the sheriff. "And there's no need for it either!" he exclaimed, frustrated. "I'll charge 'em with invasion of privacy if they have the audacity to put cameras on public property! Can't do anything about someone wanting them on their own land, but there's nothin' more to 'unearth,' so to speak." He tipped his hat again. "Well . . . guess I'll go find Parish and tell him the good news. Good day."

Although GH was obviously tired, he stayed and chatted a bit longer. Marcia gently pushed him to leave, joking that he was keeping them from getting any work done. He smiled and said, "you've made short work of lunch, but not much else!"

"We could use an extra pair of hands," Marcia agreed, "but you just get on out of here and rest!"

Jax and Winchell also wanted GH to leave, both urging GH to go so they could work in peace. "We've just got to walk away and start working or he'll never leave," Jax commented as Winchell nodded in agreement.

"Yup! See 'ya later, GH," said Winchell, giving a quick salute and walking away toward a pile of debris that needed to be loaded into the dumpster.

Jax also said goodbye to the group and walked off toward another pile of trash. After hugging GH, Marcia lingered before going to help Winchell load the dumpster. GH walked slowly across the parking lot to his car, disappointment written in the set of his shoulders. Squeezing past the flimsy gate, GH waved at Parish, who was just returning.

Parish surveyed the work already done before joining Marcia and Winchell at the dumpster. Jax started sorting through soggy piles of lumber further away from the little trio. The "itch" of energy flowing from rotting debris irritated his raw nerves. He rubbed his arms and a tiny shower of sparks rained down on the ground. Frustrated, he cursed softly under his breath.

Jax looked around quickly, hoping the sparks hadn't set fire to anything. Convinced all was secure, he knelt down and drained energy into the ground. Safely "grounded," Jax stood up and looked around again. *What's the best way to clean up the area?* he asked himself, struggling to cope with the sheer volume of chaotic energy surrounding him. The whole situation made him jittery, as if he'd eaten too much sugar or drunk way too much caffeine.

Trying to get on track and back to work, Jax walked over to another part of the store that still stood. *Gotta find something to shield myself from all the energy pockets,* he thought as he frantically rummaged around in what remained of the store's stocks. *There! That's the ticket,* he told himself, reaching over to pick up a pair of large rubber gloves. He pulled them onto his hands quickly.

Marcia heard Jax digging around in the store while she was gathering more debris to toss into the dumpster. Curious, she caught his eye and waved. Jax raised one gloved hand immediately and waved back. Satisfied, Marcia bent to her task once again. Thanking his good fortune, Jax walked away to the far side of the lot. Subconsciously, Jax realized he'd worn his heavy rubber soled work boots that morning.

Jax walked across the lot and carefully tested the effectiveness of the rubber gloves by casually swinging his arms. He let his gloved hands pass through waves of energy as he went. The rubber prevented his hands from absorbing energy, but if he passed his unprotected arms through it, the surging energy passed directly into his body. "Thank you," he whispered, trying to stretch the gloves further up his arms. The gloves kept the erratic energy pockets from bathing his skin and he didn't feel quite as jittery.

Relieved, Jax continued looking for areas that needed cleaning up; it wasn't hard to do. Everything needed cleaning up. Finding a spot where he couldn't be observed using his power – that was the hard part. The fire had eaten large holes in almost every wall, and the walls that were left standing were waterlogged and sagging. *Need a 'dozer*, thought Jax as he put debris in piles and made logical pathways through the ruins of the store.

As Jax works, Parish returned and picked his way over to him. "Slow going?" asked Parish.

"Yes, sir," replied Jax. "You know what would really help?" he asked.

"A bulldozer?" asked Parish.

"Yes, sir!" Jackson agreed.

"Already in the works; should be one over here before the end of the day. That and another dumpster," Parish finished.

"That sounds great," replied Jax.

"Just don't bite off more than you can chew, Jax," cautioned Parish. "I know you – just like your grandpa – you tend to go above and beyond. Don't want you getting hurt."

Jax smiled. "Of course, sir." He watched as his boss picked up a waterlogged board and tossed it onto one of the piles of debris. Parish stayed another five or ten minutes before saying goodbye, explaining that he was going to try to speed up the arrival of the bulldozer. It relieved him to watch Parish leave, having spent the last few minutes in a state of increasing panic. The particular pile of debris they were working on seemed to radiate more energy than any of the other piles. The longer Jax was near it, the harder he struggled to maintain control over the energy surging and flowing freely in his body. By the time Parish left, Jax's body dripped with sweat from the emotional and physical struggle against the pile's energy source.

Jax immediately peeled one large rubber glove off and laid his hand on the ground to drain off energy as fast as he could. Sparks dripped from his forearms as the power level fell within him, forming undulating puddles of fire on the ground. The fiery puddles evaporated almost as fast as they were formed. As always, the release of energy from his body relaxed Jax.

No longer burdened with the excess power, Jax became curious once again about what he could do with it. Glancing around, Jax saw Marcia and Winchell preoccupied at the far end of the lot. Parish was getting in his car to leave. No one else was in eyesight. He touched one of the waterlogged boards and let the energy flow through it, heating it. In the blink of an eye the board was dry as a bone, snapping and popping from the strain of rapid change. Before Jax thought to stop pumping energy into the board it tore apart with a loud "CRACK!!" that caused Marcia and Winchell to spin around in surprise, looking for the source of the sound. Jax looked up and saw them staring at him. He glanced to the right and left, making an exaggerated show of shrugging his shoulders to feign ignorance. They waved at him and pantomimed their ignorance as well. Winchell picked up a board and let it clatter to the ground. Marcia grinned sheepishly and turned back to the task at hand.

Jax turned away and picked up a soaking wet 2" X 4." He concentrated on slowing down the energy transfer. This time, the wood heated much slower and more evenly, allowing for a more fluid transition. Jax stopped before the board cracked from the strain. He held the board up and examined it. The result looked like a perfect kiln dried board. Satisfied, he decided to make a pile of salvaged goods. Whistling happily once again, Jax started to examine the soggy mess with a more discerning eye. He soon had enough restored boards to make a decent sized pile of good pieces amongst the debris.

Whether Winchell got tired quicker than Marcia or just got bored faster, he wandered over to Jax to see how he was doing. Since Jax was experimenting, he was making slower progress than his coworkers. As Winchell got closer, he saw the larger pile of debris. "Wow!" he said, whistling long and low. "It really does go much faster with two people!"

"Yikes! You startled me!" Jax said, whipping his head around. It surprised him that he hadn't sensed Winchell's approach. "Not much progress here, but some progress over there." He pointed to the pile of "salvaged" boards he'd stacked nearby.

"Woah!" said Winchell. "We haven't found anything salvageable. That's awesome!"

"Just a drop in the bucket, really. Are you making good progress?" asked Jax.

"Some," admitted Winchell. "Boss said he was going to get a bulldozer. That's the best idea I've heard so far."

"Yup," agreed Jax. "I'd vote to wait for the 'dozer to do any more clean up, but then we'd miss all of the salvageable items."

"Maybe that's what we should concentrate on; just dig out anything that's still useful for now, then scoop the rest up with the bulldozer," replied Winchell.

"Maybe," Jax said, agreeing. "How's Marcia doing?"

"Ok," said Winchell. "She's pretty tired, though. I've tried to get her to only pick up little things. But you know her. She'll do the hardest thing and pretend that it's the easiest and most convenient thing to be done."

"Yup," Jax repeated. "She can be stubborn."

"Ummhmm" agreed Winchell.

"Is that one of the things you like about her?" Jax asked.

Winchell blushed. He felt like he'd had a crush on Marcia forever, but she was already spoken for. "Is it that obvious, Jax?" he asked.

"Maybe only to me," Jax answered. "I do work with both of you."

"Do you think she knows?" Winchell asked, somewhat timidly.

Jax thought about it for a moment, and then said, "No, I don't think she knows. She's pretty smart, but not that smart about men." He gave a wry smile. "Just look at her current boyfriend." Marcia's current boyfriend was likeable enough, but not supportive. It was easy to look at her relationship from the outside and draw conclusions because Marcia talked openly about her life with her coworkers. She talked about it a lot.

Winchell nodded. "I thought I didn't like the way he sponged off Marcia just because I'm sweet on her."

"No," answered Jax, "I don't like that either. Hard to tell her, though. I don't want to be known as the guy who breaks up relationships. If that's going to happen, it can happen without my help."

Winchell rubbed the back of his neck and sighed. "Well, guess I'll wander back over to Marcia," he said, bending over and picking up a board to toss onto the debris pile. Jax watched him wander across the lot to Marcia, then went back to drying boards and placing them on the "salvage" pile.

The afternoon dragged on, but the sun was still far from setting when they heard the sound of a big truck. Parish waved happily at the three of them from the passenger seat as the driver pulled the truck up to the lot and parked. Hopping lightly out of the cab, Parish cupped his hands around his mouth and bellowed, "Got the 'dozer!'" Jax kept working. He knew he wouldn't be able to salvage much more without being found out. Marcia and Winchell went over to watch as the machine was unloaded.

As soon as the bulldozer was offloaded, Parish climbed into the driver seat and skillfully began scooping debris into piles. In the process, he created a large path that meandered across the lot toward the dumpster. He didn't lift any piles into the dumpster, as it was already almost full. Looking up from time to time, Jax saw that progress was being made much faster. The departure of the truck was followed quickly by the arrival of two large dumpsters. Marcia and Winchell oversaw the placement of the dumpsters while Jax and Parish kept working. The rest of the afternoon passed quickly, and dusk settled gently on the quartet of workers.

Jax worked by himself pretty much all day, Parish stayed on the bulldozer, and Marcia and Winchell kept working together. The darker the evening became, the more apparent it became that Jax was doing something altogether different. In the bright daylight, Jax hadn't noticed the boards glowing as he dried them. Tossing another salvaged board onto the pile in the near dusk, he noticed the board looked "dusty." Trying to brush away the dust, he realized it wasn't dust at all; it was light. Jax effectively doused the light by placing one ungloved finger on the board and extracting energy from inside the lumber. Glancing quickly over his shoulder, he hoped no one had seen him. Marcia and Winchell were watching Parish moving a pile of debris, and Parish was driving away from him. Relieved, Jax decided that was enough salvaging for one day and walked across the lot to join his coworkers.

As Jax approached, Marcia smiled and patted Winchell on the back. The move was both familiar and affectionate. It made Jax wonder why his two friends had never dated each other. Parish chose that moment to power down the bulldozer. The three coworkers turned and watched as he hopped down and walked over to them, a big grin on his face. Jax said, "You look pretty happy."

"Can't help but smile," replied Parish. "I love driving that thing! Even though it means I'm shifting through the rubble of my business, I love it."

Marcia said, "I guess you've just got to find the good points of the situation and focus on them. You amaze me."

Parish looked at her thoughtfully and said softly, "Yes, but there are still situations that can't be salvaged. When you're tied to a dead horse, you just need to cut yourself free," said Parish with a tinge of sadness as he glanced across the entire lot. He continued in a more positive tone, "but this isn't a 'dead horse.' Not yet, anyway. Let's call it a night, folks. No use coming back tomorrow. Not until I get those dumpsters loaded, emptied, and ready for more. Let's just plan on the day after tomorrow." He shook hands with Jax and Winchell and gave Marcia a hug.

Winchell said, "Jax managed to make a pile of salvaged boards."

Parish looked at him and asked, "Is it easy to work around that pile?"

Jax nodded, "I think so. I'll go put a flag on it so it's easy to spot."

"Good idea," said Parish. "Thank you! See y'all tomorrow."

Winchell pulled a bandana out of his pocket and handed it to Jax. "You can use this," he said.

"Thank you," Jax called over his shoulder, as he jogged quickly through the scattered debris to his pile of salvaged boards. He found a dowel and tied the bandana to it before lodging the dowel near the top of the pile. The sun had just dipped below the horizon, and though the sky was shaking off the robes of the day and slipping into the silky colors of twilight, there was still enough light to hide any glowing boards from the casual observer.

Carefully, Jax scrutinized the pile and double- checked for any lingering evidence of light. Satisfied that the boards looked like ordinary lumber, he walked back across the lot to his truck. Marcia and Winchell had already left so he closed the makeshift gate at the edge of the parking lot.

Looking up as the light fought to maintain a foothold on the sky, Jax watched the wind tear at the large cottony masses of clouds. Torn free of the main body, each bit of fluff was snatched and colored swiftly by the changing light. Jax's mouth started watering as the clouds became tufts of grape, cherry, and blueberry cotton candy. His stomach growled loudly, protesting its emptiness. Startled at the rudeness of his own body, Jax ignored the gentle pull of hunger and kept staring at the sunset. Everywhere he looked, colors were changing, blending together and finally drowning beyond the horizon. Jax wondered how the world could go on being so beautiful when his life was being so violently changed. He sighed. This wasn't something he would figure out anytime soon. He hopped into his truck and headed home.

21

The Storm

Jax considered himself a happy guy. He couldn't remember any truly "bad" days. The good things in his life were always stacking up. Listing things in his head, he reviewed his blessings. One – he had just seen one of the most beautiful sunsets imaginable, one that left him in awe of creation. Two – his boss was currently paying him full time to work part time. Three – his grandparents were the best people anyone could know, much less claim as family. Four – he was envied for the quality of friends he boasted, and so on and so forth. So *why* did he feel so out of sorts?

Jax drove slowly home. He paid close attention to the familiar streets. A sprinkle of lights blinked on inside almost every house and illuminated most of the front porches. Although it was easy for him to drive in this town out of habit, with an almost careless attitude or an air of neglect, tonight was different. Jax's inner feelings inexplicably put him on edge. There was nothing unusual about the traffic. No one he passed on the road was speeding. No "road rage" in sight. No outrageously loud music stealing past tightly rolled up windows. People trying to cross the road didn't run carelessly out into the street as if – whether or not they had the right of way – every car would and could stop under any condition. Pedestrians waited politely for passing cars to either stop or get out of their way. So why did he now feel like a million eyes were watching him? Why did it feel like he needed to crawl out of his own skin or hide under a rock to get comfortable?

About halfway home, the familiar routine of his hometown started to soothe Jax's nerves. The "rush hour" traffic, for lack of a better phrase, was over and he had the streets mostly to himself. He rolled down the windows and heard children playing. He could greet people (and knew a lot of them by name) as they passed on the street. These were some of the things he really liked about living in a small town.

Jax could see down the block to his home as he turned onto his street. Fabric that looked like it had been dipped in the sunset floated on the breeze at his garden gate. He slowed to a stop and saw Mamere talking to a beautiful young woman draped in the vibrant colors. Evie was hugging Papere and Franklin was in the garden, facing the street. Franklin waved when he saw Jax.

Jax pulled over and stopped as he called out, "Welcome home!" Franklin sauntered over to the roadside, leaned into the passenger window of the pickup and shook Jax's outstretched hand. "Seems like only yesterday you were a single man," Jax commented to Franklin. "Marriage looks good on you."

"Everything looks good on me, Jax," Franklin boasted playfully. "But thank you."

"True, my friend, too true," agreed Jax. "Come on over here and give me a proper hello, Evie!"

Evie just kept hugging Papere and said, "Go park that truck and we'll see you inside, Jax. You need to come and meet our new friend," she finished, turning to look at the young woman speaking with Mamere.

"Yes ma'am," said Jax as he winked at Franklin and whispered, "Still bossy." Franklin stepped back onto the curb as Jax pulled away and went to park his truck.

Jax stopped to wash the grime from his hands and forearms at the kitchen sink before joining everyone. The low murmur of conversation was momentarily masked by the sink's running water, but as he turned off the tap to dry his hands, he clearly heard Papere saying, "Jax would be a great choice. He stays proficient in martial arts. I think he'd be open to the idea."

"Wonderful," said the young woman. "But I need to leave the final decision to my father. He's letting me choose the applicants on the condition that he has the definitive word."

"Absolutely," replied Papere, "I'd like to meet him. He sounds like an interesting man."

"Yes, I think he is," she answered, smiling and nodding her head in agreement.

Jax walked through the kitchen toward the front room and was met by Evie in the hallway. She gave him a big hug and said, "Hello! Be on your best behavior," she admonished, leaning in closer to whisper in his ear. Electricity snapped as she kissed him on the cheek. "Ouch!" she exclaimed, pulling away and rubbing her lips with her fingers. "Didn't realize there was so much static in the air," she said with a grimace.

"Of course, I'll behave! Listen, Evie," whispered Jax. "A lot has happened while you were away. We have got to talk," the urgent tone in his voice unmistakable.

Stepping back, Evie raised one eyebrow quizzically. "Ok, but it'll have to wait," she said, then took his hand and led him into the front room. "Lyla, I'd like you to meet Jax. Jackson, Lyla," she said as they entered the room. The visitor turned and Jax was face to face with one of the most beautiful women he'd ever seen.

Lyla was shorter than Jax, but still tall. She was dressed in what he thought must be some sort of sari. The fabric of her dress fell lightly from her shoulders and hips, whispering and shifting with the slightest movement. The whole effect flattered her slight figure. Her hair hung about her face in long, glossy black strands that fell just past her shoulders. Her eyes were so dark he couldn't tell at first if they were brown or black. Her skin was the color of warm honey and nutmeg. As she smiled at him, Jax thought the light in the room physically brightened.

"Hello, Jax," Lyla said, "I've heard so much about you."

Jax could feel and see the energy building in the room; it looked like rivers eddying around everyone before reaching out across the room to splash into him. He cleared his throat uncomfortably and rasped, "Nothing awful, I hope. Nice to meet you, Lyla."

"A pleasure to meet you," she replied, shaking his outstretched hand.

The energy amped up rapidly and he pulled his hand back, almost too quickly. An uncomfortable silence oozed into the room as Jax just stood there, staring at Lyla. She blushed. Lowering her eyes, the dark fringe of her lashes brushed her newly pinked cheeks and made Jax catch his breath. She was really beautiful.

"I'm sorry," whispered Jax. "I don't mean to stare. I've spent all day cleaning up a burned building and my manners are a bit raw," he added in a clumsy attempt to cover his own embarrassment.

"Jax," Evie said, frowning at him as she sat on the couch. "Sit down." She pointed to a chair across the room. "Lyla, come sit next to me," she added, patting the cushion on the couch next to her. "Jax's manners are usually finer than that."

"Perhaps my intrusion into your home is too unsettling," Lyla proffered, not moving to take a seat.

"Nonsense!" Papere exclaimed. "You are our welcome guest." Mamere nodded her head in agreement.

"Maybe y'all should keep talking like I'm still in the kitchen washing my hands," Jax said.

Lyla smiled again. "How about I just tell you what brings me to town?" she asked. When Jax nodded affirmatively she said, "Then I'll come straight to the point. I need a bodyguard and Evie has convinced me that you would be perfect," she said, never letting the smile leave her face.

"Bodyguard? Me? And Evie said *I* would be perfect?" he asked, surprised.

Evie nodded her head vigorously. "Of course! You know *krav maga*, you're easy to talk to, you're smart, *and* you're available," she said, counting on her fingers as she listed his qualifications.

Holding up his hands in protest, Jax said, "Hang on, hold up a minute! I'm flattered," he elaborated, laying one hand on his chest, "but I don't know the first thing about being a bodyguard."

Lyla spoke up, "Well, what I really need is an escort that can act as a bodyguard, if needed. There will be a lot of travel, so you'll need a passport. I hope you're as easy to talk with as Evie says. The long trips can be very tedious without good company."

"Long trips?" asked Jax.

"Yes," she began, but was interrupted by Evie.

"Would you both please sit down?" Evie asked.

"Ok, how about we start from the beginning?" Jax asked, motioning for Lyla to take the seat next to Evie. Fearing that the energy building within him might snap if he got too close to anyone, he sagged into the rocking chair across the room with almost palpable relief. Gently, he drained more energy into the old wood – just enough to take the edge off without harming the chair. Feeling instantly at ease, he smiled more naturally.

Lyla started talking and Jax lost track of time, caught up in the way she spoke, the way she talked with her hands, and how she looked. It was difficult for him to concentrate on what she was saying. Even the way her lips formed each word distracted him. *Wow,* he thought to himself, *I am totally smitten!* Whatever this job was, he wanted it, just to spend time with her! Jax discretely covered his mouth and cleared his throat, trying to ease the tension building in him again. "Pardon me," said Jax.

Lyla paused and looked at him questioningly, "Yes?" she asked.

Jax was now truly uncomfortable. The last thing he'd wanted was to become the center of attention right now. He thought quickly, then blurted out, "Mamere, could we finish this over dinner?"

Mamere stood up quickly, "My Lord! Look at the time! Where *are* my manners? Why of course, child. Lyla, you'll stay to supper?" she asked, though it was more a statement than a question. Without waiting for an answer, Mamere headed into the kitchen and started pulling pans out to make supper.

Papere also stood, intending to follow Mamere and said, "Excuse me, but I'd better make myself useful in the kitchen."

Lyla looked questioningly at Evie. "Is it ok if I stay?" she asked almost apologetically. "I hadn't planned on being an inconvenience."

Evie smiled. "Yes, please stay. It's not an inconvenience. Mamere is a wonderful cook and she'd be insulted if you left without eating."

Franklin piped in, "If you haven't had down home Louisiana cooking, you're sure in for a treat tonight."

Jax stood and echoed, "Please stay. I'm very interested in this job proposal. If you'll excuse me, I've got to change into some clean clothes. Cleaning up a lumberyard is dirty work." He left Franklin, Evie, and Lyla in the sitting room and leapt quickly up the staircase, eager to not only shower, but to drain off more energy.

Safely in his room, Jax shed his clothes. They were so covered with filth and grime that he felt cleaner just taking them off. Looking at them, he was surprised Mamere had let him into the sitting room at all! He dug around in his desk drawer for some batteries and wondered again what was wrong with him. He'd been flirting with Patrice just yesterday. Last night he decided to put romance on hold. And yet here he was, finding himself attracted to another woman he'd just met! Frustrated and confused, he slammed the drawer shut on the fruitless search for batteries.

Panic and energy built as Jax glanced around the room desperately. Inspiration struck as Jax, focusing on the surging energy, channeled it into his right index finger. He aimed at the wick of the candle he kept in the room for power outages, and "fired." Jax smiled when the flash of energy jumped and successfully lit the wick. For a minute, he watched the flame intensify before blowing it out. He lit the candle again, this time with a larger jolt of energy. The flame guttered out quickly, snuffed by the ceiling fan. He relit and blew the candle out over and over, which helped alleviate his panic and drain the excess energy. Each successive attempt gave him a greater release of power. This was much better than burning up the little batteries.

Showering quickly, Jax wondered why he'd never thought about lighting a candle before. It made perfect sense. It was controlled, easily hidden, and effective. He could hardly wait to tell Augie about the new "fix." Feeling much better about his future in general, he dressed and walked lightly down the stairs to rejoin the group.

The aroma of Mamere's wonderful cooking wafted through the house; it met him long before he got to the formal dining room. The dining table was already laid and everyone else was in the kitchen. For the moment, Jackson stood alone in the room. It was formal but not impersonal. He, Mamere, Papere, and Evie had enjoyed holiday after holiday in this room; it was full of happy memories.

Jax pulled open a buffet drawer to get some fresh candles and place them on the table. He focused his energy and lit them with a series of tiny lightning jolts. Lingering in the dining room before retreating to the kitchen, he watched the flames bounce happily on their wicks. Unknown to Jax, Evie was standing in the doorway; her mouth flung open and eyes wide. She'd seen Jax work some of his wick lighting magic.

Before he could say a word, she breathed, "Wow! Do it again! When did you pick up magic?" she asked.

Jax hesitated before answering. He was torn between blurting out the whole story and keeping it completely under wraps. Quickly deciding that now was not the time for that revelation he simply said, "I've been working on it for a while. I don't have it mastered quite yet, so keep it under your hat."

Evie shook her head from side to side and said, "You have *got* to do that again!"

Jax crossed the room and took her hands in his. "Seriously, Cuz," he whispered with an air of both gravity and apology. "Forget about it for now. I really need to talk with you, and I'll tell you about the magic then."

Evie shrugged her shoulders. "What is wrong with you? I've only been back a few hours, but I can already tell that something is different." Evie stared at him as if she was trying to see under his skin. Getting nowhere, she finally said, "It's cool to have a magic trick like that but OK, OK! I'll change the subject." She smiled conspiratorially and asked, "What do you think about Lyla and continent hopping with a beautiful girl for a living?"

Jax shook his head. "What's not to like? I just don't know that I'm the best man for the job."

"James Bond isn't available," Evie deadpanned, "and, he's probably a little too old."

"Well, I *am* available, and a little bit younger," he agreed.

"And you don't have anywhere near the mileage," added Franklin as he carried a platter of steaming food in from the kitchen. "Cher', would you please bring the sweet tea?" he asked Evie.

"I've got it," said Lyla, hot on Franklin's heels with a large pitcher balanced in both of her slender hands. "Ooohh, the table looks beautiful, Evie!"

"Thank you," Evie said. "This room reflects Mamere's personality perfectly." Franklin and Jax nodded in agreement.

"I'll go see what else needs to be brought in," Jax said, deftly stepping around his cousin to duck into the kitchen. Papere and Mamere were already on their way to the dining room, each with a platter of food. Jax gave Mamere a kiss on the cheek and took the platter from her as they all entered the dining room. "Smells delicious, Mamere," he said.

"Thank you," she replied, wiping her hands on the apron at her waist. Per their routine, Papere sat at the head of the table and Mamere sat immediately to his left. They'd never liked staring at each other down the long table, preferring to sit at one end of the table together. Evie sat next to Mamere, and Franklin chose the place next to his bride. Jax sat on Papere's right and Lyla took the next seat, across from Evie. After everyone was settled, Franklin said grace and they all started eating.

Throughout the meal, Lyla asked what each dish was, commented on how wonderful everything tasted, and asked about the spices. Mamere enjoyed elaborating on what she had done in the kitchen. By the end of the meal, she glowed with pleasure, basking in Lyla's overt, honest appreciation of her cooking. Evie's comments both inspired more questions from Lyla and got Mamere to go into even greater detail about this or that cooking technique. The years of practice led Mamere to take for granted much of what she did out of habit in the kitchen. While the women reveled in cooking chatter, Jax, Franklin, and Papere mostly ate in silence and let the women carry the conversation.

Jax was truly grateful for the chatter. It gave him a chance to observe Lyla without drawing attention to himself. Franklin and Papere both caught him staring at Lyla several times, making them smile knowingly at Jax while he tried not to blush.

Thank God Evie hasn't caught me staring, Jax thought with relief. He knew she'd tease him unmercifully if she was the one who caught him mid stare. A few times, he'd glanced up and caught Lyla staring at him. Each time, Lyla immediately dropped her eyes, and an adorable blush colored her cheeks.

By the end of the meal, the storm that flirted with them all day long was developing in earnest. Sensing the changing energy pattern, Jax realized the storm would be large. Jax was grateful for Papere's insistence that the men do the dishes; it gave him the time he needed to drain off some excess energy. At the first opportunity he ducked out of the room, up the stairs, and into his bedroom to light his candle about a dozen times. Finally breathing easier, he rejoined Papere and Franklin in the kitchen.

Mamere and the girls were already sitting on the front porch enjoying the cooler air. Franklin made a fresh pot of coffee and took a tray of steaming cups out to the porch. The changing weather made it nice to have a hot cup of coffee outside. The stars were hidden by dark, heavy clouds that released occasional sheets of raindrops that swirled about in a breeze that was colder and stiffer than the one that morning. During a normal lull in the conversation, a dense rain started. Feeling the raw intensity of the storm building, the irritation put Jax's nerves on edge.

Off in the distance, the storm coughed up a throaty roll of thunder. To Jax, the sound was menacing. Before he could suggest that everyone move inside, the wind gusted, raking leaves off branches with cold fingers. The large tree limbs swayed and bent obediently. Suddenly, the screen door blew open and slammed shut with a startling bang! Without a word, Franklin stood up and took Evie by the elbow, protectively pulling her close to him.

"I think we should move back inside," Papere stated. In apparent agreement, the screen door slammed again, this time as if violently possessed. The whole chaotic scene completely startled Lyla and she stood abruptly. Nodding mutely to the others, she followed Evie and Franklin inside. Papere helped Mamere rise from the rocker and escorted her into the house. Jax brought up the rear.

Just before Jax reached the door, lightning flared, much closer than the last time. Jax's veins glowed in response to the electrified light. Turning to look at the sky one last time before going in, Papere saw the answering glow building in Jax's veins. He hurriedly shut the screen door and held up his hand to keep Jax from being seen by the others.

Jax knew his arms were glowing without needing to look at them. The now-familiar pulse of energy that made every single inch of him feel alive told him everything. He nodded to Papere and sprinted quietly to the opposite end of the porch before dropping lightly down into the garden. He jogged quickly over to a spot with the most open sky and looked back to be sure he couldn't be seen from the door. Satisfied, he closed his eyes and stopped fighting the energy surge.

The next bolt of lightning hit the ground about two blocks away. It was so close that thunder peeled before the flash could fade. The lights in the house and along the block flickered and went out, pitching the town into darkness. Papere picked up a flashlight and handed it to Franklin, and Evie ducked into the dining room to retrieve the candles. Papere directed everyone to the basement. Evie led the way with Papere bringing up the rear.

Relaxing his hold on the energy, Jax let it surge through him. The light coursing through his veins and arteries intensified with each successive heartbeat, no longer waiting for lightning to call it out. He closed his eyes and traced the flux of energy with what he was starting to think of as his seventh sense; his "energy sense," for lack of a better term. With his next heartbeat, Jax glowed white hot. A cushion of energy formed beneath his feet and he started to float on an invisible cloud of sizzling ions. *Up,* thought Jax. Then, instantly, he was above the clouds, impossibly alive with energy, racing from horizon to horizon! The thunderclap in the garden rolled out from where he'd stood and bounced back and forth between the tight walls. The merging swells of noise were a cacophony as the sound waves collided again and again in the small garden, like waves generated by a pebble dropped in a square bowl of water.

All day long, Jax kept a tight lid on the surging power within; now it felt so good to fly! He was absorbing energy from the atmosphere and discharging it without worrying about being discovered and without hurting anyone. He felt like he was finally able to take a deep breath and truly *live!* He stayed aloft only until he felt sure that enough energy was dissipated to be able to finish the rest of the evening without further incident. Releasing energy at the lumberyard earlier, and again when he lit those candles, had helped, but nothing worked as well as moving like lightning itself.

Jax landed lightly in the garden, feeling like a new man. He walked through the din of thunder that his return caused without truly noticing it and jogged lightly up the stairs into the house. He knew everyone would be in the basement by now, so he headed straight for the basement and the fuse box. Dark shadows provided visual covering as Jax deftly crept down the stairs, carefully avoiding the creaky steps. Franklin, Evie, Lyla, and Mamere were huddled in the far corner of the cellar away from the fuse box.

Cardboard boxes stacked sporadically around the basement helped make an effective screen. One box was full of scrap cloth that Mamere saved for quilting on rainy days. A second box was full of old toys and clothes designated for charitable donation. Yet another box was full of old pictures and albums that still needed to be sorted and labeled. There was even a sewing table in the corner with its own chair. Jax saw that someone had dug around for a few more chairs so that everyone could at least have a seat while they waited out the storm.

Papere was across the basement by the fuse box, speaking in a loud voice to an imaginary Jax, pausing an appropriate length of time for a response, then speaking again. He jumped, startled, when Jax laid a hand on his shoulder in the dark. "Lord, son," Papere whispered with a grin, "give a man some warning next time!"

"Sorry, sir," Jax replied. "Shall we fix this?" he asked. Jax laid a hand on the fuse box and motioned for Papere to step back. He closed his eyes and traced the energy path, seeing the ebbs and flows along the line. He stopped and took his hand off the box a few moments later and said, "There's a crew working on the line about a mile away. They've almost got it fixed. I'd better not interfere right now."

Papere nodded in agreement, and said loudly, "Well, Jax, looks like we just have to wait this one out in the dark."

Jax matched his volume and said, "Yes, sir" as they both walked across the dark basement to join everyone past the screen of boxes. They all shifted a bit to make room for Papere and Jax. Evie was absently shuffling a deck of cards. Jax pointed to the deck and asked, "Are we going to play cards?"

Mamere, who managed to sit down in the old rocker kept in the basement, shook her head negatively. "Wouldn't do much good. It's not a full deck. Can't even play old maid because two queens are missing. Only good for shuffling." Just then, the lights flickered and came back on. "What good luck!" exclaimed Mamere.

"I was hoping to kiss you in the dark," Papere remarked with a crooked grin. "Put some romance into the blackout."

Mamere responded by standing, planting a kiss on his cheek, and saying "Don't need a blackout for romance, but that's about enough 'romancing' in front of the children."

Papere held her for a moment and then feigned a sigh, "You are such a sexy woman, I can't help myself!"

Evie rolled her eyes and said, "Ok! Ok! Enough sugar! My teeth will rot!" She took Lyla's hand and led her across the basement to the stairwell saying, "They are always this way, even in front of company. I *do* apologize if they've embarrassed you."

Lyla smiled and said, "It's not embarrassing! It's adorable!"

"You hear that, Mamere?" asked Papere. "I'm adorable!"

"Don't let it go to your head," Mamere remarked. "Let's get these young people upstairs out of this damp basement."

They climbed the stairs single file and settled back down in the sitting room. Jax trailed behind, grateful the light-hearted conversation was one he could just listen to without joining. He didn't really feel like talking right now. He was enjoying the peace of mind and body the release of energy gave him. While everyone else settled down, he walked over to the window and looked out at the storm. The heaviest clouds had moved off, taking most of the wicked weather with them but leaving a steady rainfall. The lightning now only flared at the horizon. He hoped the evening would end without having to deal with another energy surge. Papere came and stood next to him at the window.

"Better, Jax?" asked Papere.

"Much," Jax replied.

"That was something to see," Papere whispered.

"It's . . . " Jax whispered, "I . . . don't know how to describe it yet."

"Don't try," Papere said, "no need to even try."

Jax felt a change in energy as Mamere walked over to the window to join them. "Papere," she said, "it's time for me to call it a night."

Papere nodded and said, "Of course." He walked over to Evie and gave her a kiss. "Good night, sweet girl, glad you're home safe." He took Lyla's hand, held it gently and said, "Feel free to stay and visit as long as you like. It was a pleasure to meet you."

Franklin took his hand and said, "We're headed out, Papere. I want to get the ladies home while there's a break in the weather."

Turning reluctantly from the window, Jax nodded at Franklin, "Good idea. Lyla, it was very nice to meet you."

"You'll consider my offer?" Lyla asked Jax.

Jax rubbed his chin with the back of his hand and said, "It's very tempting. Could you give me twenty- four hours to think about it?"

"Of course," Lyla replied as she offered him her hand. "Thank you for considering it."

Jax walked them out to Franklin's car, holding a large umbrella over Evie and Lyla. This was the first time he'd seen the vehicle since the wedding. "Car looks pretty good," he commented.

Franklin nodded in agreement. "Weirdest accident ever," he said.

Evie shivered. "I almost lost you," she said quietly.

Franklin brushed off the sad remark by saying, "Not a chance!" He held the door for the young women as they ducked into the car, trying to stay dry. He shut the door and turned to clap Jax on the back. "Thanks, buddy."

Jax gave a quick salute, holding the umbrella as Franklin got into the car. He watched as they drove off, lost in quiet thought. The rain had started up again in earnest, turning the driveway into a little river and soaking his feet. He looked down and said to himself, *time to go fishing*. He went inside, setting the umbrella down by the back door before taking his shoes and socks off. Padding softly through the house barefoot, he pulled the cell phone out of his pocket and texted Augie: "Time to go fishing."

Augie texted back almost immediately, "Yes!! I'll be over first thing in the morning!" Sighing with a mix of excitement and determination, Jax went to bed. When Mamere needed to think, she sat in the rocker and chewed tobacco. When Jax needed to think, he went fishing.

22

Going Fishing

Jax spring out of bed almost before his alarm went off. He was ready to go! It had been far too long since his last fishing trip. Slipping into jeans and a t-shirt, he grabbed the backpack that was kept packed and ready for times just like this. He stopped at the door of Mamere and Papere's bedroom before going downstairs. Hearing Papere's soft snore and the rustle of sheets as Mamere, still half asleep herself, nudged him to make him quit snoring, made him smile. When they woke and found him gone, they'd worry, so he decided to leave a note for them near the coffee pot.

Tiptoeing quietly down the stairs, he made a pot of coffee in the kitchen and waited for Augie to arrive. He didn't have to wait long. Augie slipped quietly in the kitchen door just as the coffee finished brewing. He was just as eager to go fishing as Jax. Augie toasted bread and scrambled a couple of eggs while Jax put the fishing gear, the backpack, and a cooler in the back of the truck. Packed, they sat down to eat their breakfast and drink some coffee.

"Ready, Augie?" Jax asked, hastily getting up and almost knocking his chair over in the process. He picked up his dishes and put them in the sink. Although Jax spoke perfunctorily, his words bubbled with anticipation in the quiet kitchen.

"Always!" Augie replied eagerly, tossing back the last of his cup of coffee. He followed Jax's example and put his own dishes in the sink. "Papere or Mamere know we're going?" he asked.

Jax slapped a hand to his forehead, "I need to leave them a note!" He dug up a piece of paper and pencil and quickly scratched out a message while Augie turned off the coffee pot. That done, they went out, careful not to let the screen door bang shut behind them. Jax's truck purred into life and they headed out of town toward the scrub. Their usual fishing spot was not far from where Jax caught the boar. Neither one spoke for a while. Knowing Jax as well as he did, Augie realized that this spur of the moment invitation to fish meant Jax needed to think, so, Augie just enjoyed the early morning drive with his friend in companionable silence.

Jax parked the truck off the road in the scrub where it couldn't be easily seen by passing cars. Taking the hunting rifle off the rack, Jax slung it over his shoulder before unloading the rest of their gear. Augie draped the backpack over one shoulder and carried the fishing rods. They started walking and Jax soon found himself unconsciously leading them back to the still. Augie noticed they weren't headed for their usual fishing hole but didn't say anything. Now that they were closer, it was harder to keep from stating the obvious. He had just about decided that Jax had enough time to think when they arrived at the ring of stones around the clearing. Jax put down their gear and sat on the low wall.

Plopping down next to him, Augie asked, "Penny for your thoughts, Jax?"

"Guess I've been quieter than usual," Jax replied, looking at the ground.

"You could say that," he agreed.

"Evie and Franklin brought a friend over yesterday, a lady named Lyla," he started to explain. "She offered me a job." Augie raised an eyebrow but didn't interrupt. "It sounds amazing. I'd be a travelling companion for a beautiful woman."

"They don't want me? I've got some medical training . . ." Augie said eagerly.

"Maybe *you* could be *my* travelling companion. Should the need arise, I'm supposed to double as a bodyguard," he said.

"Would you carry a weapon?" Augie asked.

"We haven't discussed that. Probably not. Too much paperwork in too many countries," Jax replied.

"Countries?" Augie asked incredulously.

"Countries," Jax affirmed. "It'll be international travel."

Augie whistled. "Good thing you trained in hand-to-hand stuff and not fencing."

"Could you imagine me with a sword?" asked Jax.

Shaking his head negatively, Augie chuckled, "You're scary enough with a fork and knife. Are you going to do it?"

"I'm not sure, Augie. What do you think?"

"Jax," he sighed, "I think we need to do some fishing."

Jax nodded affirmatively. "I have a taste for salmon. . ." he began.

"We're not fishing at the grocery store," interjected Augie.

"How about Alaska?" asked Jax. "I think some cold, fresh air would do me good."

Augie just sat there with his mouth hanging open for a moment. "Alaska?" he asked. Then he smiled. "There are some definite travel advantages to your 'condition.' Let's go!"

Jax stood and handed the rifle to Augie, then moved the cooler closer to his feet. Augie stood facing him, holding the rest of their gear. Jax held his arms straight out and closed his eyes. The air around them started shimmering. A moment later, they were lifted off the ground. Augie could see the outline of a "bubble," and they were at its epicenter. Staring at the shining barrier, it got brighter and harder to see through. Suddenly, he felt heavier, as if he were in an elevator that was climbing too fast. The sensation was followed quickly by a feeling of weightlessness, and then he felt lighter, as if the elevator were now descending. Jax dropped his hands and the shining border faded. Augie now saw they were standing in a thick forest. Augie didn't realize at first that the buzzing in his ears wasn't the sound of electricity fading; it was the loud murmurings of a river.

"Sweet!" Augie exclaimed.

"Worked better than I thought! I might be getting the hang of this," Jax replied. He picked up the cooler and started off toward the sound of the river. Augie followed him without hesitation.

The rugged terrain was painstakingly difficult to traverse, and they were both breathing hard before reaching the riverbank. Mocking them and their struggle, the river knifed mercilessly through the rough Alaskan backcountry; effortlessly carving a swath through the same terrain they stumbled across.

The entire scene was majestic and breathtakingly beautiful. Mountains rose on the horizon, their tops cloaked in snow, green showing only at their bases. They hadn't seen any large wild animals, but Augie was glad Jax brought the rifle. Bracingly brisk, the fresh air scrubbed their bare skin, cleansing Jax and peeling away at the heavy shroud of uncertainty weighing him down.

The raging and roaring of the river was mesmerizing and made casual conversation impossible. Staring at the fast-moving river, Jax locked his eyes on the whorls, dips, and crests churning in the water sweeping past them. Pantomiming to each other, they decided to start fishing where they stood.

Jax set up and cast his line out about half-way across the river. Watching the bait being teased and pulled by the current until the line was taut made him happy. The familiar rhythms of the sport slowly relaxed his entire being. Patterns in the water tugged the strings of chaotic memories that stacked up so recently. It pulled them out one by one, untangling them, turning them into cohesive patterns he could grasp and finally understand. The power he now held was previously unimaginable. He shuddered, realizing that to use this power was an even greater responsibility. Eventually, out in the clear air, Jax came to grips with the fact that it was a burden he had to carry.

Glancing over at Jax periodically, Augie was relieved to see Jax's shoulders relax, the tension in his friend easing. Fishing in silence was therapeutic.

Augie had also felt stressed lately. High school graduation was a fading memory, and he was already back in school, no summer break there. He loved his mom, but sometimes she could be frustratingly hard to understand. Sometimes he felt like *he* was *her* parent, having to encourage her and support her. Even working up the nerve to ask Jessica out on a date was stressful. The river's throaty growl was like a frothy sponge, audibly scrubbing everything clean in ways no ordinary soap and washcloth could.

Jax and Augie fished in silence for an hour or two before either one of them got a bite, but when it came, it was beautiful. Shouting excitedly, Jax got Augie's attention when he felt the first nibble. Augie watched as the fish leapt from the water in a desperate attempt to free itself from Jax's hook but turned his attention to his own line as it was stretched taut by another fish. Both men landed their fish effortlessly and were soon gutting the fish.

The specimen Jax pulled out of the water was multicolored with an odd-shaped mouth. "What the heck kind of a fish is that?" Augie asked.

"I have no earthly idea," Jax answered. "Looks like it belongs in a museum next to some dinosaur fossils. These colors are unreal!"

"Why don't we cook yours and put the other one in the cooler?" Augie asked, sizing up both fish.

"Sounds good," Jax replied.

Jax finished gutting and filleting both fish while Augie scouted around for firewood. Making a small depression in the rocks along the bank of the river, Augie soon had a nice little crackling fire going. Jax pulled a grate out of the supplies and propped it over the flames. The sound of sap hissing and popping in the greener branches and the smell of fresh fish roasting made Augie's stomach growl loudly.

"Woah!" Augie exclaimed, rubbing his belly. "That fish can't be ready soon enough!"

"I know," replied Jax, "just being here, breathing this air, seeing those mountains, it all makes me want to *jump* into living, and that makes me hungry."

"I know what you mean, Jax," said Augie as he slapped at a pesky mosquito. "The only downside of being here is that we are also prey. I've lost track of how many times I've been bitten today."

Jax nodded. "I think it's better out here in the breeze. Back through those trees it seemed pretty thick with mosquitoes," he commented, scratching at a bite on his own arm. "Your blood must be sweeter than mine, though."

"Should have packed bug spray," sighed Augie, agreeing regrettably. He looked at the mountain in the distance. "It's so beautiful out here. That fish smells so good! Is it ready yet?"

Jax nodded as he pulled two plates out of the backpack and divided the fish between them. Eating, they silently appreciated the comfortable weight of hot, fresh fish in their bellies. The breeze drew the smoke from their fire into gentle eddies that bobbed and weaved in harmony with the rushing of the river. Sighing contentedly, Jax licked the last bit of fish from his plate. Looking at Augie, Jax saw he was also staring at the smoke patterns, lost in thought.

"Augie, I think I need to take this job," Jax said.

Augie chewed the bit of food in his mouth and continued to stare at the smoke for a minute. "If you don't take the job, I will," he said finally, smiling.

"Be serious!" Jax almost shouted.

"Serious?" asked Augie. "I'm totally serious! It's an awesome opportunity. Worth dropping everything else. You can always come home and work in a lumberyard. You *can't* always go globetrotting with a beautiful woman on someone else's dime." He paused. "School will always be waiting for you. You could even study online while you're travelling. But I probably wouldn't." He put his plate down and stretched his legs out in front of the fire. "I'd let school wait for me, too, and just enjoy the ride for a while. See the world. Soak up life!"

"What about Jess?" asked Jax.

"I'd miss her," Augie said, "but if it's meant to be, then she'll also be here when I get back. She'd understand about me being handed the opportunity of a lifetime. And unless I don't know her at all, she'd want me to take it."

"Cold," said Jax.

"Not cold. Realistic," countered Augie. "But you do agree with me, don't you, Jax?" he asked.

Jax was silent for a while. "Yup," he said. And that settled the matter. The final threads of heaviness slid from his shoulders like an unwanted cloak and he smiled. "Want to fish some more or do you want to go home?"

"I want to catch another one of those dinosaur-looking fish," he said, yawning, "but I also want to take a nap. It feels like I haven't got much rest lately," finished Augie.

"Go ahead and nap. I'm going to fish some more." Jax stood up and walked back over to the bank of the river to fish again while Augie dozed lightly by their campfire.

Twilight stained the western horizon before Augie woke from his nap. Jax was grilling another fish on a freshly fed fire and the aroma was even more tantalizing than the first time.

"Why did you let me sleep so long?" Augie asked, stretching and yawning.

"Looked like you needed it," replied Jax. "You wake up hungry?" he asked.

"Yup. Even if I wasn't hungry, I'd eat that fish. It smells fantastic!" He rubbed his stomach as it growled. "Hear that? Proof positive."

"Too bad I didn't bring any veggies," said Jax.

"Whatever," Augie replied. "My backwoods knowledge of Alaskan field greens and mushrooms is slim to none, so I won't be suggesting we eat anything we don't recognize today."

Jax shook his head and said, "I'm good with that. Fish for supper!"

They ate ravenously even though they'd eaten only a few hours earlier. The rest of the light bled from the sky quickly and they finished their meal staring in awe at the multitude of stars bursting through the dusk to dominate the night.

"Have you ever seen a more beautiful night sky?" Augie asked.

"Nope!" Jax whispered, awestruck. "It would be even better if it was the season for the Northern Lights."

"Man," breathed Augie, "I've always wanted to see them."

"Maybe next time," suggested Jax.

Augie turned to look at him and said, "You know, I'm starting to see some definite perks to this friendship." Then he spread his arms out wide, threw his head back and said, "you can bring me back here anytime!"

Jax snorted. "I'm still waiting to see some of those perks myself, Augie." He ducked, letting the pebble Augie threw at him sail past his shoulder and land somewhere in the darkness. "You've *got* to work on your aim."

Sipping the last of the bottled water Jax had tucked into the backpack, they marveled at what seemed like millions of stars they'd never seen before. Without the sun's warmth, the night air was markedly colder. The chill put a sharp edge on the starlight, making the stars appear to bite through the darkness as their light conquered the deep blackness of space. Augie shivered as the breeze picked up again and cooled the campfire. The moon was a pale silver sliver on the far horizon when he rubbed his arms and said, "Right about now, I could really use a cup of coffee. It's getting a little brisk."

"I don't feel the cold," Jax replied. "Look," he pointed to his arms. They were glowing slightly. "I can ramp up the energy just enough to keep myself at a comfortable temperature."

"You did that on purpose?" Augie asked, incredulous.

"Not at first," he said. "I felt the energy building and was going to just discharge it into the pebbles, but then I thought . . . I should be able to use some of this in a productive way."

"How . . .?" Augie asked in amazement.

"I don't know," admitted Jax. "Are you ready to head home?"

"Nope," he sighed, "but I guess we oughta go. I was *hoping* to see the Northern Lights. Wasn't there supposed to be a solar flare recently?"

"Yup," answered Jax. "The flare makes me feel a little jittery, but that's all."

"Poop," Augie almost pouted. "Is there still a fish in the cooler so we can feed Mamere and Papere?"

"Yup," he said, "two."

"You worked while I slept! Another thing I like about you," Augie said with a smile.

"I guess that makes two things in one day," grinned Jax. "Slow down, or it'll swell my ego."

"We . . ." Augie started to say but stopped mid-word as the breeze momentarily died and they clearly heard heavy panting from the tree line. They both froze. Augie had a clear view of Jax and the area where the panting was coming from but couldn't see its source. Jax closed his eyes to decrease distraction and willed himself to concentrate on the energy patterns around them.

The campfire dominated his senses at first, and he saw nothing except the fire swirling and changing between himself and Augie. Next, he picked out Augie's familiar pattern of clear, steady energy on the other side of the fire. The breeze picked up again, and the raw animal energy of a bear brushed across his face. He could almost taste the hunger and determination driving the animal this close to a fire. Jax opened his eyes and leapt towards Augie, clearing the small fire with a hurdler's stride. Augie scrambled to stand when Jax started toward him, inspired by the twin fears of the unknown and Jax's unexpected move.

"Hang on," Jax whispered, and wrapped Augie in his arms.

Augie sucked in his breath as he watched the bear emerge from the tree line and charge across the brief distance to their campsite. Then, light blossomed, obscuring everything from his view.

The confused bear skidded to a stop. Light and thunder filled the now empty clearing, overwhelming the stunned animal. Panting heavily, its jaws dripping with saliva in anticipation of the meal, it snorted in frustration and pawed at the remains of the cooked fish, ignoring the tightly closed cooler. The hungry bear stiffened, hunched its shoulders, and roared in frustration.

They were standing by Jax's truck before Augie could breathe. With the thunderous sound reverberating in the scrub, Augie couldn't hear what Jax said, but he instinctively ducked, closed his eyes, and covered his ears when Jax jogged to the other side of the road. Light flared in front of Augie's closed eyes and he pressed his hands tightly over his ears in an attempt to protect his hearing. Before the noise could fully subside, lightning flashed three more times.

Augie hadn't dared to open his eyes or remove his hands from his ears. He jumped, startled, when Jax touched him on the shoulder. Opening his eyes to mere slits at first to verify that it was Jax made Augie feel foolish. *And just who else would it be?* Augie asked himself. Augie stood up straight, opened his eyes fully, and removed his hands from his ears. "Wow!" he shouted. "I need to bring earplugs from now on. What happened, Jax?" he asked, still speaking as if he'd just attended a loud concert.

Holding his finger to his lips, Jax said just as loudly, "You're yelling! I had to go back to put the fire out and get our gear."

"What about the bear?" Augie asked, still yelling.

Jax grinned and said, "Seemed pretty pissed."

"Isn't that why we brought a weapon?" Augie asked.

"Yup, but since we could get away without hurting it, I thought why not? Could you imagine explaining bear meat in the freezer?" Jax asked.

"I guess Mamere would go through the roof if she thought this was getting that dangerous," agreed Augie.

Jax nodded. "Let's load the truck and get back to the house. I could use a cup of coffee now, too."

"Maybe with a shot of whiskey in it for my nerves," suggested Augie.

"Whiskey?" Jax asked quizzically. "I didn't think you ever touched the stuff."

"I don't," quipped Augie with a wry smirk on his face.

23

Aurora

Back in the scrub, they packed up their gear and stowed it in the bed of the pickup. Jax drove the first mile in the dark without headlights, easily navigating by moonlight alone. Augie just stared at the night sky. "We grew up here and I always thought the stars were amazing . . . now they look muted."

Jax nodded in agreement and commented, "With all that's happened these past few days, I'm starting to think that nothin'll ever look the same again." Jax didn't need to turn on the headlights until they reached the intersection where the dirt road met the paved road. The tiny "click" as the lights came on, and the familiar noise of the road, were the only sounds made, making it easy for Augie to fall asleep again. As the truck rolled to a stop in Jax's driveway, the crunch of tires on gravel in the alley, and the gently protest of the brakes, woke him.

"I'm sorry about the bear," Jax sighed, reluctantly breaking the silence in the cab.

"Sorry about the bear?" Augie echoed quizzically, stifling a yawn. "Dude, how could you be sorry about a bear?"

"I should have been paying attention. We were in bear country. I let my guard down," replied Jax.

"Don't waste your time trying to take the blame for something mother nature threw at us. That's just silly," he replied.

Jax was quiet. He finally said, "I guess." He rubbed his hands on the steering wheel and asked, "Ready to face the music?"

"It's all sweet for me," Augie smiled. "You know they love me more than they love you."

"Augie," Jax asked, "these things you delude yourself into believing . . . do they make you happy?"

"They *have* to love you," he replied. "You're family. They *choose* to love me."

"This is the first time *I* talked *you* into doing something and I'll probably still get the blame," sighed Jax with a crooked smile on his face. Growing up together, it was not in Jax's nature to suggest highly questionable, but undeniably fun schemes that they usually only survived by the skin of their teeth; that was Augie's contribution to their friendship. Nevertheless, Jax was routinely reprimanded as the instigator. Augie's protests that he was the culprit always fell on deaf ears.

"I can't help it, Jax," joked Augie. "And I'm not going to try, either. Let's do it."

They got out, unloaded, and went inside to stow the fishing gear. Jax carried the rifle; Augie brought the cooler. The delicious aroma of Mamere's cooking met them in the driveway. Mamere and Papere were seated at the kitchen table finishing their supper. They both turned to watch as the boys shuffled into the kitchen. No one said a word as Jax unloaded the rifle and locked it in the gun rack. Augie set the cooler on the floor near the sink and was the first to break the unusual silence. "Wow! Something sure smells good, Mamere," said Augie as he smiled and rubbed his hands together.

"Thank you, Augie. You boys hungry? You need to eat?" she asked.

Augie patted his belly and said, "Thank you, but no, Mamere. I couldn't eat another bite. But if *anything* could convince me to overeat, it would be your cookin'."

Mamere looked at him sharply. "Don't you try to sweet talk me, August," she said, the sternness in her voice unmistakable.

"No, ma'am," he said, too quickly. Thinking it sounded odd, Augie quickly added "I mean, yes, ma'am."

"What's up? You seem upset," asked Jax, sensing her tension.

Papere leaned back in his chair, folded his hands and answered Jax by addressing his wife, "Mamere, we need to remember they're not six years old anymore."

"True," answered Mamere, so softly it almost wasn't heard. Tears instantly welled up in her eyes and tumbled down her cheeks. She brushed them away roughly with the back of her hand.

Jax crossed the room and put his arms around Mamere. "What is it, Cher'?" he asked. "Didn't you see my note?"

"'Course we did, Cher'," she said, her voice sad and soft, muffled by his shoulder. "But then we saw the lightning. *So much lightning!* I knew it had to be you." She paused, relaxing enough to wrap her arms around him. "I thought I'd grown out of frettin' 'bout you *long* ago . . . worrying about you now is just a shock to my system."

"I'm sorry, Mamere," said Jax, holding her tighter. "But I don't think I can fix that."

Pursing his lips, Papere drew in a deep breath and said, "It is what it is. No one expects to have this kind of thing thrust on them. She'll be fine." He shot a sideways glance over at Augie and asked, "Augie, what did you talk Jax into doing this time?"

"I am wounded, sir, truly wounded!" Augie replied, placing a hand on his chest, eyes widening and mouth dropping open in a mock display of shock.

"It really was *my* idea this time, sir," Jax interjected, releasing Mamere and standing up to bear the full brunt of his admission.

Mamere smiled through her tears and watched them as Papere said, "It was always fun to tease Jackson about your dare-devil plans, Augie."

"Figured you always knew," responded Jax.

"We just kept hoping you would get smart enough not to fall for the next crazy idea of Augie's, Cher'," said Mamere.

"Not sure I'll ever want to do that," Jax said, smiling.

"Whatever," Augie sighed, still pretending to be hurt.

"So, where did you go fishing?" asked Papere.

"Alaska," responded Jax.

"Alaska?" Mamere echoed, quizzically.

"It was pretty cool," said Augie, dropping the pretense of injury in favor of expressing excitement about their trip. "I've never seen the type of fish we caught, but they were delicious! Fish always tastes better fresh out of the water."

Jax crossed the room to grab the cooler and brought it to the table. Opening it, he pulled out the fish he caught during Augie's nap. He'd only gutted it so he could show his grandparents what Augie meant. "See?" he asked.

Mamere said, "Ooh," and Papere reached out to stroke the scales, making the colors dance. "Almost too pretty to eat!" Papere just nodded.

"I've never thought *anything* was too pretty to eat," joked Augie. "That's why I have to work out so much. If I didn't, I'd be super fat."

"*Whatever,*" Jax said, throwing Augie's favorite expression back at his fit friend, making Mamere roll her eyes and Papere shake his head.

"What's Alaska like?" asked Mamere. "Did you see the Northern Lights?"

"No Northern Lights; we missed 'em. But it was so cold that the air kind of tingled," said Jax.

"Beautiful," said Augie.

"No one around us. Probably for miles and miles," Jax added, his eyes no longer seeing the people in front of him but seeing Alaska once again. "Perfect place to think things through. The river was loud. The water was clear and bone-chilling. And so powerful! The land was so rugged that it was like the river was actively tearing a path through the ground – wrestling with the earth – just to tumble down the mountainside. Not like the rivers here."

"What do you mean, 'not like the rivers here?'" asked Papere.

"You know. Rivers here mostly just pass on by. They look lazy, their beds are already made. This river was gouging a place for itself . . . as if at any moment, it was afraid it would lose its fight with the land," Jax elaborated.

"It sounds wild and beautiful," whispered Mamere, a catch in her voice. As she listened to them speak, she realized their little boys had turned into men.

"Yes, ma'am," agreed Augie.

Mamere cleared her throat and changed the subject, "I still don't understand how you can bring anyone with you, Cher'."

"I don't either," agreed Jax. "The first time my clothes got singed!"

"What?" asked Mamere. Papere smirked.

"Right?!" Jax exclaimed. "Thank the Lord I had some clothes in the truck or it would have been an interesting ride home."

"I'm sure glad you got some of the kinks worked out," Augie interjected. "You should let him make you an astronaut someday. It's a life-changing experience."

Mamere shook her head negatively. "No, Cher', not me."

Papere stared hard at Jax. "Space travel," he finally said. "Seems like only yesterday I was teaching you how to ride a bike."

"I'm glad I finally got that right," Jax said, absently rubbing his knee as he remembered a particularly horrific spill.

Augie suppressed a chuckle.

"What?" asked Jax, offended.

"I just . . . " Augie hesitated, "It's just . . . I've seen you ride. I don't know that I'd be as quick to say that you got it 'right.'"

Hanging his head, Jax shook it side to side and said, "I don't fall down. I get where I want to go. What more do you want?"

"Nothing!" Augie answered, smiling. "Let's just say it's entertaining to watch you ride a bike."

"Be nice!" Jax cautioned.

"Hummph," Augie responded. "That is nice."

"How about we change the subject?" interjected Mamere.

"Good idea," said Papere, agreeing. "Make any progress besides catching some pretty interesting fish?" he asked.

"Yup," Jax replied. "Had a chance to think. I'm going to accept Lyla's job offer on the condition that I can give Mr. Credeur two weeks notice."

"That sounds good," Papere said.

"I think it sounds exciting and romantic!" Mamere said.

"I think she should give the job to me," grinned Augie.

"Okay then," Jax said. It felt good to have their support. "I'll ask Evie for Lyla's number. Don't know why I didn't think of getting it yesterday."

"Maybe I'll get to meet her sometime," said Augie.

"She's nice," said Mamere.

"You'll like her, Augie," Jax reassured his friend.

"What matters more is whether or not *you* like her, Jax," Augie replied. He sighed and said, "You know, I think I'll have a cup of coffee too."

"That sure sounds good right now," agreed Jax as he poured them each a cup of coffee and sat down at the table.

Mamere smiled. It warmed her heart to have them all here at her table. The space left by Evie ached, but knowing she was happy with Franklin eased that ache some. She realized suddenly that Jax would be leaving soon. She reached across the table to pat his hand. Smiling back at her, he picked her hand up and brushed it with his lips. Tears sprang up in her eyes again, making her dab at them with the corner of her napkin.

"What is it now, Mamere?" Jax asked.

"Nothing, Cher'," she replied. "My heart is so full with y'all sitting here at this table. Augie, you'll need to come by once-a-week *bare minimum* after Jax leaves with Lyla. No need to make yourself scarce."

"You can count on it!" Augie agreed. "I would probably die without your cooking to sustain me. Have you ever eaten anything I've cooked? Dangerous territory," he warned.

"I've eaten your cooking and survived," Jax deadpanned.

"You've got a cast iron stomach. You're not like this delicate southern flower," replied Augie. Leaning over, Augie put a hand up to shield the side of his face and whispered loudly, "Don't ruin it for me now, Jax!"

"Wouldn't dare!" Jax whispered loudly back, nodding, and winking conspiratorially at Augie. Papere and Mamere just chuckled.

"That's it for me, folks," Augie said after polishing off his cup of coffee. "I've got a long day tomorrow. Thanks for the coffee, Mamere. Jax, thanks for the fishing trip."

Jax got up to walk outside with Augie. The moon still hung low, skimming the horizon, and bathing the streets with an orange glow as the two of them stood staring up at the night sky.

"Awesome," Augie breathed. "Too bad we missed the Aurora Borealis, but this moon kinda makes up for it."

"Right?!" Jax smiled, nodding in agreement. "But, you know, I think Papere is right. Best to lay low. Do you think I'll be able to stay anonymous?"

"Well," Augie thought for a moment. He took a deep breath and said, "No."

"What?" Jax asked, offended. "Why not?"

"I don't think you'll be able to stay anonymous, buddy," he said, almost apologetically. "And – not that you asked – but I don't think you'll be able to resist using these new powers either. It isn't like your power is 'quiet.' Most of what you do *is* accompanied by thunder. And, well . . . it's *too cool* to not use. Will you tell Evie before you go?"

"Harsh, dude," Jax sighed. "I'm not sure. I was all set on telling her, but I think it might freak her out if I tell her and then leave. She saw me light a candle in the dining room. She thinks it was a magic trick."

"Sweet night!" Augie said in an exasperated tone, slapping his forehead with one hand. "You can't even be sneaky in your own home!"

"I know. Pretty pathetic, huh?" he asked, kicking at the ground. It was more of a statement than a question.

"Then *definitely* not possible for you to remain anonymous. It's more a question of how long before the rest of the world knows about you. I think you'd better tell Evie before you leave. It'll freak her out for real if she finds out from anyone else," Augie concluded.

"Yup. You're probably right." Jax was silent for a minute. "The next two weeks will be kind of busy. Want one more view from the 'top' before everything changes?"

"Seriously?" asked Augie, incredulous.

"It's probably not the *best* choice, but it's a *fun* one . . . What do you say? Are you up for an adventure?" Jax asked.

"Yes, sir! One superhero sidekick at the ready!" said Augie, standing up straight, squaring his shoulders, and attempting his best military salute.

Standing close to him, Jax stretched his arms out to either side. The outlines of a sphere instantly encompassed them, glimmering faintly at first, but quickly thickening into the familiar opacity they knew so well. Rivers of light began coursing through Jax; they were carried by his arteries to each extremity, and back to his heart through each vein. With every beat of Jax's heart, the glowing rivers intensified. Jax smiled at Augie, tilted his chin up, and in a flash, they were gone! As the light dimmed in Jax, the sphere expanded, and the opacity thinned to a translucent sheen.

They were floating above the Earth again; this time Augie thought they were somewhere near the North Pole. He could see bands of color fluxing across the atmosphere below them, sparked by plasma from the recent solar flare finally reaching into the Earth's atmosphere. The solar energy was pushing and pulling at the Earth's magnetic fields before pooling at the poles. The atmosphere, excited by the energy, was responding with the phenomenon known as the Aurora Borealis.

Lightly touching the sphere, Jax steered it down into the colorful sea of activity, allowing the rim to "dip" into the solar plasma stream. Color blossomed from the point of contact and danced around the sphere until it met Jax's hand. Augie watched in amazement as the white light within Jax flared, then faded as it was dominated by undulating colors. An entire ribbon of dancing light appeared to be splashed onto the sphere and sucked into Jax.

"Wow, Jax," Augie breathed. "I guess we didn't miss the Northern Lights after all."

Jax was drawn to the solar energy like a moth to a flame. About a day ago he sensed the plasma make contact with the earth's outermost magnetic fields but didn't understand what was putting him on edge. To him, it was like the buzz of an espresso coffee brewed in the next room – something just out of reach – that he could smell but couldn't get to. Now in contact with the energy, the plasma stream's intensity initially overwhelmed him, demanding his full attention. Once Jax decided that he actually liked it, he sucked it down like a baby drinking its mother's milk, absorbing the new power through his connection with the plasma stream. The surge made him start to physically grow.

Fascinated by the interacting colors, Augie didn't notice that Jax was growing. Jax's physical evolution happened so gradually that it was almost unapparent. But it soon became evident that Jax was actually getting larger. The longer the colors wove in and out of him, the bigger Jax became. Augie reached out and tried to touch him, but his hand passed through Jax. Quickly recoiling, Augie's hand dragged back swirls of color that eddied away from Jax. The colors wrapped tightly around Augie, sparkling gently on his skin, depositing tiny white and blue stars on his bicep that burned briefly before being extinguished.

Jax's familiar bright white rivers on dark skin were revealed only temporarily when those few colored ribbons left him and wrapped around Augie. The mini northern lights display floated sinuously within the sphere, eddying until it coalesced into a tiny star system that floated around Jax. Color was stealing back over the exposed area that Augie tried to touch just as Jax turned to look at him. That was when Jax realized he was growing larger.

Jax was surprised at how small his friend appeared. Wrestling his attention away from the nourishing surge, Jax placed one abnormally large hand on Augie's shoulder and said, "Woah!"

"Dude!" exclaimed Augie. "What's happening?" he asked.

"No idea!" exclaimed Jax, his voice booming within the sphere as he held up his hands for a closer look. He clearly saw the multicolored play of plasma on his skin. Jax closed his eyes and did a quick self-exam. The growth stopped when he pulled his hands away from the sphere, but the sphere itself continued to absorb the energy, its edges becoming more opaque and thickening with color. "Crap!" exclaimed Jax.

Concern etched on his face, Jax tried to steer the sphere up and out of the plasma stream, but the solar power held it fast. Jax concentrated and searched for the pure white lightning stored deep in his core. *I'm losing control!* Jax thought. Suddenly, a bright white explosion of light sprang from his chest! Capturing the colors soaking the sphere, a shockwave of multi- colored light pulsed in all directions.

Satellite communications were briefly interrupted as the wave of energy and light saturated their sensors and illuminated the nearest planets. The light chased along the Aurora's colored plasma streams, away from Jax and the sphere. A second explosion of white light from Jax overpowered them completely and sent a white-hot pulse toward the sun. The powerful concussion propelled the sphere up and out of the atmosphere's edge, away from the Earth, and into the shadow of the moon.

Jax and Augie weren't looking for danger as they watched the Aurora from their perch above the North Pole. Fascinated by the events within Jax's own sphere, they were oblivious to an obsidian, sensor-like tendril lurking at the far reaches of the plasma stream. When Jax's power overwhelmed the Aurora, the surge of brilliant white energy infused the tendril and it recoiled in shock, shrinking back into a celestial sphere that was hidden in the shadow of the moon. The sphere shuddered and shrank, absorbing the energy from the shock of white lightning. The sphere convulsed a second time, became smaller, and its gravitational pull magnified with the exponential increase in density. The sphere, a twin to Jax's, bobbed wildly in the shadow of the moon.

Both spheres spun wildly in space. The opaque border of Jax's sphere became sheer again as the pulse fled the solar system and bathed everything it touched with Jax's personal energy signature.

"What the heck?! Does it look like I've stopped growing? I mean, now that I've um, since I, um, unplugged . . . yeah?" Jax asked Augie.

"Ok, Alice," prompted Augie, "do you eat the cookie to shrink back down to normal, or do you drink the potion?"

"Ha, ha . . . very funny. And I don't know," Jax replied, frowning.

They stood staring at each other. Jax looked like a giant adult next to Augie's "tween-size" form. Augie scrutinized his friend from head to toe, looking for any other changes besides physical size. With Jax disconnected from the plasma stream, the white rivers of light that normally coursed through his dark skin regained their dominance. The tattoo on his arm was "dancing" and changing colors. New star-like designs were sprinkled along his bicep, and there were new tracings laced among the old. One errant tendril snaked out and touched Augie's bicep and "zapped" him, leaving a tell-tale green stain.

"Ouch!" Augie yelped. "Watch it, man! Can you control that?"

Jax just stared at Augie. "Seriously?! After everything that's happened, do you think I've got that kind of control?"

"Sorry, dude. I spoke without thinking. How do you feel?" Augie asked.

"Big. Strong. Relaxed." Jax replied matter-of-factly.

"Relaxed?" queried Augie.

"Yeah, relaxed," he said. "Like I've been on edge for the past few days, and . . . *finally* things are beginning to fall into place, you know? Make sense."

"This is making sense now?" Augie asked, pointing at the moon and the stars.

"Yup," Jax said, smiling happily.

"Anything in particular you'd care to share with the group?" prompted Augie.

"Nope," replied Jax.

"It's a wonder that anyone wants to be a sidekick. Ever. Y'all are so mysterious and tight-lipped," Augie almost pouted.

"I just don't really know what else to say about it," Jax mused.

"Did you notice that you not only got larger, but you were multi-colored? Like a string of Christmas lights?" asked Augie.

"Yeah, but at first I didn't know," Jax answered, looking down at his arms again. "Cool!"

Augie just shook his head in disbelief and turned away to look out at the chaotic Aurora dancing in the atmosphere. Sometimes, the obvious escaped Jax. The colorful plasma flares spiked over and over in Jackson, but minute by minute, they lessened in intensity, appearing to fade in sync with the plasma stream and the waning Aurora. Jax gradually shrank back to his normal size.

Augie stopped watching Jax, preferring to stare at the Aurora, so he didn't realize at first that Jax was shrinking back to a "normal" size. Jax didn't notice the change either, and they both lost track of time watching the light show. Augie yawned loudly. "Sorry, dude. I want to stay up here forever, but I'm bushed," Augie admitted sheepishly.

Smiling, Jax reached over and laid a hand on Augie's shoulder and channeled energy into him for a fraction of a second. "This ought to help."

"Woah!" Augie exclaimed as his body arched gently, eyes widening in disbelief. "What the heck?! Feels like I just got up from a killer nap! What did you do?" he asked.

"Umm . . . think of it as draining energy into those rechargeable batteries," Jax started to explain.

"What?" screamed Augie. "Dude! You could have 'fried' me like you did those batteries! Be careful!"

"No, dude, I've got much better control now," Jax said, holding his hands up in self-defense. "And I was *really* careful. You are in safe hands."

Augie looked down at his own hands; then, out at their improbable situation, hanging out in a transparent sphere somewhere above the Aurora Borealis in true outer space. Living. Breathing. No spaceship. No spacesuit. Smiling, he admitted, "Yeah. I *am* safe with you. Thanks."

"Don't mention it. But you're right. It's time to go home." Jax held his arms out and the sphere began to shrink in around them, becoming more opaque as it touched his hands. When they could no longer see beyond it, Jax closed his eyes. A moment later, they were standing in the driveway next to the pickup. The sphere faded completely from sight.

"Wow," breathed Augie. "What happens to the sphere when you 'let it go?'" he asked.

"I'm not sure. I don't think it's ever really gone. It's just so thin that everything passes through," answered Jax. "You cool?"

"Yeah," replied Augie. "Better get ready for work."

"Work," sighed Jax. "I'd better get Lyla's number and square things with Mr. Credeur. It's gonna be a busy day," he smiled.

"Yup," agreed Augie. "Later!"

"G'night . . . um . . . morning," Jax said. Jax lingered outside and stared up at the sky after Augie left. It was still dark, but he knew the stars were fading, being washed out by the light of the rising sun. Though he couldn't see the Aurora from this part of the world, he could still feel the delicious tingle of plasma feeding into the atmosphere. Even from this far away, it energized him. Finally, turning to go inside, he realized that Mamere and Papere had cleaned up long ago and gone to bed. He wondered just exactly how long they'd been away but wasn't curious enough to actually stop and look at a clock. Jax, suddenly melancholic, slowly climbed the stairs to his room. Emotions vied for dominance in him: excitement about the prospect of a new job and curiosity over these amazing "super" powers. Those thoughts stopped him short.

Superpowers. Hmm. I'm using Augie's words for it now, he thought to himself. Jax took a deep breath and was swamped by a sudden pang of homesickness even though he was standing on the landing in front of his own bedroom. His eyes welled with tears as he shook his head. Jax squeezed his eyes shut to prevent those tears from spilling down his cheeks. *Don't be such a baby!* he scolded himself. Closing the bedroom door, he laid down without changing clothes. As he drifted off to sleep, Jax thought he'd rest for just a moment before getting up and starting his very busy day. Above him, in the shadow of the moon, Jax's energy signature finally penetrated the border and reached the core of the dark sphere suspended there, gently waking the alien form inside.

24

Cocoon

While Jax slept, long before sunrise flushed the night from the Louisiana sky, communications satellites rocketed noiselessly above the Earth. In geosynchronous orbits, at approximately 22,000 miles above the Earth, these man-made platforms of modern technology were unequipped to detect Jax's presence. The moon, about 235,000 miles away, rotated quietly on its axis. Beyond that, in the deep shadow of the moon, a dark sphere also slumbered. The increase in solar flare activity touched it, too, and color flared briefly around the sphere before being absorbed.

Bathed in the solar plasma stream, the sphere sporadically danced with color. Again and again, color and light were absorbed into the sphere and extinguished. The inexorable pace of the moon's orbit finally pulled the sphere beyond the sun's range, and the ebony field within the sphere became even more intense. Tiny star-like fires glittered and burned coldly throughout the sphere's depths and made the moon appear to shudder.

The sphere's long slumber over, it sprouted shadowy tendrils that arced hungrily into space, seeking sustenance. Unsated, each tendril returned to the sphere before groping out in a new direction. The thirsty tendril, that finally extended far enough to touch the plasma stream that was puddled at the Earth's northern pole, was briefly lit with color.

Jax and Augie didn't see the danger as they watched the Aurora from their perch above the North Pole. Fascinated by the events within Jax's own sphere, they were oblivious to the tendril lurking in the far reaches of the plasma stream. When Jax's power overwhelmed the Aurora, a surge of brilliant white energy infused the obsidian tendril and it recoiled from the shock into the celestial sphere. The sphere retracted its tendrils and became dark again in response to the shock of white lightning. The sphere convulsed and shrank even further, its gravitational pull magnified with the exponential increase in density.

Jax and Augie were back home before the nearest heavenly bodies moved toward the malevolent orb. There was a barely perceptible shift in the universe as stars moved slowly toward the sphere. The gravitational attraction on the nearest stars ripped trails of light that slowly whirled toward its dense center and were smeared like skid marks. Before the solar system could move more measurably, the sphere exploded with a murky ferocity that masked the stars around it! The black balloon heaved massively and expanded to half the size of the moon before collapsing back to its original size.

The orb spasmed at the epicenter of its own explosion yet remained inexplicably intact. Tiny stars reappeared on the sphere's surface and twinkled with a maddening vehemence. It expanded again, and the sphere's opacity thinned to translucency. A lone figure, a celestial Sentinel, was revealed, resting at the sphere's core. The brilliant white energy that touched the orb stirred the Sentinel from his centuries-long slumber. He woke, and slowly uncurled from a fetal position.

Blue and white flowers floated, flared, and popped around the Sentinel. He allowed them to bob and weave without disturbing them, and they eventually settled on his bicep, tracing a tattoo much like the one on Jax's arm. He smiled menacingly. He closed his eyes, held his arms out, and beckoned the sphere to contract around him.

The sphere became impenetrably black on the side that faced the moon and angry little stars glittered icily on the side that faced away. The sphere momentarily flared with the intensity of a supernova when the outer edges touched his hands and sent an incandescent beam of light that pierced the far reaches of space beyond the named planets!

In the opposite direction, one inky black tendril sliced unerringly through space, toward Jackson. Light and power swelled in Jax's bedroom as the alien invader surrounded his sleeping form. Thunder trumpeted violently in Jax's bedroom! The sound waves jostled Papere awake and shook the house's foundation.

The malicious enemy wrapped around Jax in his bed and attempted to siphon power from him. The latent energy within Jax ramped up instinctively to protect him. Jax woke, about to wrestle for the life being stolen from him by this unknown, previously unimagined assailant.

Hmmph . . . Jax yawned and flopped uncomfortably in bed. He tried to turn over and reach for his sheets but his hands hit the inner edge of his protective sphere.

What's happening? Am I dreaming? Jax asked himself, struggling to wake up. Still half asleep, Jax opened his eyes and saw his protective bubble as it glowed and solidified around him. A wiry filament snaked around Jax's sphere, licked at Jax's energy, and left sticky jet-black stains in its wake. Jax glanced sleepily at the stains, his light-infused gaze easily erased them as he intuitively repelled the assault. Jax felt the energy within him surge.

Gotta drain some energy, he thought, not yet fully awake. He bumped his head on the narrow confines of the opaque boundary as he tried to sit up.

What the . . . ?! he wondered. *That's not right!* He felt suddenly claustrophobic. He pushed at the sphere to enlarge it and fully extend both arms out to either side of him. White lightning flared brilliantly and seared the inner boundary as he exerted himself, thickening and protecting him further but without increasing the inner space. Jax jolted fully awake and earnestly tried to assess the situation.

Twisting around Jax's orb, the maleficent filament deposited more tar-like stains and tried to feed on Jax's power. Steam billowed as the alien touch annealed Jax's sphere and formed an energized calyx that further protected Jax. Unable to see beyond the brilliant inner surface, Jax felt his energy level fall as power was used to protect him. Jax panicked! He pushed his energy level as high as he could and attempted to free himself of the unidentified assailant. Magnificent flashes of white-hot lightning flared, echoing Jax's increasingly frantic heartbeat; but he couldn't free himself. The incorporeal intruder absorbed Jax's energy surges and engulfed the bedroom. It prevented light from escaping the room to bear evidence of the epic struggle.

Papere rolled out of bed and got up to check the house when the thunder woke him. He opened his bedroom door but saw nothing out of order; the dark hallway betrayed no evidence of the battle or the extraterrestrial presence in Jax's room. *Must be some strange dream Jax is having,* Papere thought to himself as he shrugged his shoulders and quietly closed the door on the empty hallway.

Jax realized subconsciously that he was losing this battle. He attempted to protect himself by conserving his energy. He relinquished control to the source within him and was pulled into a semi-conscious state. Jax's chaotic heartbeat slowed and normalized, his mind now completely unaware of external influences. An eerie calm permeated the chamber, his power level stabilized, and Jax slept.

In the bedroom, a brilliant white energy flared again, this time from more deeply within Jax's core; it tempered the calyx and cocooned him in an impenetrable shell. The hard shell repelled his attacker and prevented it from stealing any more of Jax's energy, preserving him before his heart could be silenced with an unrecoverable finality.

Cut off from the precious energy source, the tendril raged! It constricted and powerfully squeezed Jax's cocoon, the tarry grip tightening and twisting as it sought to crack open the energized calyx. In frustration, the Sentinel directed an energy pulse infused with murky colors along the Earth-bound filament, which flared eerily but only succeeded in staining the white cocoon without weakening it.

The Sentinel opened its eyes, two unfathomable light absorbing pits in its misshapen face. What could best be defined as frustrated maleficence directed his next action. He clapped his hands together in front of him and the tendril was yanked away from the Earth, back into space, bringing Jackson and his protective cocoon with it to the Sentinel.

Hovering gently in the zero gravity of outer space, Jax's cocoon glowed in mute defiance of the Sentinel's failed assault. Occasional ebbs and flares of brilliance from the cocoon were the only evidence that a viable life remained within. Jax, suspended in his energy's attempt to preserve him, rested in a dreamless stupor.

The Sentinel floated within its dark sphere next to Jax's cocoon. He curled back into a fetal position and lapsed back into slumber. The angry star-like fires that littered the sphere were extinguished and the sphere became opaque. Now increased in mass by Jax's energy and presence, the darkened sphere absorbed light, bending it just enough to allow a measurable change by distant viewers, if they were even bothering to look.

Lucy Claire Jones - Author

Jack of a Few Trades - Lucy Jones earned her first degree from the United States Air Force Academy and fulfilled her commitment as a captain in the 1st Space Wing at Eldorado, AFS, TX. Refocusing to a more personal form of service, she changed careers and became a registered nurse. An avid reader, she started writing poems and songs for personal enjoyment. She is fortunate to have four of the most amazing people in the world as her children.

Lucy hopes you enjoy getting to know Jackson.

Michael Marcades, PhD - Publisher, Executive Editor

Author, Choral Music Professional, Founding President and Executive Editor of PENIEL UNLIMITED, LLC - Dr. Marcades completed his PhD in Fine Arts (Choral Conducting) at the Texas Tech University School of Music in May 1999. His dissertation, *Benjamin Britten's Ad majorem Dei gloriam (AMDG): A Musico-poetic Analysis and Performance Guide for the Choral Conductor*, was nominated for the 1999 Julius Herford Prize and is housed on request in the Britten-Pears Library, Aldeburgh, England. Throughout his career, he has served on faculties at Texas Tech University, Columbus State University, and Southern Union State Community College.

Additionally, he has devoted extensive time to in-depth research and writing about the mysterious life and death of his mother, Melba Christine Youngblood Marcades (aka Rose Cherami). Cherami is known to the worldwide President John F. Kennedy assassination community as the woman who knew in advance and tried to warn authorities about the pending assassination plot. Marcades has authored two books under the title: ROSE CHERAMI: Gathering Fallen Petals (Revised Second Edition, 2020)

Michael is married to Kelly Casey Marcades, a music educator, vocalist, and PENIEL UNLIMITED, LLC CFO and Marketing Director. As a couple, they work on many projects, including their recently launched podcast, *3N1: God, Politics, and Music*, with Robert Wilson of Florida. Michael and Kelly reside in Georgetown, Texas. They celebrate their seven grown children, five grandchildren, and three dogs - Lucy, Molly and Sadie.

CPSIA information can be obtained
at www.ICGtesting.com
Printed in the USA
BVHW070120030921
615904BV00013B/1452

9 781736 718506